Crows on a High Wire

Paul John Hausleben

Cover design by Paul John Hausleben
Cover concept by Paul John Hausleben
Cover art and graphics by Paul John Hausleben
All photographs by Paul John Hausleben
Copyright © 2020 by Paul John Hausleben
Published by God Bless the Keg Publishing LLC
Henrico, Virginia, U.S.A.
All rights reserved
ISBN: 978-0-9986300-8-3

This is a work of fiction. Names, characters, businesses, places, events and incidents are either the product of the author's eccentric, strange and unusual imagination or used in a fictitious manner. Any resemblance to actual persons, living or dead or actual events is purely coincidental, and it was not the intention of the author.

Dedication

To all the crows that I sat on a high wire with, chatted with, and tipped a few with, in my seemingly endless adventures.

Crows on a High Wire

Paul John Hausleben

Contents

Acknowledgements

A special thanks to the crows on the high wire that sat outside the front door of my favorite pub on that warm spring evening. I have no idea of what you were squawking about because I do not understand your secret language. Regardless of the subject of the discussion, the squawking and the communal gathering of the murder of crows inspired me to write this novel. In addition, I send out a warm thank you to the brilliant Mr. Ian Anderson of Jethro Tull for the song, "Another Harry's Bar."

"Life tiptoed on quiet but still audible footsteps while sneaking up behind me. In fascination, I turned around to look back, but sadly, it was gone."

Paul John Hausleben

05 March 2020

Prologue

Mr. Gregory Coates turned the key in the front door of the building. It was his first day as the new owner of whatever this business was going to be. He had a vision and his wife had faith. Blind faith. He knew he was going to build a pub here and while he did not have a name for his pub yet; he had a very clear vision of what this all meant for him, for his wife, and for the family they dreamed of together. It was a gamble. A huge gamble. Their life savings stood before him. Sometimes, we plant our faith and it just needs to take root and to grow. Regardless, Mr. Coates, or as most people called him, "Coatsie" was going to make his wife proud of him.

As he turned the key in the door, he heard a few crows cawing, and he looked up to see what the chatter was all about from so high above his head. Shielding his eyes from the sun, Coatsie looked up and watched as a few crows landed on the wires out on Main Street in front of the pub. Then a few more crows flew in and landed on the high wire, too. Not on the lower electric wires, but on the high wire far above those wires. Closer to Heaven. They bobbed their heads and made the calls and then a few more crows answered the calls. They flew in and landed on the high wire and together, they all scanned their world from their high perch. Mr. Coates captured the visions of the crows and he admired how their calling and chattering gathered in the flock for a social gathering right there on that high wire hanging above the city. The crows and their social behavior remained in his mind's eye. He slipped into the building and he closed the door behind him. His face broke into a wide smile as he first stared at the bar and the stools lined up in rows there. A dusty bar that had not been occupied in forever and a little more. Now he had a vision. Crows on a high wire combined with the barstools all lined up in a row. The chatter, the gathering, the camaraderie.

He took a deep breath and mumbled aloud, "Crows on a High Wire Public House. Hell yeah, we have a vision and we have a name and we have a plan."

Yes, indeed, he was going to make his wife proud.

In fact, he was going to make all the crows proud. Very proud.

Chapter One

Xavier "Gilly" Gilford

Psychology Rules

I am not exactly sure how this all came to be and why I am doing what it is that I am doing right now.

Life is a funny thing, for sure. Years ago, I set out with the best of intentions for my life, admittedly; I was a dreamer, but I set the bar high for my dreams. My father was a petty officer in the United States Navy, and my sister and I were military brats. We were both born in San Diego, California, then we moved to Norfolk, Virginia, then to the Philippines, a stopover in Spain, a bounce here and there in various countries in Europe, another stop over for a few years in Germany. . ..

My sister, who is two years younger than I am, seemed to enjoy it more than I did. She made friends rather easily, and I did not. I am a big guy, almost as round as I am tall, and with the first name of Xavier, it was not always easy. To top it off, I am a carrot top, a redhead, so I have heard all the jokes from the schoolyard bullies in our many stops along the way. The only good thing, when I began to sprout up, the jokes stopped because I can kick some major ass. By adopting the nickname of Gilly with a play on my last name, I slowly pushed the Xavier name to the sidelines, and I became a careful observer of life and of people. That is where I felt as if I excelled. I could pick out a jackass a mile away. Just the smile on a person's face, their body language, their interactions, the way they walk, and the way that they talk and I nail 'em. It is not as if I don't like people or enjoy them. Au contraire, (we had a stop in France too) it is just that by being a quiet observer of people, I became quite good at it. Now, in my adopted profession, the skill comes in very handy too, while I flow through my life and my career. This brings me back to where I began this story before the digression. I am not exactly sure how this all came to be and why I am doing what it is that I am doing right now. When my mother and my old man sat me down and had the talk with me of what my career plans would be, the first thing out of my mouth was that I sure as hell was not joining the Navy or any other branch of the military. Nothing against serving our country or anything, but I had no desire to move around anymore and I had seen enough of the world to decide that I had no desire to see much more of it.

No, I wanted to go to college and study psychology. Since I enjoyed studying people from a distance, I felt as if I wanted to get into their minds too, and maybe even go on to pursue teaching at some level. I love history and feel that it is the one subject that our widely politically correct modern world messes with more than it messes with any other subject out there. Modern spins of history piss me off. It is not the Revolutionary War any longer because it makes us seem as if we were rebels and revolutionaries. Well, duh, yeah. Now, it needs to be the War for Independence. Get the hell outta here! Bullshit! We were revolutionaries. Anyway, you get the picture.

Off I went to college in Pennsylvania. Not a huge school, not a small school, sort of a midrange school. However, it was so expensive! In retrospect, it was a good thing that I took that bartending job in my junior year of college when the tuition costs were running over my parents and I stuck with the bartending gig even though I nailed the psychology degree. With my strong opinions spouting off within the liberal world of education, I would never have made it as a teacher. No question that they would fire my big ass in the first year when I bagged the standard curriculum and taught the conservative and historically correct, "Gilly" version. I would refuse to brainwash students with revised bullshit. How the hell do you revise history? Friggin' history is history. It is what it is. We did not write it and have no right or legitimate reason to rewrite it. We created a generation of pansies and politically correct idiots, and now, we have to live with the creations we made. Sorry, in this world, there are losers and winners and I have yet to find a boss or an employer who will reward me with a paycheck for participating at my job but not succeeding in earning the company or establishment money and helping to turn a profit.

Anyway. . ..

My wise old mentor in the bartending world, at the little gin joint just off campus in the college town where my alma matter is, and where I began my bartending career, when he heard what my major was, nodded his head and accurately predicted my future.

On my first night and at the end of the training shift, my mentor told me, "All psychology majors become bartenders. It is sort of the same thing. Ya make more money than working at that psychology stuff, or at teaching, or working as a social worker. Ya would be lousy at that because you don't kiss ass with the pansies. Ya tell it as it is. Ya are a good talker, ya kinda cynical, but realistic, ya know a little 'bout a lot of things, like sports, history, politics, sex, cars, fixin' shit. Besides, ya big e'nuff to throw drunken clowns and ass pinchers of the pretty gals out of here if ya need to. In fact, ya big e'nuff to do two at a time.

Hell yeah, ya gonna be just fine. Ya gonna be a good one."

It turns out that he was right on. One or two nights with a packed joint after a home football game and with the tips flowing gloriously and overflowing from the tip jar, easily convinced me of my ultimate fate.

One night, in my senior year, right before graduation, I met a little cutie who wandered in for a few drinks on my late shift and she captured my heart. She overlooked my six-foot-five frame and my scale tipping two-hundred and ninety pounds and the fact that my formerly lush carrot top head of hair now had faded to such a small patch that I shaved my head clean and bare. This gorgeous little gal ignored my weird first name and all of my many flaws. We fell in love over glasses full of beer, booze, and wine, and we married after graduation and in sharing our love, we made a miniature cutie and life moved on. The degree hangs on the wall in our house and my wife dusts it off every week. Her accounting degree hangs next to it. Anyway, the degrees make for a nice decorative touch in our home office. After a careful study, I would not say that my education was a total waste, no, no, no, quite the opposite. Totally overpriced . . . hell yeah! However, a total waste . . . no. Not only did I learn my profession while going to school, and it was where I met my glorious wife, but I also learned a great skill by attending college and earning the degree. It was a skill to pick out bullshit from the first word uttered out of a person's mouth. When you are a bartender, it is an awesome skill to possess. You see, I learned from my first day on campus and in my first class that most, if not all, of what the professors taught was total bullshit and it was actually very easy to pass all the courses. I agreed with what they said on paper in order to pass the tests and then did the opposite in real life. It was awesome. A breeze. Nowadays, these colleges and universities offer degrees in every subject that you can think of, so I think they should simply rename the psychology degree, "Bullshit Detection and Interpretation."

I truly believe that doctors, lawyers, teachers, nurses, engineers, architects, nuclear engineers, guys and gals who are discovering and making shit to blow up the world or find a cure for cancer all require higher education. The rest of us—nope! I think that you are better off being smart, being practical, saving the dough, learning a hands-on trade or skill and knocking the world over like bowling pins. Most of college is a total fraud. A falsehood, shouldering young persons with mortgages without houses and without equity to recover their investment. In my progression through my life and my career, I have become a rather perceptive businessman. I seek a return on my investment. Okay, I am going to pay you . . . how much? What are you going to give me in return for my investment? Or what is the potential earning for my investment? Oh, okay, I am going to spend over one-hundred-thousand-dollars to earn the right to earn a salary of thirty-thousand dollars and have a wife, a child or two, raise a family, pay off a mortgage and a car and a house. I don't think so! I mean, why does a college football coach earn millions of dollars in salary? Colleges exist for one purpose. To make tons and tons of dough! Oh no, Gilly, you are wrong! They "care" about the success of students and student athletes too! Get the hell out of here!

See, I told you that I have a great bullshit detector. Now, that alone was worth the price of the degree.

I think.

I apologize if I am coming across as being cynical or being slightly tainted in my demeanor, but old Gilly is a factual dude and years of standing behind a bar counter slinging drinks and meeting all kinds of people and whackos from all walks of life, tends to make you that way. Now, after spewing all of that long-winded drivel laced with touches of hyperbole, we finally arrive once more, to where I began. Here I stand, Xavier (we need to use my actual first name for legal reasons,) "Gilly" Gilford, the new proud owner of an establishment known as Crows on a High Wire Public House. Once more, I am not exactly sure how this all came to be and why I am doing what it is that I am doing right now.

Life is a funny thing, for sure.

Backtracking . . . for this story's sake, my wife was from Bloomfield, New Jersey, and after our daughter was born, she wanted to return home to New Jersey. We landed in Bloomfield to be close to her family and friends and other than being expensive as all hell—it seemed as if it was a decent place to put down roots. When you are Mr. Xavier "Gilly" Gilford and you lived all over the world, at this point, it did not matter where we lived.

Whenever a person asked me the common question of, "Where are you from, Gilly?" I always answered that question with some stupid-ass rhetoric such as, "Where am I not from?"

Bloomfield, New Jersey, seemed as good a place as any other place was. It was close to New York City, and to Newark, and to Jersey City, and to Paterson and to wherever. . ..

So, there we were in Bloomfield and with the responsibility of a child to feed and a wife to take care of, I needed a solid job that paid me enough to take care of my family. Every man's goal and dream. Well, a large majority of men's goals. Some are just born losers and lazy idiots. More on that subject later. Employers were not exactly doing somersaults over each other in order to offer me a job and my wife and I really wanted for my wife to stay at home and take care of our daughter. At least for the first five years or thereabouts.

I grew tired of the endless job application rejections, and I was feeling down on my skills and obligations as a father and a husband.

I knew that my strong, conservative opinions would

keep me out of the teaching field, and returning to school was not even a consideration. We were, for the most part, broke. I had a gig in a local supermarket, but it barely kept us fed and put a roof over our heads. With my bartending and conversational skills and aggressive attitude, I felt as if I could make a ton of dough in the right place. In my heart, I knew that I needed to return to my roots, back to what I knew the best, and paid me more than just decent money. Therefore, when the unpaid bills piled up, I stopped sending in applications to mindless corporations and I decided to punt downfield and take the safe play out of the end zone. I looked for a job in bartending.

Shortly after rethinking my job search goals, I mentioned to a friend of a friend of a friend how I was looking for a bartending gig and the gent suggested to me, "You should check out this local pub. The owner is looking for a bartender and a shift manager. I bet you will nail the job in the first interview. He is a good guy and for a Jersey guy, a very honest guy too. Nice guy. His business is thriving, and it is very successful. It is close to the new downtown renewal projects, there are many office buildings in and around there and they do a knock-out business."

From here on in, I can recall all of these events and the words spoken as if they were the screenplay of a movie. Word for word and frame by frame. It is all too clear to me. Please, let me recount and recall the entire scene and all that passed before this and all that brought me to where I am right now.

A few days later, after taking the suggestion of the friend of the friend of the friend, the owner of the Crows on a High Wire Public House, Mr. Gregory Coates, looked first at my application papers and then at my résumé. I nervously looked around the interior of the pub while the owner checked out my paperwork. It was clean and well-lit with a combination of high-top tables, booths, dining tables and small nooks to sit and relax and enjoy the visit. A stage lined the front wall; the bar was toward the rear. The walls held an assortment of artwork, and I found the interior to be warm and inviting.

After a careful perusal of my paperwork and with a peering of his eyes out of the top of his glasses that remained perfectly perched between his nose and his forehead, Mr. Coates asked, "Is your first name really, Xavier?"

"Yes, it is," I said with a nod and added, "if I had to guess, I think that my parents smoked a ton of weed years ago when they decided to name me. I prefer Gilly for obvious reasons."

Mr. Coates only nodded and asked, "Ya have a degree in psychology, huh? That is why you ended up working as a bartender. Best education ya can have in order to detect whacky customers and bullshit. All bartenders have psychology degrees. Some earned by passing coursework of nonsense in a fancy or a not-so-fancy-college and some are simply earned in life. The life degrees are the best ones." I nodded at his wisdom and with his intense and peering eyes; Mr. Coates retreated to the paperwork. "Ya can mix anything? Can you deal with jerks, punks, drunken and horny chicks, wanna-be-mobsters and general lunatics and nutcases?"

"I can. Yes, sir. I've seen it all. I have seen the people who choose to allow booze to ruin their lives and their health and seen the people who allow it to give them peace and a sense of joy. I can handle the most crowded bar you can dig up and any mix of looney-tunes . . . believe me . . . look at the size of my ass, I can throw the jerks out on their ears."

"How about the drunken punks, who decide their hobby is to pinch the asses of all the cute chicks?"

I made a cutting motion across my throat, but did not say a word.

Another nod, a hint of a smile, a quick perusal of the

papers, and finally, a full and wide smile.

"Okay, Gilly, let's give ya big ass a test drive." He cleared his throat, and quickly added with a hint of a smile upon his face, "That is figurative, not literal."

"I understand. Thank you, sir," I said with a smile.

"Ah, please, there really is no reason to use the sir, bullshit. Coates is the name, or Coatsie. I use a nickname too. Ya know, in order to keep it light. Life needs to be light and not heavy. The heavy shit comes too often and when it arrives, it is generally, kinda ugly. Okay, so, Gilly works for you and Coatsie works for me. All bartenders develop nicknames over the years and I might be the owner of this joint, but I am still a bartender at heart. Can you start working tomorrow?"

The use of his nickname stumbled out of my mouth, "I can . . . Coatsie."

"Good. Be here by ten in the morning. We get our booze delivery on Tuesdays and I want to show you the check-in procedure and explain the inventory check sheets. Do you have any questions, Gilly?"

I decided to ask the question that was on my mind since the first moment that I read the sign on the outside of the building, "Only one. Why did you name your business, Crows on a High Wire Public House? It is so unusual." I turned and pointed to a menu sitting on the table where they sat, and I directed his attention to the logo for the establishment and added, "Don't get me wrong. It is super cool, and the logo is awesome."

Mr. Coates broadcasted a hint of a smile across his face, and he picked his glasses off his nose and he set them upon the top of his head. He took a deep breath that seemed as if it began at the tip of his toes and finally finished near the top of his head. For a few seconds, he seemed quite pensive and then after the passing of the elements of pensiveness, the words arrived.

"It is not quite as obtuse as it appears to be, Gilly.

Actually, it is quite simple. I bought the place, and it was a dark, dingy, failing, business at the time and my wife thought that I was crazy. I quit my steady job as a foreman in a garment factory in Paterson and tried my best to sell my wife on a vision and a dream. She loved me with all of her heart and soul and went along with it, but still felt as if I lost my mind and was crazy. We were both frightened as to where our next paycheck was coming from, but with a dollar and our dreams, we pushed ahead. Love will do that to you. The greatest motivator is love. It is a product of your mind and of your faith. It is not lust, it is not desire, it is love that causes a person to believe in you and to trust you and to have pride in you and to honor you and support you. My wife and I have that and I hope that you do too in your relationship. My wife was correct because I did lose my mind and I was crazy. In many ways, I think that I still am. Her love was, and is, so deep and so strong that it is not within my comprehension. If love such as that kind of love does not light your fire, then your wood is too wet, or your matches don't work."

Mr. Coates gazed over at me and I felt his eyes studying my face for a reaction, but after seeing none, he continued.

"Wishful dreams, often, are not measurable. Nor do they make much sense because they are a part of your heart and your soul and are not derived or contrived, nor controlled by any aspect of common sense. Anyway, e'nuff of the profound bullshit, but I had no idea what I was getting into, but when I obtained the keys to the establishment and turned them in the door for the first time, I heard the hollering and yelling of a high wire gathering of many of the neighborhood crows. I looked up and spotted a row of crows sitting on a high wire, high above the street, and they all clamored and called and carried on in such a manner that they stuck in my mind forever. If ya think 'bout it . . . a row of barstools with customers yakking away and drinking are the same as those crows were while they all sat together on the high wire that day. Right then and there, the name for the public house came to me in a flash and here we are . . . many, many years later. Apparently, the name stuck in many other people's minds too, and if I had to guess, it was all part of the plan. Now, the plan is the true mystery. Who controls it, where it comes from, what it is all about? Well, all of that, I remain conscious of but oblivious to as to where it comes from and where it all goes? The plan. I am not sure as to why it exists . . . but it does, it is, and always will be."

His explanation astounded me. I had no other way in which to describe it. After a floundering for words and a start and stop stammer, I managed to say, "Wow, Coatsie. I think that is one of the most awesome explanations and speeches that I ever heard."

Coatsie nodded, picked up all of my paperwork and gathered the papers into a neat pile and then he looked at me and asked, "Aren't you gonna ask me the pay?"

Once more, I must have seemed like I was half in the bag, or a dope, or a combination thereof, and after shaking off the cobwebs, I smiled and answered, "Yes, the pay. I guess my wife will want to know that. Ah, yes, what is the pay?"

"Salary. Six-fifty a week. Tuesday to Saturdays. You will work four in the afternoon until closing, except on Tuesdays when I need you in the morning for the booze deliveries. Prepare for long hours, but you will split the tips with two other managers. The kitchen manager and the catering manager. Those two managers do not have any bartending duties, and this gives them a chance to earn a few bucks over their salaries. However, on Friday and Saturday night all the bar tips are yours unless we bring in an assistant to handle the crowds. Then it is fifty-fifty. How does that sound?"

I knew in my heart that this man was genuine and an outstanding man, therefore, I spoke from my heart.

"It sounds more than fair. I am very grateful to you for the opportunity. I am looking forward to working here for a very long time."

I recall how strong his handshake was for such a slight man of what seemed as if he was nearing fifty-five or so years of age. He was thin as a rail and seemed fragile. I was wrong on that assessment but not wrong about much else as far as Coatsie was concerned. He was a wonderful, honest, hardworking and sincere man, and he taught me more than any college professor did or I am quite sure even knew. He was more than a mentor to me, or a boss or a friend; he became a second father to me.

When he came to me about six years or thereabouts after the day that he hired me and told me that he was retiring and his wife and he were moving to Florida to join their children and grandchildren, I felt as if I might cry. Then, he dropped the bombshell that he wanted to work out a deal to sell me the business, and I did cry. A big, huge, giant lug of a man, sobbing with joy for what this life had dealt me.

Today is the day . . . my twenty-eighth-year anniversary of being the owner and operator of the Crows on a High Wire Public House. I look back on all that has happened and all the people that I met and all the adventures, and it brings a rush of joy to my soul. Coatsie is still alive and doing well in Florida. He is old now but still getting along fairly well. I finished paying him off for the business about five years ago or thereabouts, and now we are on a roll. I actually make a fairly good living here. My wife has put up with long hours and my daughter missed her daddy and I missed her too, but my wife was able to for the most part, stay at home and raise our daughter and that is due to this business and all that it afforded us and brought to us. Hard work is hard work and no matter what you do to earn a living, it always comes down to hard work.

Coatsie was correct in so many ways, but whatever power, fate, or force intervened to sit those crows on that wire that day and invoked the name for this pub within Coatsie's mind, sure nailed it. This business is not about the food, which is pretty damn good, by the way, or the pints or the booze or the bands that play most every night, or the cool lights behind the bar, or the interesting décor, or all the other things that make up this business—it is about the people here. Not only the staff, but the patrons and the regular crows and the visitors and the folks who come by to listen to the bands or they come by just to hang out and shoot the breeze while catching the hockey game or the soccer match, or the golf game, or a baseball game on the large screen televisions. We are not an Irish pub, nor an English pub, or Scottish or Welsh or any other specific "country" influence, but we are pure Americana here. With a heavy touch of New Jersey too! We specialize in a mixture of everything good. We have a small stage here and we have live entertainment every evening. Mostly music, but sometimes, it is a comedian, trivia, spoken word, or special events for holidays and such. Mostly local bands and entertainers following their dreams and we are happy to give them their chance to shine in the sun. Some are great, some are good, and some, well, honestly, they suck, but a stage is a stage.

After Coatsie retired and I became the publican here, I made some gentle changes to the interior of the pub and some slight renovations. First, I covered the walls with nostalgia of New Jersey; vintage photographs of Paterson, Newark, Jersey City, and of course, Bloomfield. We decorated the walls with some sports memorabilia, logos, photographs and mixed the décor with posters and banners of beers, whiskies and other related décor from the various distillers and distributors. We opened up a wall or two and divided the stage area from the game area, where the dartboards and shuffleboards are and we set some high tops over in that area for those patrons that wanted to play games, and talk and interact and have some freedom from the music and entertainment. We painted the ceiling flat black, added ceiling fans, and covered the walls with rustic wooden planking. The bar area had a railing divider from the main dining room to give it an authentic pub-like feel, and we upgraded the brass railings at the bar. Not too many changes, but just enough. As far as the menu goes, it was pub food, but you could find a little of everything on the menu. From homemade soups, to fish and chips, to classic grilled cheese sandwiches and with the addition of Senor Renaldo Lopes as our head chef, we even stuck a few Mexican dishes on there too. Hell, in a stroke of genius, I put spaghetti and meatballs on there for the kiddies that might accompany their parents. Many adults order it too. We have had business meetings here, funerals, repasses, birthday parties, Christmas parties, we honor the veterans-on-Veterans Day; we celebrate Saint Patrick's Day with wild and crazy celebrations, and we jump up and down, laugh, sing, and celebrate just about every other event that you can think of here. They were all wonderful, but without the amazing cast of characters that have sat here just as those crows on the high wire did, then this place would be just a building housing a business of slinging cold pints of beer and stout and dropping glasses of whiskey and cocktails and pouring wine and serving pub food. Just another gin joint, smelling like stale beer, malt-vinegar-soaked chips, a hint of whiskey and a taste of a blob of bangers and mash. Here in this neck of the woods in New Jersey there is a gin joint on every corner.

Yet, I like to think that we are different and we are special and we are unique. We are crows all sitting on a high wire, enjoying life and watching the world go by as we all sit together.

Here, now, come on and pull on in and sit down along the bar and you too can be a crow for a bit and you can listen while I organize things, wipe down the bar and the bottles and I get ready for the opening. I need to talk about some of these special people and to tell their stories. Some of the stories are happy, some are sad, some tell of caring individuals, some rather sketchy and a few mean ones too, but they are stories that they wrote on their own. I am the narrator and the gatherer of these stories, but not the creator. First, I will give you a rundown of the highlights of the past twenty-eight years and by the time that I run out of those stories; it might just be time to tell you of another era. Who knows? Actually, what does it matter? Life is great and let's all go for a ride together. Sip a pint or two, while I spin the yarns, or just sit and enjoy, but please, join along for the ride.

Yes, indeed, I need to tell you why they came, what they shared, who they were and are, and you too can understand why it is that those crows came along that day.

Chapter Two

Mr. Clive Barrows Peepers

The Wise Sage of the Last Barstool

I am not sure of the exact date when it was that I first met Mr. Clive Peepers. I can sure as hell confirm that it was in the summer, though. Whether it was June, July, August or early September, I do not know, but I know it was in the summer. It was summer because Clive could sweat like no other human being, or in fact, perhaps any other living creature in this entire wide world could sweat. It was not an ordinary sweat, no, no, no it was an epic sweat. Clive looked as if someone sprayed him with a fire hose when he walked into the pub on the day that I first met him. The drops of sweat poured off his forehead and hit the floor of the pub with a resounding, "thud."

I will always remember that day and our first meeting. And his sweat and dislike of the heat and everything about it.

In the summer, or even in the mild heat of the spring and in the fall of the year, Clive would sweat bullets and force his body with painful and agonizing steps to make its way to a barstool. Preferably the last one on the left of the bar. My left, not Clive's left. Clive loved that stool because it was right next to the air-conditioning vent. If it was cool outside or winter, Clive would still take that same barstool or the stool closest to the end. I was not sure if it was a habit or not, but Clive loved the cold. The colder, the better.

I recall Clive settling into the last barstool, wiping the sweat away from his forehead while I stood amazed to see that someone could actually sweat that much. Clive looked up at me and smiled.

"This is all because of Matilda," Clive said, with the hint of a smile etched on his face.

It was difficult, if not impossible, for me to hide my confusion as to the meaning of his words and understand the testimony. I slowly walked closer to where he sat while being aware of the puddles forming on the floor behind the bar as the sweat flowed off his face and body, ran over the edge of the bar, and dripped onto the floor.

Please believe me that I am not exaggerating as to the level of sweat that poured off this man. Okay, well perhaps, I am exaggerating, but you get the picture. Clive sweats a helluva lot.

Upon seeing the river run, the man sitting next to Clive stood up, bowed in his honor, picked up his beer mug, and moved about five stools to the left of the river.

I stammered and caught myself while my words became a bit more forceful, "Ah, okay, Matilda? You're gonna need to give me a little more to go on there, pal."

With the smile still on his face and the air conditioning working overtime to dry up the river of sweat, his next words gave away his heritage as I clearly heard his English accent enunciate the words carefully and properly.

"Gonna. Tsk, tsk, such awful choice of dialect and chopping up of words. How do two individual words such as going to become a single word such as gonna? Oh yes, this awful heat is not the only reminder that I am here in New Jersey. The accents and complete disregard for proper English is also a painful reminder." He clucked his tongue and shook his head before continuing. "Please, forgive me. Yes, yes, Matilda. In retrospect, that is an untrue testament. And while Matilda certainly had her faults, it is unfair of me to state that she is the only reason that I am here in New Jersey. Please, forgive me and let me retract that statement and say that one of the reasons that I am here in this wretched heat and ungodly humidity is because of Matilda." I still stood silent, and Clive read my face and continued with his explanation. "Ah, yes, please forgive me for the haziness in my explanation, dear sir. The reason that I am sweating so much and I am stuck here in this wretched climate known as northern New Jersey is because a long time ago, and for many reasons, some due to love and some to many other cruel reasons and awful circumstances, I left my homeland of England to come to America and marry Matilda Worthington."

Clive rolled his eyes back in his head, removed a handkerchief from his shirt pocket, wiped more sweat from his brow, and despite his discomfort at the residual heat . . . he smiled. His voice now grew loud and somewhat intense while he explained a little more of his vague reference to the reason as to why he was sweating a river.

Oh yes, Matilda, something or other.

"Her legs were the most glorious legs that I have ever seen. They were miles long, and they were even better when she wrapped them around my waist." He cleared his throat, wiped more sweat and apologized, "So sorry, old chap, but she was gorgeous and I am factual. Too bad. She wrapped them around the local grocer who sold her bananas. Apparently, she loved his bananas. Or, perhaps in the interest of good taste—I will use the word banana in a singular fashion as a placeholder for a similar shaped item that is part of our male anatomies. Ah yes, my good man, I see your smile at learning the background of my rather inglorious fate for coming here to the colonies. And that was only wife number one. We have many, many stories developed over a long lifetime of travels, cheap booze and expensive booze, hangovers, employment, women, life, spoken and written words and a taste of a little light music. Let us be friends and please, a gin and tonic, with a lime wedge, easy on the ice and a bit harder on the gin, sir. And a glass of ice water. The house gin is fine. I am retired now and watch my pennies, to take care of the dollars. The house water works too."

I nodded, smiled, and went to prepare his gin and tonic.

That is how I first met Mr. Clive Peepers. When I dropped the gin and tonic and ice water in front of Clive and extended my hand to greet him, it was the beginning of knowing and enjoying the company of one of the most interesting persons that I have ever met. Eccentric, and sometimes downright wacky but certainly interesting.

"Nice to meet you, sir. A friend sounds like a good plan. Welcome to the Crows on a High Wire Public House. Being friends is what we are all about here. The drinks are cold and the company is good, the discussion is always lively and the barstools do not give you ass splinters." I turned and pointed to a barstool on the opposite end of the bar and explained, "Except maybe for that one over there. We try to make all the jackasses sit there. Xavier Gilford is my name. Please, call me, Gilly."

Clive's eyes lit up upon hearing my name and he laughed a little before saying, "My bum just breathed a huge sigh of relief at your statement about the condition of most of the barstools. Xavier, eh? Glorious name. It is my pleasure to meet you, Gilly. Clive Barrows Peepers is the name here on this end. Please, you may call me . . . Clive . . . because, well, I guess because it is my first name and I have not been ingenious enough to invent a clever nickname."

Clive picked up the gin and tonic, waved the glass under his nose, and then took a sip. He nodded his appreciation at the mixture and followed a sip of the gin with a long draw of the ice water.

Upon setting the glass down on the bar counter, Clive spoke once more, "I am most intrigued by the name of your establishment and I am sure over this long afternoon, you can provide me with more of an explanation as to the origins of the title. However, I must tell you more of why I wandered in here today."

"The heat?" I asked and jumped in with a dose of supposition.

"Partly," Clive took a sip of ice water and then a sip of the gin and tonic and while I waited for the answer, the man who had moved his seat leaned in to hear it too. Suddenly, Clive Barrows Peepers captured the attention of the entire bar on this previously routine afternoon. "Mostly due to the demise of wife number three . . . my dear, Dianne."

The man on a few barstools to the left gasped, and I mumbled a barely intelligible, "I am so sorry."

Of which, Clive raised his gin and tonic in the air and nodded with his head for everyone else to do the same. I quickly picked up a water glass and joined in the homage to poor Dianne.

"Oh, please don't be sorry. Here is to good riddance. She did not pass. I kicked her ass out eleven months ago and the divorce was final today. She was a royal pain-in-the-ass, and I am quite sure any royal blood she has in her veins would cause our dear Queen of England to disown her rather promptly. Cheers and long life for you and yours! Despite her flaws, a long life to Dianne, too. Let us hope that the next sucker she lures into her den of lunacy and she cons into the bliss of Holy Matrimony, is deaf, blind or a strategic combination of both."

While remaining puzzled and perhaps in self-defense, we all took a drink and shared in the toast and I promptly traded in my water for a three finger pour of Irish whiskey. After all, I did own the joint and if I wanted to drink while on duty, then I damn well could do it. Something told me my life might not be the same after meeting Clive. He was hilarious, sweaty, fun, engaging, and obviously very intelligent. The legendary English wit and humor was on full display with this character. I studied him from my post behind the bar. I guessed his age to be in and around seventy years of age or thereabouts, and his white hair was sweaty, but it was short and combed over in neat waves with a clean right-side part. His comb-over was not a bald-covering comb-over, but a hairstyle choice. This man had a solid head of hair for his age. His blue eyes were clear and bright. He was a handsome man with gentle facial features, and an engaging smile, with genuine warmth that emitted from his face and mannerisms. It only took a few minutes in conversing with him to discover how intelligent he was.

The man sitting to the left asked the question that was on my lips and I am quite sure was on everyone else's who remained within earshot of the conversation.

The question escaped his lips before I had the chance to ask it, "What happened to wife number two?"

Clive had mercifully stopped sweating now. He lifted his ice water and took a long sip, followed by a swig of his gin and tonic, and once hydrated, he answered rather succinctly.

"She is gone and living in Edmonton, Alberta, in Canada. Of all places! She met a chap at her place of employment that lived in Edmonton and decided to run off with him for a life in the frozen north. Can you imagine? I cannot recall ever meeting a single person from Edmonton, Alberta. I guess that there is a first time for everything in life. My selection of fickle women over the years proved to be quite interesting, indeed." He leaned in with both elbows on the bar and rested his head in his hands before adding a final pensive thought about wife number two, "She was my favorite wife out of the three. Quite lovely, a bit of a lush, but she was generally amicable and fun. She left me a note one morning while I was at work and explained that she grew bored with her life with me and apologized for leaving me. However, we had our time in the sun together. She high-tailed it out of here. At least she is not sweating such as I am. The summers are quite lovely there." He emptied the gin and tonic, nodded, and pointed for a refill, and I promptly did so. A few more patrons required maintenance and refills, a few more wandered in as the afternoon lingered onward and I moved about the bar, attending to my customers. The previously spooked man to the left of Clive had now slid back to his immediate left since the sweat flow stopped. I could pick up pieces of the conversation while I worked and occasionally interjected into the conversation when I was close to them. Clive was a retired high school teacher, having taught English and Literature for over thirty years in a school district a few towns over from here.

He effortlessly proclaimed in his glorious English accent, "How he did his best to correct and to teach countless New Jersey young persons from botching the English language with their wretched New Jersey speech. It was a gallant, but sadly, a fruitless effort for the most part, but at least a few students learned to use the letter r and to pronounce coffee without turning the letter o into a prolonged and awful a-w-w-w- sound."

He was born in Manchester City in England, his family moved to Trafford Park, England when he was a young boy, eventually he received his education from Leed's University, and of course, moved to America in pursuit of the now infamous Matilda and as he stated, "Many other cruel reasons other than her long legs." Recently, he purchased a small townhouse on the outskirts of the city in a newer development to spend his retirement years. He always consumed four gin and tonic cocktails, along with ice water. Apparently, Clive was a renaissance man, who knew very little, if any, boundaries. He had his long career in teaching. He wrote poems and books and papers, painted in oils to create artwork, and traveled the world while accumulating, as he reported, "A little bit of knowledge about many different things."

"I need to settle my tab for today, dear Gilly. I see the waves and throngs of a different crowd moving into your establishment, as the older crowd readies for an evening of snoozing by the telly, and most, if not all of them, will be out cold by seven in the evening. As much as I despise wandering out into the heat, I pray that most of the heat of the day has now become a bit of a memory," Clive said with a smile while he reached for his wallet. He quickly added, "First, you need to tell me about the crows."

I nodded and while pushing the buttons on the computer monitor that was now my cash register, I told him the now very familiar tale. Clive handed off cash for his tab, and when I made change and attempted to hand it over to him, he simply waved for me to keep the remaining money. I thanked him while studying his eyes. The clear blue color of his eyes reflected some of the down lights of the soffit of the bar, and he remained silent and pensive for a few seconds before commenting.

"Such a glorious tale, and I thank you for sharing it with me. The crows strategically landing on that high wire and invoking inspiration for Mr. Coates is most unique and interesting. He cast the role of the crows perfectly here. They do flock together and have a chatter all their own, they are intelligent, which I think the majority of the people here are." Clive paused and added a touch of his wit to his statement, "Well, I am sure there are a few dumb-dumb crows here and there. Anyway, crows are resilient. They improvise and adapt. Did you know that they label a gathering of crows a murder? A most unusual name, but true."

I leaned in and said, "No. Never knew that one. Thank you for sharing that fact. It is a strange name."

Clive agreed and added, "Crows even mourn their dead and conduct a funeral of sorts. Mostly, they try to figure out why one of their own met their demise. And they remember faces of humans too. Never fiddle around with a crow, or be mean to it because they make note of your behavior, recognize you, and share the information with their murder. So interesting . . . anyway, this has been a most pleasurable and memorable go-round for passing the time on a sultry and nasty summer afternoon. Your testimony of the drinks and of your establishment is accurate, and it allowed me some shelter from the heat and time to share intellect and companionship with a remarkable collection of blokes. Mr. Coates was quite wise to make note of the occurrence that the crows shared with him and he proved to be even wiser by using it to his advantage. Such a catchy name, which no doubt, lured many a folk in here over the years. As it did for me. Now that I am somewhat of a local here, my inkling is that I shall wander in here often, in fact, every Tuesday afternoon and it is now my favorite haunt. Once more thank you for an enjoyable time, but I must wander on my way. As a chap from my homeland wrote a few years back, I wandered lonely as a cloud." He slid off the stool, caught his balance and with a wave and a nod of his head, Clive mumbled, "Cheerio."

He was gone. I looked up the words he repeated, and it did not surprise me that he was quoting from one of the most famous poems of William Wordsworth, a famous English romantic poet. I would learn that literature never wandered far from Clive's mind.

True to his words, for many years, on every Tuesday and occasionally a few days in between, Clive Barrows Peepers always made his way to that particular barstool. If a person occupied "Clive's barstool," or what slowly became known as the post for the Wise Sage of the Last Barstool, often that person would relinquish it on his or her own due to his legendary status, or Clive would settle in close to his home stool and move if it became unoccupied. He always mumbled something about how his ass, or as he called it, his bum, felt comfortable in that particular stool; even if I could not guarantee that, we did not mix the stool up with the others during the mopping of the floors and the cleaning of the stools.

"It does not matter much, dear Gilly . . . it is more of an aura than it is a fact. Is that not our life? More aura than fact?"

So, of course, there is the story behind meeting Clive for the first time, and my prediction of how interesting and special the relationship would be certainly proved to be true as the years went on.

"Straight shots of Irish whiskey and no chasers of water, eh? My dear, Billy Squire, you need to hydrate my dear lad or tomorrow the Devil will dance on your brain and your stomach will spin on its axis. If I must say and comment, you have a fervent look in your eyes of deep determination. From your intense pounding on the keys of that laptop computer . . . it tells me of some type of mission for your work that has now captured your heart and soul within a vise of words," Clive commented to his drinking mate, Mr. Billy Squire, who sat a few barstools away. Clive spoke with a hint of wisdom in his voice and an intense study of Billy with his eyes. At that point, I did not know how those simple words and Clive's wise suggestion would be a prelude to a conversation and event that lives forever within my mind. Clive took a sip of his gin and tonic while studying Billy Squire carefully out of the corner of his eye. Billy nodded to me, and I read his mind. Clive was correct about keeping hydrated and I previously offered the water, but Billy refused. I guess the wisdom and the aura of Clive remained much more convincing than mine was. I poured a glass of ice water and carried it over to Billy. With a mumbled, "Thanks" Billy continued to tap away on the keys of his laptop, but with a little less intensity on the keys than he previously had typed, since Clive made his observation. I tucked a foot on the inside bar rail to take some pressure off my lower back. Standing on your feet for long days and continuous hours while weighing much more than was good for me took a toll on my lower back and my legs too. I made a vow to lose some weight and soon. In honesty, that was a vow that I made many times before and would likely make many more times more in the future.

Billy Squire was a young newspaper journalist for the large newspaper out of Newark, and he wrote pieces for the on-line blogs for the paper, made the rounds of some local radio and television shows and spread his rather strong and biased opinions on a variety of subjects. Mostly, Billy spoke of, and wrote of, politics. Ah yes, politics. The root of such intense opinions and discussions and, in some cases, the root of all, evil. I could not understand how he yielded a double-edged sword with his words. An unbiased newspaper journalist does not give the perception of being an activist and go around broadcasting his opinions. In my opinion, either you are a news reporter or you are an activist. The gate does not open and swing on both sides of the fence. Billy was well educated and highly opinionated and the epitome of an "angry young man." Deep down, Billy was a decent guy; he was simply and factually a young man who always carried a chip on his shoulder. Billy was highly antiestablishment, and it was easy to light his fuse with the simplest of opinions that he overheard. Many times, I had to calm Billy down, threaten to haul his ass out and toss him on the sidewalk and ask him to be respectful of others during his time here. Billy was short, skinny, and slightly nerdish in his appearance, but very handsome in a different sort of way. He wore his hair very short, neat and stylish, with close-cut black hair, combined with a light beard shaved to a constant array of stubble to present an ever-present five o'clock shadow. Over his eyes, he wore thick framed, oversized black eyeglasses, which appeared as if they were out of fashion for the last twenty years or thereabouts. I often overheard some of the younger females lament that despite his appealing good looks, his brash demeanor made him well, rather unappealing. Unfortunately, his short stature and lightweight frame gave him the classic "little guy" syndrome, as well as his aggressive chip. And often, those two traits were a volatile combination. I did not enjoy disciplining regular crows, but sometimes, it is a necessary job here at the pub. After all, this is New Jersey and arguing and causing some type of ruckus was an unofficial state sport. Despite his heralded status as a "celebrity", other pub-goers and the regulars that knew Billy did not like him nor did his fellow patrons enjoy his company. The exception, of course, was Clive Peepers. Everyone else tended to steer clear and sit far away when Billy was around. Politics was his number one subject followed closely by local sports, then anything else that he could argue about, or any subject that leaned toward controversial. He usually floated in on Tuesday and Wednesdays and tapped away notes on his laptop for his pieces in order to meet his Friday deadline.

I read his work, but honestly, I did not agree with most of what he wrote. He was a regular customer, so I was very careful about making any comments on his work. Long ago, Coatsie suggested that while working the bar and operating the pub, it might be best if I adhered to the motto of never discussing money, religion, and politics and especially so, since, I tended to have very conservative opinions that might not resonate with most of my customers here in liberal New Jersey. It was very good advice. The crowd of patrons frequenting the pub ranged from union tradesman, to schoolteachers such as Clive was, to local businesspersons, to the younger crowds of eclectic hipsters, musicians, artists and hippies, who wandered into the pub in order to listen to the musical acts. For the most part, all of these pub-goers tended to lean toward the left wing of politics and embrace borderline socialism as the preferred way of life these days. Looking at my tax bills, it sure did seem as if those in control in Trenton and the people running New Jersey already had us halfway there. I figured that next; they might tax my shoes for causing wear and tear to the sidewalks and my nose for breathing the common air, because virtually everything else was already subject to their incessant taxes.

Clive leaned back in his stool and folded his arms as if to signal to Billy to take a drink of the water. Billy sensed his study and stopped typing to take a drink of the ice water. He still had some whiskey in his glass and he picked that up and did not sip it, but instead, he swirled it around in the glass and seemed to ponder the status of the whiskey in the glass for a bit.

Billy could no longer hold back. The whiskey, the water, and Clive's persistence at drinking the water had lit his anti-establishment fuse. After all, Clive was acting as an authority figure over Billy and deep down, Billy knew that Clive was correct. Believe me when I told you that I am an expert on the study of human nature.

"It is this president, Clive!" Billy exploded. "He wants to build this bullshit border wall to keep out illegal immigrants, and it is bullshit!" Billy launched into what was apparently the subject of his angry typing this afternoon. After emphatically stating his opinion, Billy fervently dove back into an intense session of typing. Upon hearing the subject matter, some patrons nodded their heads and others tuned Billy out. A quick observation and a poll of the patron's faces told me it was an even split down the opinion middle. I went back to work, but kept a careful ear on this conversation. Clive seldom waded into controversial waters and he always tiptoed on the ledges of precariousness when it came to Billy Squire and his strong opinions. It seemed as if this time, Billy struck a nerve with Clive and the Wise Sage of the Last Barstool was going to jump into these particular waters.

"I see," Clive said in a low voice between sips, "I think the key word in your commentary might be the word, illegal."

Sensing a pushback out of the normally neutral and placid, Clive Peepers, Billy stopped typing and at first, he seemed very surprised to get a rise out of Clive, but after recovering and loading his argumentative cannons, he turned toward Clive and asked, "How so, Clive? I am not following you."

"Illegal, Billy."

Billy jumped into action to correct his word from a political point of view, "My apologies. I meant, to say, undocumented."

Clive smiled, and he watched as I poured a beer and dropped it in front of the man sitting next to Billy. Clive took a sip of his gin and tonic and rather quickly emptied the glass. Since that was number two, I knew what to do. I scooped the empty glass up, picked a fresh glass out of the dishwasher, and began to prepare a replacement drink for Clive. As I did so, I leaned in closely. This was getting good.

"Careful now, Billy. Playing on words is fine and well, but you know my profession and honestly, you know yours too. Wordplay can be dangerous."

I knew that Clive, in his role as the Wise Sage of the Last

Barstool, had hit home with his point because Billy lodged no protest.

Instead, Billy nodded a conceded defeat and stated, "Okay, yeah, they are technically . . . illegal." Billy held a long pause before speaking the word, "Illegal" and he almost choked on the word.

"Yes. Those that cross the border without proper authorization and admittance papers and orders are breaking the law. Spinning the descriptor word to soften the emotion distorts the fact. When you allow emotion to dictate the facts, then you get into trouble. Not only in politics but also in sports, in love, and in life. Remove the emotion and examine the facts. I love my football club and always will, but the facts remain that they are an awful club and have not won much of anything over the years. I will not distort the facts due to my love for them. Those officers stopping illegal breeching of borders, by ways and means and by using any legal and authorized method allowed to them by governing bodies are simply enforcing existing laws. Laws that have been around for a very long time. If you choose to speed and break the posted speed limit law and a police officer pulls you over and issues a ticket for your speeding infraction, then will you direct your anger at the police officer?"

Billy shrugged his shoulders and downed the last of his whiskey. He nodded to me and I put one finger up because I was pouring another beer. This was really starting to become very interesting as far as a debate goes. The wisdom of Clive versus the anger of Billy.

"I might. I might not, all depending on the circumstances."

"Why?" Clive jumped right on that comment.

"Because the speed limit might be silly in its restrictions." Billy immediately waved and nodded, because he anticipated Clive's response beforehand.

"I know, I know, the officer is just enforcing the posted

law. He did not establish the speed limit."

Clive nodded and smiled and asked, "So, this president and his administration of which you direct your anger to . . . did he create the border crossing laws? I seem to recall the same restrictions when I came into this country many years ago and I chose to obey them. If I recall basic government structure in America, of which a few parts and pieces are similar to the United Kingdom's structure, the president does not pass laws . . . I think it comes from Congress. Nor does he enforce them. I think the Attorney General is the ultimate law enforcer, eh?" Billy nodded, and his temples throbbed. His anger was mounting because his defense position weakened. "Billy, it seems to me that you are taking it out on the monkey for dancing to lousy organ grinder music. The organ grinder is playing the tunes, not the monkey."

"But these poor people are fleeing despair and strife and have little economic options. Where is the compassion of humanity? When you came to America, you had an education and were not fleeing turmoil and strife and despair."

In all the years I knew Clive, I never saw him grow angry or raise his voice, nor did he ever disrespect any one person. His humor was always present, his mannerisms gentle, and while he might have had three wives and assorted complaints about them all, he seemed to have elements of love when he spoke about them, or rarely, but occasionally, other family members.

"One of the major troubles with your generation and a few others behind you is that you have forgotten history. On the other hand, perhaps, in your defense the trouble, dear Billy, is with this present education system here in America. A system in which I was intimately involved in for most of my time here in America. I often debated heatedly with the history teachers in my school and with my fellow faculty members, because nowadays, we teach history with revisions. How can you revise something historical and based upon facts? It is ludicrous!"

Clive took a sip of his gin and tonic from the glass and slammed the glass down upon the bar counter and his eyes glowed as everyone in the pub jumped up and nearly shed their skin.

Clive Barrows Peepers was heating up his burners.

"To set the record straight and factual, the Germans did not exactly treat us too kindly, in the big wars, Billy! On the other hand, did you forget that part or perhaps, your teachers, educators and professors decided to skip over that part?" Clive's eyes narrowed and you could sense his anger at the facts. "They feel as if it is too intense of a subject to teach young people. Besides, it makes the world seem as if there are evil people living in it. These modern-day educators enjoy sugarcoating the truth. Well, guess what, the world is full of evil people, Billy." Clive lowered his voice a little and for a second or two, he lowered his head and hovered over his gin and tonic before lifting his head and continuing to state his thoughts. It seemed as if the pauses provided Clive with strength and allowed him to gather his thoughts.

"Regardless of the anguish that we were fleeing from in my homeland, I chose to come into this country legally. Despite the fact that we were Allies in the wars, and the authority that was in charge of regulating admittance to this great country knew very well of our circumstances in England and the entire United Kingdom, the admission officials here in America turned away my lover and I two times and sent us back to England. When she finally gained admittance on the third attempt, and I did not, I returned to my homeland without her. It took me four tries before I finally gained admittance. And, I could work and had a higher level of education! Other than a short stint in Australia, I have stayed here for all these years. I kept dual-citizenship for a long period of time, before becoming an

American citizen, but regardless, I never broke laws and I worked diligently, paid taxes, produced, and provided many, many children a decent education. Are there massive large-scale invasions by evil countries in Mexico, or in Central America?"

Billy cleared his throat and offered a rebuttal, "No wars, but, Clive, many are fleeing evil drug cartels and economic conditions that ravage their lives."

Clive responded, "A little different from my situation, but if they are truly victims of terrorism and poor economics, then, fine, go ahead and follow the correct process, state your case, apply for admittance as I did and see how it goes. Do not break laws and then cry foul! I am sorry, Billy, there may be some people fleeing tragic situations, but the overwhelming majority of these people only seek rainbows and unicorns. In my opinion, it is all horseshit because the large majority of people simply want to come here to America because they want everything for free. They are mostly takers and not producers." After speaking, Clive studied Billy for a reaction or words, but Billy remained silent. Clive's emotions continued to overwhelm his spirit and after a careful study of Billy, Clive spoke once more.

"You used some words that stoked a fire that long ago went out, dear Billy."

Billy seemed puzzled and said, "Words. What words?"

Now Clive lit it up, "Strife and despair. Strife you say! Despair! Ha! You think that I simply chased long legs and a skirt across the pond. You know nothing of my situation. However, dear Billy, now, I will share it with you since you claimed that when I arrived here in America that I was not fleeing turmoil and strife and despair. Good chap, look up the Battle of Britain, or better yet, the Manchester Blitz or Christmas Blitz on that laptop and you will see strife and despair. My family moved to Trafford Park right before the war in order to find work and they found work indeed.

Trafford Park was where various manufacturers produced engines for the RAF aircraft, and the city and the entire area remained strategic shipping ports as well as key manufacturing areas. The Germans showed us no mercy. They mercilessly bombed the city and the area in and around Christmas in 1940 and leveled it. Hellfire rained from the skies. My hometown was in rubble during and even after the war and many people died in civilian functions, as well as in combat during the war. Many. Too many. All of my family . . . gone. Every, single, one of them." Clive lowered his eyes and then raised them again before saying, "For some reason, I was spared. Now, I am just a young man, actually, just a child and my family members are all dead. Dead from evil bombs dropped by an enemy flying above us in the sky or they were killed later on during service within the military with bullets and bombs and grenades and other awful weapons while serving in combat action. My grandmother, my mother and my father, my sister and my brother, all died while decorating our family Christmas tree, my uncles, aunts, and cousins were sleeping in their beds. Our homes were dust. I was the little boy asleep in his bed while dreaming of Christmas magic. I survived. Why? I do not know. I am all alone now. Can you pause, push aside emotions, concentrate on the facts, and imagine that? What would you do, Billy?"

Clive now stood up from his barstool, and I stood by, watching the scene carefully unfold. This was disruptive to the other patrons, but we are a family here, and Clive earned his title of the Wise Sage of the Last Barstool for good reasons. I knew that he deserved to share his story and his opinions and his experiences. The emotions ravaged his normally eloquent speech, and his body shook as the pain chased away from it. His lower lip quivered in passion, and in an effort to steady it, Clive bit his lip and forcibly held it closed. He pointed his finger and waved his hand across the bar, and then, he pointed to the entire pub, while silence slowly fell over the pub. Out of respect for this great man, televisions and music turned down in volume and conversations stopped. Clive slid out of his barstool and wiped the tears away from his eyes. He waved his arms across the entire population of the pub and encompassed each and every person. Everyone respected Clive enough to listen and realize the poignancy of the moment and the unimaginable horrors of which he experienced to create such emotion. I could see from the looks on many faces and the body language that not all the patrons agreed with his opinions, but they did respect him. Perhaps, when he delivered the final element of his speech, then many more would agree with him. I am not the judge here, just a Publican, but there was no doubt that his story drilled into many hearts and souls on this monumental afternoon.

Clive raised his voice while asking, "What would any of you do if the sky above you right now here in Bloomfield, New Jersey filled with enemy planes and they dropped bombs on your houses, killed your mother and father and grandparents and a sister and a brother, your cousins, and some of your neighbors? If they dropped bombs on your workplaces, on your streets and on this pub? If the streets here were piles of rubble and the houses and buildings and places of business were piles of smoke and dust and the bodies of your neighbors and your friends and your loved ones were inside of the rubble holding them as if they were fortresses of death. Tombs constructed of evil. The German bastards even destroyed the pitch and leveled the football stadium for the Manchester United Football Club! What would be your reaction to seeing your famous and beloved Yankee Stadium in ruins? What would you do? I humbly ask of you all." Clive lowered his head and shook it, and in retrospect, he turned away to hide his tears and emotions.

"What would you . . . do?" Clive's question was barely

audible even above the ensuing silence.

No one dared to move a muscle in the entire pub as his question resonated within all of our hearts and minds.

Clive nodded, waved, and slid back onto his barstool while saying, "I know what you would do," Clive answered his own question; "you would do what we did and even the score. We did not start that wretched war but with the help of America and the Russians and other great nations, we damn sure helped to end it." Clive waved his hand in the direction of the population and bowed his head and in a low whisper said, "Please, my apologies for the interruption and disruption of your glorious time here at the pub today. Gilly, I am very sorry for allowing my emotions to capture me. My sincerest apologies, dear chap."

"No apologies are required, Clive. None at all. My condolences on the tragedies inflicted upon your loved ones and friends. My sincerest condolences upon hearing of the loss of your entire family," I said.

Now I knew why, other than his ex-wives, he never mentioned any family.

He had none.

It was very easy to see that the dark and heartfelt testimony of Clive, profoundly affected Billy, and many, many other patrons too.

Billy lowered his head, sipped his whiskey and mumbled, "Clive . . . I am so sorry. I had no idea."

Regret embraced his posture, and tears filtered within his eyes.

Oh, this glorious pub, the discussion it brings, the people that meet here, the world that we share, and the insight that we learn.

Clive recovered and the entire pub remained silent as he closed his rebuttal to a now speechless Billy, "Please my dear, Billy, with all due respect and I mean no malice, but please, don't you dare ask me ever again about the whereabouts of the compassion of humanity. Furthermore, my dear Billy, I ask you . . . do you want to be an activist or a journalist? Only you can decide what to write and what you feel in your heart. Please, decide soon, because you cannot be both and serve your readers fairly and without bias or remain true to your own soul."

Clive finished his drink, smiled and nodded at me and said, "Please, my final cocktail, Gilly, and a glass of water too. Thank you. Excuse me. I need to visit the loo."

Off Clive went, and Billy downed his whiskey, peeled off more than enough money to pay his tab and to provide a tip, and he dropped the cash on the bar and pointed at it.

"Thanks, Gilly. You are the man."

He finished his ice water, closed his laptop, and tucked it under his arm. Billy looked at me for a few seconds, then his eyes stared at Clive's empty barstool. Without speaking another word, Billy executed a slow slide off the stool. His feet hit the floor, and he quickly headed for the front door.

Billy Squire changed after that day and as a result of that conversation. He no longer was an angry young man. I thought that in my opinion, he became a writer and a journalist. Either his strong opinions and activist tendencies remained tossed aside or he kept them to his own mind and soul and he chose not to share them and stick them in people's faces as he once did.

When I anxiously opened the newspaper on that Friday morning to read his column, I almost cried out in shock at the subject matter.

It was a glorious piece entitled, "The Wise Sage of the Last Barstool."

Now, in my mind there remained little question which career path that Billy Squire chose.

The article paid great homage to a history lesson about an awful war and the commitment that so many made for us to be able to sit here in this pub, and to debate, argue, compromise, love, learn, share in each other's lives and be free to do so.

A history lesson that rather shamefully, if not for Mr. Clive Barrows Peepers, we might have all lost along the way.

There were many other stories of adventures with Mr. Clive Barrows Peepers and profound and wise statements that he told us, words that he shared that stuck in our minds forever, and other wonderful aspects of his life that he shared with us. Clive taught us more than just about life and love, he also taught us about our hearts and our souls. I could go on and on over countless pages, sharing the words and wisdom of Clive. Suffice it to say that he was much more than just a colorful character. He exuded the essence of what the Crows on a High Wire Public House represented. He was one of the crows. The last one on the far left of the high wire.

His humor pervaded most of his presence. A great example of his deep and profound humor was the time when Father James from Saint Peter's Catholic Church, stopped in for an after-mass celebration, and the good priest launched into a drink-induced mini-homily of why Clive required religion in his life.

Clive, who mentioned God quite often, but never shared his deep religious thoughts, told Father James over sips of his gin and tonic, "Careful now where you tread, Father James. Religion is the world's second oldest profession."

There was the time that he told a horrified mother of a solo singer performing one night that, "Her daughter's singing reminded him of when he howled in pain when he caught the skin of his male parts in the zipper of his pants."

In a meager defense of Clive, the mother did ask for his opinion of her daughter's performance and Clive was three drinks into his session.

Not only did he share humorous moments with us, but he also shared his wisdom and his intelligence and his love of words and literature and his many stories of travels and best of all—he shared his love of life with us.

There were many sides to Clive, and we were lucky to have him with us for a very long time.

A time that sadly, one early autumn day, came to an abrupt and sudden end.

It was on the third Tuesday in a row that pub-goers, and I realized that we had not seen Clive for a number of weeks. That in and of itself was not unusual, but if Clive was going on "holiday" as he would call it—he usually told us. He shared his address with me. On birthday cards, Christmas cards, and such and when a month went by, I stopped by his townhouse to find it vacant and a for sale sign posted on the lawn in front of it. I inquired about his status from some neighbors, but no one really knew Clive, or knew a specific reason as to why the townhouse was for sale. His immediate neighbors on each side of his home were not at home, and his status was disturbing and puzzling. Why would he not have said goodbye? Clive wouldn't have left us like that. We all feared the worst.

His pub family all hoped and prayed for the best.

Our questions were answered a day or so after I visited the home when a gentleman stopped in the pub shortly after I opened for the day at three in the afternoon.

"Mr. Xavier Gilford?" the man asked, while taking off his hat and tucking in under his arm. He was dressed in a fine suit and a tie and certainly, he did not look as if he stopped in for a quick nip or an afternoon drink. In his other hand, he held a large, felt cardboard box with an envelope taped to the front of it.

"Yes, I am, Xavier Gilford. I am the owner of this pub.

How might I help you? Please, call me Gilly."

"Oh, okay, Gilly. Well, I am Laurence Goldstein, ah, ah, Attorney Laurence Goldstein and my legal firm and I represent the estate of Mr. Clive Barrows Peepers."

I am sure that my face turned ashen at his words and the realization that the worst fears of the status of Clive came to fruition. I held onto the edge of the bar counter to steady reaction.

Seeing my reaction, Mr. Goldstein nodded and affirmed the worst.

"Yes, I am very sorry to inform you of his death. Mr. Barrows passed on about a month or so ago. I know that he always told me you were one of his greatest friends. He did not have many, but Clive counted you, Mr. Gilford. Ah, I mean, Gilly, amongst them. In fact, you are at the top of the list. Here are my credentials." Attorney Goldstein handed me his business card, as well as a lamented placard of some sort with his picture, information, and a legal seal imprinted on it for an official identification. I examined the placard, nodded, and handed it back to him, but I slid the business card into my shirt pocket.

"This is awful. So terrible. Clive was a genuine legend here. More than just a friend, a customer, or an acquaintance. He was a special man. I wish that I knew of his passing. I, as well as many others of his pub family here would have liked to attend his funeral."

The attorney shook his head and explained, "There was no service. Just a cremation. Mr. Barrows was a very private individual. He left my firm with very specific instructions about his passing. His ashes were spread over the campus of Leed's University back in his native England and a handful on the street outside of his boyhood home."

"Oh. I understand. Thank you, Please, excuse me. I need to pour a whiskey to steady me out a bit. This news is very upsetting and quite sad."

"Of course, I understand. I can see how upset you are. I

am very sorry to deliver the sad news, but Clive lived a long and glorious life. If it is some consolation, he passed very peacefully, in his sleep one evening. His cleaning lady found him in his easy chair, with a book in his lap. Just the way that Clive would want to leave this world. Immersed within a world of words."

I nodded in affirmation and even felt a bit of a smile break across my mouth at the situation of his demise. "I agree. Words were his life. We all should meet such a peaceful end. Still, it is sad. Mr. Goldstein, do you want a shot too?" I asked. Then quickly added, "In his honor."

At first, Attorney Goldstein held his hand up and shook his head, "no," and he mumbled something about working, and then when he heard the word "honor," he nodded and pointed at the Irish whiskey bottle that I was pouring my drink from and he held two fingers up and smiled while saying, "Sure. Please, make it a double. In his honor."

I poured the drinks and handed Mr. Goldstein the glass. We held our drinks in the air, and I proclaimed, "To Clive Barrows Peepers. A great man, a great mind, and an even greater friend. Here! Here!"

We touched glasses and downed our drinks in honor of the great Clive Peepers.

"Please forgive the formality and legalities, but I am an attorney and there are items bequeathed to you in the settling of his estate. Please, Gilly, do you have your identification?"

I nodded and said, "I understand."

I pulled my wallet out and tried to hide my surprise at the news that Clive had left me something from his life. I handed Attorney Goldstein my driver's license. He carefully examined it, and after copying the number and information down, he handed it back to me.

"Thank you. I will need you to come to my office in the next few days to sign many papers and such, but at first, I wanted to give you these items and this note from Clive in a more informal setting. It was in Clive's instructions to inform you of his passing, his wishes and his intentions right here at your pub."

My shift manager, Ashley Stokes, wandered out of the back room and when she saw the sadness in my face and saw that I was engaged, she excused herself and whispered, "There is a delivery in the back. I have it. You okay, Gilly? Is this bad news about, Clive?" Ashley was brilliantly smart and her mind quickly surmised what the situation was. She gently touched my arm, and I rested my hand on hers while she studied my face for a reaction.

"I am, okay. Yes. Thanks for handling that for me, Ash. It is Clive. He passed away." Sadness crept in over Ashley's face, and her eyes brimmed with tears.

"I did not know him as well as you did, but Clive was so cool. I am so sorry, Gilly. He was such a special person. I know how close you two were. I will take care of the delivery."

"Thank you, Ashley. I will be there shortly."

Attorney Goldstein handed me the flat box, and he tore the card off the front of the box and handed the card to me, too. With his eyes, the attorney begged me to open them. I opened the box and slid out an elegant black picture frame of considerable size. Holding it up, I saw that it was a beautiful reproduction print of Clive's favorite poem, "I Wandered Lonely as a Cloud" by William Wordsworth. I carefully studied it and marveled at its wonder.

"He often quoted from this poem. It is glorious. It will hang over the bar." I turned and pointed at the last stool where Clive usually sat and added, "Over there is his barstool. I will add a brass plaque to the bar too."

Attorney Goldstein nodded and said, "It is a beautiful piece. It hung in his living room. He treasured it. His house was rather barren of pictures and decorations and such. He had many books and papers but that was just about the only wall hanging. Please open the card."

I slid my finger under the flap and pulled out the card and for some reason, because these were the words of Clive, and we were together for the last time in The Crows on a High Wire Public House, I felt the need to read it aloud.

"Hello Gilly. By now, you know that I have met my demise. Please do not be sad. Now, I can wander through many clouds and read many books. There might not be any gin or much tonic, but there is peace. Of that, I am quite sure. There are endless books too. I am quite sure of that because a world without books is the equivalent of Hell. I hope you find a nice spot in the pub for the poem. The words always gave me comfort. I left a small gift for you and one for your daughter. Mr. Goldstein will take care of it.

Thank you for being such a wonderful friend and allowing me to be one of the crows. You are a brilliant man, my friend. You hide your wisdom in a strategic disguise that is opaque and covert. Nonetheless, I was able to see through it. You do not just operate and own a pub; you realize that it is a haven of bliss. A niche for friends to become a family and you nurture that and grow it. Of course, your soul is kind and caring and that, my friend, is worth more than any other human attribute is. My wandering into your pub on that hot summer day of what is now many years ago was a stroke of luck for me and it brought me such joy in my life. I hope that the next occupant of the last barstool will invoke some glorious memories and enhance the world of the crows, as you have done for me.

Regards and cheers,

Clive Barrows Peepers."

I wiped away the tears.

More arrived.

Attorney Goldstein left me with a handshake and instructions to make an appointment with his assistant to meet him in his office in order to sign papers and learn of the rest of the will details. A few days later, when meeting with Attorney Goldstein in his office, the shock of learning that Clive left seventy-five thousand dollars to my wife and me in trust for our daughter's college education was more than overwhelming. It was unworldly.

Our daughter, Connie, was now in high school and she had aspirations about writing and literature. About eight months ago, when I shared some of her works with Clive, his eyes glowed and his excitement and praise of Connie's work was something that I will never forget.

"Your daughter has amazing talents. We need to encourage these talents. I will make it my mission, with you and your wife's permission, to assist in her education and endeavors right now. And beyond."

Of course, my wife Erma and I agreed. Surely, there was no better teacher for Connie than the amazing Clive Barrows Peepers. He offered assistance, tips and education in the ways of writing and Connie sat with him many times, and leaned on his wisdom, his words and his encouragement. I now understood the "beyond" aspect of Clive's statement. Clive also left ten thousand dollars to put toward maintenance of the air-conditioning systems of Crows, to, in his words, "Keep the bloody awful heat at bay." The reminder of his money was a donation to Leed's University.

The framed poem sits above the bar on the overhanging soffit, right above the last barstool on the right side. There is an elegant brass plaque screwed to the edge of the bar at the last barstool location. About a week later, after the estate settlement reached a conclusion, I closed the pub for the day. Except for all the regular crows that all knew, Clive Barrows Peepers. Crows always gather and they mourn a loss of their own. We held a memorial service for him around his barstool. It seems corny as hell, but it was actually touching. We shared "the best of Clive", we laughed, and drank and ate, and most of all we shared some of the wise words that he taught to all of us. We shared our love for an amazing man and gave thanks for the fact that he wandered into the Crows on a High wire Public House on, as he said, "That bloody awful, miserable, hot day."

Billy Squire read the Wordsworth poem in its entirety while I screwed the special brass plate in place on the edge of the bar, right in front of his stool.

All that the plate has printed on it is an engraving in script-type print that proudly and simply proclaimed, "Mr. Clive Barrows Peepers."

Actually, that is all that it really needs to say.

Chapter Three

Ms. Noel Walker

Love, Peace, and Rock and Roll

It was a quiet and lazy Wednesday afternoon, when I first met the eclectic but gorgeous and intriguing Ms. Noel Walker. Ashley and I were working at the bar, with only one or two servers on the floor. It was late summer, nearing the Labor Day weekend, and many regular crows and not so regular crows were fleeing town to head to the Jersey Shore for a last gasp at sand, surf, fun, and glory. Hence, the reason for the quiet and lazy afternoon.

You have to live in New Jersey and understand the shore culture to understand what it means to the state and what it represents. Those living in the northern part of the state envy the shore dwellers and those living along the shore envy the northern dwellers. One has the proximity to New York City, the other large cities, and the nightlife, the sports, the restaurants (and pubs) the music scene and other activities and attractions and the other has the aforementioned, sand, surf, fun, and glory.

I had just dropped a glass of Irish whiskey along with a glass of ice water next to the now reformed Billy Squire, who had his head buried in a notebook while feverishly making pencil notes on the paper with various ideas that he had for his latest bestseller. Billy left the newspaper business shortly after writing the piece about Clive Peepers and Billy used his publishing connections in order to assist him while he struck out on a new career as a fiction writer. The piece that he wrote brought much critical acclaim to Billy and brought him to the crossroads of a decision. It was much as Clive predicted, where it was time for Billy to make a decision on his ultimate career path. In a lean to his formally volatile ways and his strong political opinions, Billy began to pen political thrillers. His first novel hit the big-time and the book quickly rose to near the top of the bestseller's list. It was a nail-biting storyline about a murder plot against the President of the United States with a complex and contrived plot of the higher ups in the president's own administration being the culprits behind the murder plan and resulting intrigue. These types of books were not my particular favorite, in fact, until I met Clive Peepers, reading was not high on my valuable and limited leisure time list, but now that Clive taught me the value of words and the mystery of books, I read quite a bit. My favorites were romantic novels, and I covertly downloaded them onto my e-reader while hiding in the closets or the bathrooms of our home, in hopes that my wife would not catch me reading sappy romantic bullshit, but I suspected she knew.

Wives know everything.

I did read Billy's book and found it a great taste in escapism, fun, and well written, but once more, I was this giant man with a huge belly, and a softie heart for teary-eyed, romantic weepiness. Anyway, Clive is proud of Billy and I guess even if it is teary-eyed, romantic weepiness that has me immersed in the magic of books; I imagine that he is proud of me, too.

After dropping the drinks for Billy, I turned away, and that is when I first saw her make her way through the front door of the pub. She caught my eye, and it was like some sappy scene from those silly romantic novels that I spent some of my leisure time with my nose in. The sun shone all around her while it leaked past the shades on the front windows, and it created a display of rays of sunlight around her as she swayed and bounced down the main aisle of the pub and made her way to the front area where the bar was. A few male patrons stopped in their conversations and in mid-sips of their drinks in order to catch a glimpse of her while she made her way through the maze of tables and chairs. She was that kind of woman. Her dress was long and flowing, and it gently wisped around her ankles while she walked. No doubt that she was that kind of gal. To clarify, she was a head-turner with her mere presence. Her dress had a red and gold paisley pattern printed on a primarily white background. The dress had a high neckline trimmed with frilly and elegant white lace, and sleeves trimmed with the same. Despite the loose fit of her dress and the high neckline, there remained little doubt of the glory hidden within the dress. She swayed and flowed and her hips moved alluringly, and her generous breasts bounced underneath the frill.

Now, my gorgeous wife is certainly the most beautiful woman that I ever laid my eyes upon and I never wander, not that any other woman other than my wife would ever care for entertaining me. What my wife sees in a giant, overweight glob of a man with no hair and two pierced ears with golden hoops, I will never understand, but regardless, she loves me and I love her. Forever. Yet, as I watched this lovely woman make her way toward the front of the pub, I felt my entire body twitch. Remember, I am an observer and detailer of people; it is part of my job.

It was more than her beauty; it was her style, her persona, the way that she walked, and the way that she carried her body. Her hair was a golden color, similar to honey, and her hair was long, almost to her waist, but braided into two even braids that tumbled down over her shoulders and along her back. The sunlight from the front windows still surrounded her while she walked. She slung a brown macramé type of purse over her shoulder that appeared as if it was homemade. In fact, her dress could have been homemade, too. Even the open-toed sandals that flapped on her feet while she walked appeared homemade. Around her neck, she wore a necklace that gently rested upon her breasts. The necklace was a red ruby shaped in a heart, hanging upon a golden chain. It was a unique and unusual piece of jewelry and it, too, shone as she did. She approached the bar, smiled at me, and I shook off the awestruck, dopey behavior . . . or I tried my best to shake off my fascination. Her facial features were a study in perfection, soft and sculpted, and forever memorable. Her lips were pale and had the appearance as if they were soft pillows. Her lips were void of any lipstick, as her face was void of makeup. This woman was a natural beauty; she did not require any enhancements. Her nose was thin and long, but perfect for her face and her eyes were brown and the edges rimmed with tiny gold specks . . . I guess, that you can tell that I was struggling in the "shaking out of the fascination" behavior.

"Hi, there. I am Noel Walker and you are?" Her voice was soft yet sultry in its lower end resonations. She extended her hand, and I reached out from over the bar and clasped her hand. Her hands were warm and, for a petite woman, her grip was surprisingly strong.

"Hello, Noel. It is nice to meet you. I am Xavier Gilford, but please, call me, Gilly. Everyone does. Xavier sounds like an elegant name, but I am sure that it is a product of some very bad weed that my parents smoked in the early nineteen-eighties. I am the owner, the chief bartender, the maintenance man, as well as the bookkeeper and the general all-around schlep here at The Crows on a High Wire Public House."

A wide smile revealed perfect white teeth, and the smile remained until the words arrived, "Nice to meet you, Gilly, I have no comment on your parent's choice of recreation that might have led to the origin of your first name of Xavier. Regardless, it is a very cool name and I find it fascinating how perfectly that your nickname fits you."

Her eyes studied me and I have to admit to studying her for a few seconds, too.

"Anyway, I am here to scout out the pub for the band tonight. I am with Slippery Slopes."

I now noticed that all eyes were on us. I think the entire population of pub-goers now focused on our discussion. Especially the male patrons, including Billy Squire. This gal must be something special in order to pry Billy's eyes away from his precious notebook.

I caught myself and yet, I still stammered a bit. No, not a bit, I stammered a lot!

"Ah, yeah, okay, a band, huh? Ah . . . who? Did you say that we are on a slippery slope? I think we are all on a slippery slope, Noel. Some more than others, but slippery nonetheless."

Noel laughed, and when she did so it seemed as if the world stood still. It was that type of laugh. It was not a belly laugh or a forced laugh, it was the type of laugh that projected joy and innocence at the same time. I guess you could use the word "genuine" to describe her laugh, but I prefer joy. It only took a few brief moments in Noel's presence to determine that this woman was all about joy. While Noel laughed at my ineptness and my use of humor to offset the fact that I might be the owner of this joint, but most of the time, I am a clueless dope.

"The band's name is Slippery Slopes, Gilly."

As further proof of my point, I expanded on my stupidity.

"Okay. Gotcha. I think. I need to confess, Noel . . . that I did not know that a band named Slippery Slopes was playing this evening. One of my managers, Ashley, performs the booking for the acts and I tend to allow her the freedom to do her job. Are you a musician? How can I help you?"

Noel shook her head and said, "No, I am not a musician. Well, I tinkle the keys of some keyboards a little but not well enough to be on stage. I am the band's official and unofficial consultant of sorts. I set up the gigs, I do the soundboard and the set lists and handle the administrative and business stuff. I would like to check out the systems because this is our first gig here."

"Okay, cool. We can get you rolling. Please let me check on all of my folks here at the bar and then I will show you the board and the lights and such and give you a crash course in how it operates. Believe me—if I can do it then I assure you that it is not too sophisticated." I turned away, then stopped after a few steps, and then turned back toward Noel. I could not help but to ask, "Official or Unofficial consultant, huh?"

After asking, I looked at her out of the corner of my eye, while now moving to check on Billy's drink. Her gorgeous face filled with a warm blush. She fiddled with her hands and then picked up the ruby necklace, and she toyed with the stone.

"Yes. I guess. After all, life is all about peace, love, and rock-and-roll. Peace, such as you have in your heart, soul, and mind, when you hear the rain gently beating on your window in the middle of the night, or when the wind shakes the leaves in the trees in the autumn. Leaves that cling onto branches for dear life in a futile effort to linger just a little while longer to the place where they were born and grew up. Just as we often do when the wind rattles our homes. Love that is contained within your heart, soul, and mind, such as when your lover's heart beats in unison with yours after you make love and cling to each other. Or love as you feel when you hug your mother. And rock-and-roll, well," her smile was simply amazing and the beauty in her eyes almost brought me to my knees, "you have to dance to rock-and-roll, lose yourself in the words and in the pulse of the beat and make rock-and-roll music a religion. Otherwise, life is just too damn boring. Right, Gilly?"

I smiled and held onto the edge of the bar for dear life. We did not need my almost three-hundred pounds falling down on my big ass. It might take a crane to pick me up. I stole a quick glance at Billy Squire, and I found him writing intently in his notebook. He was writing feverishly and without pause, scratching out words as if his life was in the balance. I surmised from his intenseness that he was taking notes on what Noel said. I shook off the impact of her words and the magic of her presence.

While refilling Billy's ice water from the bar spout, I said, "Hell, yeah, Noel. Those were some amazing words. Works for me. Can I get you a drink? Drinks are on the house for the band and helpers . . . or official or unofficial consultants."

Her smile lit up our small world again. She slid on the barstool next to Billy and pulled her purse over her head and tucked it over the back of the stool. Her voice arrived on sound waves that waltzed sweetly and gently into our spaces, "Sure, thank you. Just some of that ice water. I will have something stronger later, but right now, water works. Hydration is the key before libation."

This chick was ultra-cool.

While filling the water glasses, it was then that I noticed the intense and unworldly stare of Billy Squire in the direction of Noel. His eyes were nearly bursting from his head and I never knew much of anything to pull Billy Squire out of his notebook when he was deep in thought. Before his reformation, a good political argument could do it or a debate over the New York Yankees versus any other team but a woman. No, no, no.

Then again, it was blatantly obvious that this was no

ordinary woman.

Noel glanced in the direction of Billy, and I surmised that she felt the burn of his stare. I mixed a bourbon and cola for a regular crow and casually glanced in the direction of their interaction while preparing the cocktail. I might have strayed from my mix of the concoction and lost count of the bourbon pour due to my interest in the interaction. That might be one helluva stiff-ass drink. If the regular crow lands on his ass and crawls for the front door, then I will know that I might have poured a little too much. Something inside of me, perhaps; it was the years of time behind a bar, or watching people, or a touch of my education, but I felt that this might be the beginning of something very special. Perhaps I will be right, or perhaps I will be wrong. Only time will tell.

"Hi. I am Noel. And, who might you be?"

I smiled as Billy stammered in his response. Billy never, ever stammered. He was cocky, self-assured, the master wordsmith, the man with the plan. The man on top of every syllable, every enunciation, and a man that only the words and poignant speech of Clive managed to set down on his ass.

Until he met Noel Walker, that is.

"Ah, yeah, ah, I am Billy. Ah, Billy Squire."

Her eyes danced across Billy's face, and then she focused on his ever-present notebook.

I thought while I delivered the cocktail to the regular, 'Hell, yeah, Billy has a chance.'

"Whatcha writing there, Mr. Billy Squire?"

Billy held his notebook up in the air demonstratively, as if to proclaim his purpose.

"General notes and an outline for a novel. My second novel. I am a novelist. My first book was a bestseller."

Noel blinked a few times, and her smile illuminated the bar counter more than any light fixture ever could.

"Okay, Billy Squire, very cool. Your first book was a

bestseller! That is awesome and now you are working on the second novel. So, let me ask you . . . what is the genre?"

"It *was* a political thriller. A follow-up to the first novel. This one was . . . you know . . . stereotypical with foreign spies that are working to steal military blueprints for an ultra-secret jet engine that can fly . . . ah, ah, you know . . . fast. Really fast and really high. As in damn high and damn fast. Outer Space high and, I dunno . . . it can fly super-fast. The engine is a game changer for dominance in air power amongst the world's superpowers. It becomes a struggle between good versus evil. How is that for a description?"

Poor Billy was losing his words and his mind in love at first sight.

Another blink from Noel, and her reply was in a voice just above a whisper. Her words drifted as if they were part of the air.

"Was? You speak as if it is all past tense now. It *was* a political thriller. What is it now?" Noel asked, and then she tucked a stray strand of hair behind her right ear while she waited for the answer. Billy held the notebook in the air once again, and I held my breath.

I thought, 'C'mon, Billy, you can do it! Geez, man, you are a writer! Find the words! Don't blow it!'

"I just now changed the plot to a romance. Ah, ah, it is going to be my first attempt at romance. I wrote down your explanation for love, peace, and rock-and-roll. Those were the most amazing words that I have ever heard. I am going to need your permission to quote them. I am also going to need your phone number and full contact information." He paused and winked at Noel and messed with his already unruly hair and made it more unruly, and then he pushed his thick frame glasses back up his nose and said, "Ah, not only for the book. I want your phone number . . . for me."

When I heard Billy's words and his response, I covertly fist pumped the air under the bar.

I thought, while concealing my fist pumping and

enthusiasm, 'Hell, yeah, Billy. You just nailed it! On a cloud somewhere, Clive is fist pumping too.'

Noel tugged at her ruby necklace and adjusted the stone upon her breasts, and I tried hard (in vain) not to focus on her chest and the white frilly lace of her dress. Her voice changed to become a little deeper, a little sultrier. And I am sure that Billy Squire's pen was almost ablaze in his hand.

In fact, I am surprised that the damn pen did not evaporate in flames of burning love!

"Well, now, I think we can arrange an exchange of contact info. You are quite the cutie, an adorable nerd all engrossed in words by scribbling in your notebook and creating your novels, and now, your sudden change in genres. We must get to know each other tonight, because I want to be your number one fan, and maybe, just a little bit more. A nerd and a hippie gal . . . this relationship promises to be awesome. I promise to be back. Right now, I have to meet Gilly and learn this soundboard. Please . . . do not go anywhere, Mr. Billy Squire."

"I am glued to the barstool, Noel."

She looked up at me and asked, "Are you free to show me the ropes, Gilly?"

I double-checked the bar, nodded, waved in the direction of the stage, and made my way from behind the bar. Noel slipped off the barstool, pulled her purse off the back, and winked at Billy as she made her way to the stage. When I passed Billy, he grabbed my arm, looked quickly to check on the whereabouts of Noel, and he pulled me in close for a quiet discussion.

"Gills, I am not as worldly as you are. . . I live in words on pages and in my characters and in a world, which is a product of my own mind. Tell me, please, is there such a thing as love at first sight?"

I studied his pleading eyes and patted his arm while the words came to my lips like an eruption.

"Hell, yeah, there is, Billy. I knew when I saw my wife at

her first glance at me that she was the one for me. My heart melted. It still melts when she looks at me. I guess it always will."

Billy smiled, looked over his shoulder at Noel, and he whispered, "Thanks, Gilly. You da man."

"I try."

Confession time! Xavier "Gilly" Gilford is not an overly religious man, but I have to think that God smiled upon me to be able to witness these events, to narrate them and in some obscure way, be a part of them. All because crows decided to hang out on a high wire. How awesome is this life? In my opinion, it is pretty damn awesome. Sure, there are vicissitudes, but for the most part, it is pretty damn awesome. Love, peace, and rock-and-roll. What the hell . . . it does work for me. It should work for everyone. C'mon now, be happy, don't unnecessarily tread on others, respect them, love them, appreciate them, and dance like a mad fool if they watch and dance even harder if they don't.

I showed the soundboard to Noel. I showed her how to adjust the lighting controls and how the other various functions of the electronics and controls for the stage worked and within a few minutes of lessons, Noel was the master of the systems. As well as being very easy on the eyes, she also was very smart and her enthusiasm at not taking things too seriously was contagious.

I left Noel to set up and to test the band's equipment because a large evening crowd began to arrive and Ashley now required my assistance behind the bar. This band had a large following and once they played a few tunes, I high-fived, Ashley for booking them, and we never stopped pouring and slinging for almost three solid hours. We did an amazingly brisk business, and it was near the end of their first set, when I realized that Billy Squire had abandoned his notebook, as well as his laptop. And most of all, his introverted ways. I noticed Billy at the soundboard sitting next to Noel, and when the band broke into a very well performed cover of the song, "Brass in Pocket," I spotted Billy and Noel dancing together to the music. Even Ashley was slightly dropped-jawed at the sight of those two wiggling around out there.

Once more, I stated that there was such a thing as love at first sight, and I was not the only one who thought Billy and Noel might have fallen for each other on this magical night. I know that Ashley agreed with me, and when Billy and Noel finally wound up the evening and sat at the bar for a nightcap, I noticed a very familiar lick in their eyes. It was the same one that I had all those years ago, when I first saw my lovely wife.

Love at first sight?

Hell, yeah.

"Hey, Billy. How have you been? I have not seen ya around in quite a bit of time. Have you been all right?" Billy Squire shrugged his shoulders and pulled out the barstool at his usual spot. I paused and studied him for a few seconds and it was easy to tell that he was far from all right. He looked as if some obnoxious son-of-a-bitch had peed in his whiskey. The whiskey that I had not even served him yet. Worse than a stray and ill-aimed whiz would be, perhaps, a publisher rejected his romance novel. Still, even worse, something derailed his promising relationship with Ms. Noel Walker. Judging by my years spent slinging drinks and pouring brews while standing behind this bar and studying people in a variety of states of behavior, either while straight and while three sheets to the wind . . . I am betting my favorite bar rag on trouble in the love department. His books were too good ever to obtain a reject label and I usually manage to throw out the losers who might pee in drinks.

"Hey, Gills. I have been 'round. Just not here. Hey, please, my usual."

His morose demeanor hung over his head like a black cloud of doom. I nodded and looked over to Ashley, and my faithful assistant looked over at Billy, sensed his glumness and knew that I wanted to spend some time with one of our regulars. After all, time had proven that Gilly Gilford was a part-time bartender, a part-time psychologist, a friend, and a pastor to the murder of crows.

I decided to begin the conversation from a neutral position by spewing a bit of babble, "Been finishing up the romance novel, huh?" While I waited for Billy's answer, I decided by his body language and facial expression that I had better make it a double whiskey pour.

"Yeah, and that turned out to be the trouble. I finished it for sure. Emphasis on the word *finished*."

"Okay, now, let's hear more about this situation. Here is a whiskey for you. A double pour neat. On the house. Specifically, on me." I dropped the drink rather dramatically in front of Billy. Propped one foot up on the inside bar rail and studied him.

"Ah, thank you for the double pour, Gills. I need it."

"Hey, it's all very cool. Ashley has the bar covered for a few. I am all ears. So, spill the beans. Why so gloomy, my friend? Should I deliver your next drinks on a painted tray?"

Billy took a deep breath and when he heard my words and the slick reference to the painted tray, at least, I managed to induce a little smile and an "almost" laugh of sorts. "No painted tray required, Gilly" . . . his smile was a little welcome relief. "Gills, your ears are all that I need right now."

I leaned in close and just above a whisper, I said, "I have a feeling this is all about Noel, but I confess to not understanding the relation to the new book and the trouble it caused and the emphasis on the word, finished. So, I will pull up a rail and if I can help, here I am, Billy."

"Ah yes, my statement is mired in a shroud of ambiguity. I apologize. Things were going great. In fact, they were unreal until she read the draft of the book. The romance novel. The novel that I began on the night that I met her. Here. Do you remember?"

I nodded so much with an acknowledgment of each question that I felt as if I was a "Gilly bobble-head doll."

Billy received the message loud and clear and after a sip of whiskey, he continued with the now slightly cliff-hanging clarification, "Well, Noel read the proof of the book and cried her eyes out and expressed that she knew that this book, on the heels of my bestseller, would be an even bigger success. I combined some intrigue with the romance plot. I think it is a great book too. I remained puzzled until she told me that she needed to confess that she has a very shady past. As in, a past full of bad mistakes and poor decisions. She has lots of baggage." Billy studied my eyes for a reaction and I readjusted my considerable weight on the bar rail and shifted my posture in order to focus on the trouble at hand.

One of our many crows . . . was astray.

"Ah, don't we all? I know that I do. So, what the hell does that matter?"

Billy's face lit up. He sat up in his stool, snapped his fingers in response and said, "Exactly. We all do! Bless you, Gilly. You understand, but sadly, my darling, Noel, does not. Apparently, her past . . . well, it runs the full gamut of ugly baggage. Drugs, abusive boyfriends, multiple lovers, a little stint in jail, things that she is now embarrassed about and things that she deeply regrets. Now, Noel feels as if when I am a big superstar author that she predicts will happen because of this new book, I will inevitably happen upon limitless success that her awful past will return to haunt us and somehow, tarnish my image. Even more so, Noel, feels as if, I will move on from her and her lowly past because of the spotlight shining on me. Noel thinks that I will have my pick of women. Me! C'mon, Gills, I am a nerd. Noel is gorgeous. Inside and outside, gorgeous. You understand. I cannot comprehend what it is that she even sees in me. She has the men chasing her right and left and some women too! Not me. Noel feels that I am on the cusp of greatness and that I deserve better. Because of her past, she is somehow unworthy. She broke off our relationship on this supposed resurrection of her past! Can you imagine that? What a load of bullshit! I have not even achieved any great level of success, yet. Oh sure, the first book was a bestseller. I made a good buck on it. It still sells a ton of copies, but this book . . . it is a different direction. Because of her. I wrote it for her, and now, it has come back to bite me in the ass."

Oh boy, I felt for him as he buried his head in his hands. Now, I needed a shot too, so I poured myself a double Irish. A quick tilt, and I had to admit that the burn of the whiskey felt rather good.

"I totally understand. My wife is a stunner too, and she picked my fat ass out of the lot of men chasing her down. We shared some stuff from our pasts. Stuff we aren't proud of, but honesty prevailed, and we moved on in our life and in our love. You know my wife, Erma. Right?"

"I sure do, and yes, she is a stunner."

"I have to tell you that it has been my experience over these many years, that the beautiful women always have some level of baggage. They attract a ton of attention and usually have hordes of men chasing them down and vying for their affection. It is understandable. Practically unavoidable. Noel is gorgeous beyond description, but Billy," I grasped his hands and he lifted his weary eyes and looked at me, while I searched for the correct words, "she is worth it. Right? To fight for her with all your heart and soul. All of your conviction, all that you have to give to her. For all the marbles and a few more in a jar in a closet somewhere? I bet you have marbles in a jar from when you were a kid. Am I right? Shooters and the smaller marbles. Draw a circle in the dirt in the playground and play the game, Billy."

Billy nodded and forced a smile while choking out the words, "Yeah, she is, Gills. I love her beyond words. I loved Noel from the very first moment that I saw her. No offense to you, Gilly, you are the bomb-dot-com . . . but how I wish that Clive were still here. He would know what I should tell her. How I should exactly phrase it. How to convey how much she means to me. How the past means nothing. That the future is all that matters to me. To us. I could never in my wildest dreams, conjure up words such as the words that Clive could write, or speak, or envision. Clive could pluck perfect words out of the air as if they were puffy clouds floating within clear blue skies." Billy tilted his head and then looked at me out of the corners of his eyes and said, "That is a writer's dream to do so."

Upon hearing those words, I settled back and folded my arms across my chest and I did not take offense at his words. Instead, I channeled my inner Clive Barrows Peepers and thought, 'Okay, Clive, what the hell would you say to Billy right now?' I looked over in the direction of the bar stool where Clive always sat, and I swear that Clive was sitting there. He was smiling at me and he was nodding his head in support. And, of course, he was sweating. Sweating and smiling.

I grabbed my glass and tossed the rest of the whiskey and when the burn left my throat, I recovered my voice. The words arrived in my mind, maybe from Clive, or maybe, just maybe, they were my own and simply "Clive Inspired." It might be time to give old Gilly a little dose of credit.

I think that Billy sensed the power of my words even

before they arrived.

"Oh yeah, Clive, would know what to say, huh? Well, guess, what there, Billy? Clive is still here. He never left us. He never will. Oh, well, Clive, might not be here where we can see him, or touch him, but we damn sure can hear him. Clive would tell you exactly what I am going to tell you. You are an author. A damn master weaver of a maze of words. What the hell, man! You write fantastic words! You are a best-selling author. Out of the entire world of bazillions of people, how many people can write words as you can? Very, very few. So, take that talent and use it! Use your words for love and steal her heart forever. This is all very simple. Noel always wears a ruby shaped like a heart around her neck and it shines with her love, with her heart, and with her soul. It glows with her existence. You need to glow even brighter within her existence, too. Be her ruby, Billy. Nothing that happened before the two of you met even matters. Think about it, before you met, you never knew of each other's existence. It is all before Billy and Noel, and it is ancient history . . . irrelevant. Now, it is a new day, a new love, a new hope. All that matters in this life is how much the two of you love and adore each other. Tell her what she told you . . . that life . . . it is all about peace, love, and rock-and-roll. Tell her that she is the only woman in this wild and crazy world for you. Dance together to the music of life. Dance now and dance forever, but for the love of all things pure, and all things right, just friggin' dance. What anyone thinks or says about youse guys, or does to youse guys or gossips about youse guys does not matter. Just dance with your woman, my friend. Until the end of all time. Dance. The rest of it . . . is just bullshit."

Billy's eyes lit up, and they glowed with recognition.

Some things in this life are unspoken but clearly conveyed.

Billy smiled while tossing the remainder of his drink

down. The entire bar of patrons stood up and clapped with a standing ovation of applause. Until now, I did not realize that we even had an audience. Nor did I realize that everyone abandoned their own worlds, and they all tuned into the Gilly and Billy channel.

Ashley sauntered over, her hips swaying and her tight jeans enhancing her glorious figure and, specifically, her rather cute ass. Ashley was a looker. Not that I was looking, mind you.

She was short, and I was tall, so she motioned for me to bend down and with a little blush to her cheeks, she leaned in and kissed my cheek while whispering, "Right now, you are not my boss. You are my friend. You are indeed, the bomb-dot-com. That was amazing. Clive is very proud. I love ya, Gilly. Thank you for you."

Well, now, a kiss from a gorgeous young woman could always make old Gilly blush . . . and my wife would agree. I think.

When Billy and Noel approached me with the idea of having their wedding ceremony and reception right here at The Crows on a High Wire Public House, there was no way that I would, or could, refuse. We closed the pub once more, as we did for Clive's memorial service, and regular crows slipped in along with Billy and Noel's family and friends. We moved all the tables out and lined the dining area in front of the bar counter to form a makeshift chapel setting of sorts. As if a pub could be a chapel. But then again, we never follow any rules here and never will. Besides, I think that a pub and a chapel are interchangeable. A pastor friend of theirs performed the ceremony right in the very spot in the front of the bar where they first met and fell in love.

Yes, indeed, it was love at first sight.

Billy honored me by requesting that I serve as his best man and my wife and daughter laughed at how uncomfortable that I was while wearing a suit, but later on that night, my wife said that I looked hot and that I cleaned up quite well.

We kind of proved our love later on that evening when we returned home . . . but now, I digress.

It was an amazing ceremony. Other than my wife, Noel was the most gorgeous bride that I ever laid my eyes upon and poor Billy was weak-kneed at the sight of her. Luckily, his best man was a mountain of a man, and I held him up under his shoulders.

Yes, the ruby around Noel's neck glowed brightly, but in my opinion, Billy glowed even brighter than the ruby did. Then again, what the hell do I know? I am just a bartender and owner of this joint.

It was a rip-roaring good time, with Slippery Slopes providing the music and some dancing and partying late into the night, and in fact, into the next morning. The bride and groom danced to Brass in Pocket and I had to admit, especially, when Ashley caught me lost in my emotion, that I had some tears in my eyes while watching them dance together. To think, love at first sight, right here at the bar counter, two souls met, recognized their bond and destiny, and they fell in love. To the joy of everyone, they worked out their issues, and they happily married. Off to a happy life full of wonder.

We added a few more crows on the high wire.

Billy and Noel live in New York City now. His romance novel was another best-seller and so was the book after that one and the book after that one too. The man is a legend. There is some talk of movie rights and such. They have little Billy Junior now and come by occasionally and say hey to Ashley, the gang, and me, and drop off free autographed copies of his books for us. Their love fills the entire world, and little Billy is a spitting image of his old man. His hair sticks out in all directions just as Billy's hair does, and the kid wears black, thick-framed eyeglasses, just like his old man. The kid is cute as a button. It is awesome.

The little kid even carries around a toy pencil and notebook and mimics his dad. Now, when the three of them stopped by one night and danced to Brass in Pocket out on the dance floor, with Billy and Noel holding the little guy's hands, while he laughed and shook his little doodle, old Gilly had to duck in my office and wipe away the tears. I had to think that Clive stopped wandering on clouds and that he must have wept a little too.

Now Noel had three rubies that glowed.

There is a brass plate mounted at Billy's post at the bar. This one says, "Noel and Billy Squire. Love, Peace, and Rock-and-roll. Love at first sight."

What the hell, I am not ashamed to admit that I am a romantic at heart. Besides, I love when the romance novel ends on a happy note. You know, two jokers fall in love, one does some dumb bullshit, and it causes all kinds of conflict, then they iron it all out and it ends with a happy conclusion. I have to admit that I always cry like a big boo-boo, when the couple breaks up, even though I know that I just need to read two more chapters, and they will make up and live happily ever after. It works for me, and while I think about it, I go through this life, and run this joint. Well, I gotta think that it works for many of the crows on the high wire too. Maybe someday, I will write a romance novel. Yes indeed, I can see me, old Gilly, the romance novelist. Let me think of a catchy title for my first gig. Okay, here we go, 'Love in a Martini Mix.'

I am gonna mix it dirty with extra stuffed olives.

Wink, wink.

Chapter Four

Totally Scandalous

What a Tangled Web We Weave

Xavier Gilly Gilford is many things, but he is not overly judgmental of a person's lifestyle and choices and the decisions that they make to live their own lives. I read somewhere that people chart their own courses in life and I thoroughly agree with that statement. If what a person says or does or how they live their lives does not hurt, embarrass, disrespect my family, friends or me, or influence my own life, my family's lives and my business, then do your own thing. Gilly might be conservative in many ways, but as far as other people's lives, I can hang loose. Very loose.

That statement which borders upon a disclaimer brings me to tell the story and the rather lascivious adventure of Mr. Dino Costa and Mrs. Carlotta Mulatto. I should also include that this storytelling might also include a mention of Mrs. Irene Costa and Mr. Mateo Mulatto.

"What can I get ya?" I asked while I leaned into the bar counter and focused my eyes on a lean, dark-featured, black-haired woman. I would guess her to be middle-aged or thereabouts. Certainly, she was no older than forty-five years old. Her shoulder length black hair was pulled back in a single ponytail behind her head and her hair had a deep sheen to it in the glow of the bar lights. Her nose was long and narrow and her eyes were dark and deep set and almond-shaped. She had trimmed her eyebrows until they barely existed. Her brows were just tiny wisps of hair hovering above her eyes. I thought that was weird. She was the kind of woman who was not overly attractive, but she was not unattractive either. Then, my eyes covertly moved to her dress and the plunging neckline that revealed eye-popping cleavage. The happily married owner of this establishment had to be careful when he checked out women patrons. Her breasts desperately gasped for air inside her dress, and the slightest movement threatened an embarrassing escape. This gal would never drown, that was for sure.

Those fun jugs would keep her afloat for hours. They also made up for the weird eyebrows. Honestly, any red-blooded male's gaze would certainly not focus upon her eyebrows. . ..

"Ah, ah . . . please, maybe just a glass of red wine," her voice sputtered out of her in short bursts. While she spoke, her eyes wandered around the interior of the pub, while she checked out fellow pub-dwellers and the patrons at the bar. Her fingers also nervously twisted a small gold wedding band around and around on her ring finger.

"Sure thing. Do you have a preference or is the house wine okay?" I asked, while carefully studying her reactions. This chick was really nervous about something and old Gilly was once more going to borrow from his years of experience in studying people and use a touch of his overpriced, but every once in an empty shot glass worth it education, and guess that she is meeting someone for drinks and lunch.

And, perhaps, something else.

"The house wine is fine. Thank you."

"House wine it is," I said, while wandering down to the wine cooler.

It was around two in the afternoon on a late fall Tuesday and this was the usual dead time for Crows on a High Wire Public House. In fact, Tuesday and Monday both were usually quiet during the day and did not pick up until after the workday ended and some of the local businesses closed. The pub's business came in waves here during the day. We opened the pub up at eleven o'clock in the morning, on Monday to Thursday, and closed around midnight. On Friday, Saturday, and Sunday the opening time was at nine o'clock in the morning and we closed shortly before the local ordinances yelled at us. We had the usual gang of local retired men flow in to meet, drink, play shuffleboard and darts, argue about the assorted sporting games on the televisions, (it did not matter whether it was baseball, football, hockey, golf, or basketball, or whatever. Arguing was a sport here in New Jersey) and to hide from their wives. We had a few regular businessmen who ate lunch and drowned some bad business pain and bad deals in a few cocktails and then we usually went through a dead time until the workday ended. Then the retired gang went home to nap and listen to their wives yell about the booze on their breath, and the younger crowds came into drink, party, and get ready for whatever band was going to play at seven o'clock. We also had a fairly solid flow of non-regulars, visitors, first-time-pub-goers, travelers, vacationers and then . . . we had this chick.

"Here ya go. Welcome to Crows on a High Wire Public House. I am Gilly Gilford. Owner, bartender, maintenance guy, bookkeeper and general all-around schlep." I stuck my hand out and thought some general chitter-chatter might loosen this gal up, along with a few sips of the wine. "I don't think you have ever been here before . . . but I could be wrong."

I almost let it slip that I would recall breasts such as hers were, but in the interest of not being a creepy sexual predator, and recalling my role as a responsible business owner, as well as hoping for a repeat customer, I kept my big trap shut. She reached out her hand and touched mine in a gentle clasp. My huge size, my enormous belly, the shaved head and the two gold hoop earrings in my ears might have given her some pause. After we shook hands, she seemed to relax, and I smiled in an effort to make her feel at home. After all, the pub was a home away from home for all of us.

"Nice to meet you, Mr. Gilford. I am Carlotta Mulatto. You are correct in that this is my first time visiting here. The interior décor is wonderful. I must say that . . . this is such an unusual name for a pub. Very catchy but unusual."

"Please call me, Gilly. My actual first name is Xavier. There is no way that a bartender needs to prance around back here behind the bar, with a name like Xavier. Besides, a guy of my size does not actually prance too well. Prancing is more like thumping in my case."

Carlotta smiled and took a sip of wine and I felt as if I had reached my goal of loosening her up a little bit.

"So many patrons asked about the name of the establishment that I had the background story of the name written up and printed on the back page of our menu." I turned around to where I kept the menus on the side of the cash register, reached for the piles of menus, grabbed one, and handed it to Carlotta. "I don't know if you are just going with the wine or if you are grabbing a bite to eat, but here is a menu for you to check out the food and to read the story. I might be biased but I think that it is a kinda cool story and background. Anyhoo, check it out and I hope that you enjoy the story. Please let me know if you want to order any food. Our master chef, Renaldo, is in the kitchen and he is so bored that he is counting peas out of a can, while sitting on his ass. I think a food order would do him some good right now. I need to check on these guys at the end of the bar, but I will be right back."

I put one finger in the air, while Carlotta picked up the menus and glanced at the rear page before she looked up and asked, "Ah, ah, Gilly." More sputtering. "I am joining someone, ah, ah, a coworker. Can I save this barstool next to me here? We will order some appetizers, but mostly, it will be drinks." Her face turned a tiny shade of red blush, and then Carlotta forced a very weak smile.

I waved to imply an informal air to the setting and said, "Sure . . . of course."

In my mind, I knew that Carlotta's companion might indeed be a coworker for sure, but it was going to be a little deeper than just that. I never needed much in the way of television or other means of entertainment with the assorted cast of characters that floated in and out of Crows on a High Wire Public House. Besides, now I share these stories of all these many years and many characters! It has been a fun and wild ride.

Carlotta made quick work of her first glass of red wine, and I should be ashamed of my own thoughts, but I could not help to think that if she was filling up her two fun jugs with red wine, then this will be a rather lucrative afternoon for red wine sales. She politely signaled me for a refill. I placed another glass of red wine in front of Carlotta; I was preparing a bourbon and cola cocktail for a patron, when I spotted a middle-aged man walk in through the front door of the pub. He took a few steps inside the front door, turned, and took his sunglasses off while he scanned the interior of the pub for what I already knew was the whereabouts of Carlotta Mulatto. Her "coworker" was not exactly what I expected.

Since my relocation and marriage to a native New Jersey gal, I adopted in my speech much of the slang, some of the accent and most of the idioms of being a New Jersey dweller. One glance and this guy was what we called around these parts, a "Guido." Now, I am not sure if that is a disparaging remark or not, I am only using the classification in an effort to blend into my adopted home. Maybe.

He tore his sunglasses off and posed for the limited audience of snoozers occupying the pub at the moment. These old guys hanging around the pub today did not even give him a glance. In fact, no one other than me even noticed him walk into the pub. It was easily detectable that this guy was a movie star, only in his own mind. Not that the group of retirees might be a fair barometer of the Guido's presence. Hell, Carlotta waltzed by with her amazing chest and these guys never even noticed her twin peaks of glory. If those bouncing jugs of joy did not awaken this group of good old boys seldom used male parts then, this Italian want-to-be-stallion did not have a prayer. Besides, right now, such-and-such was trying to make a putt in the golf game.

The Guido spotted his prey at the bar, and with his pointy-toed shiny shoes making a rather annoying click on my tile floors, he made his way to the bar. I wondered if his stupid shoes were making black scuff marks on the floor. Around his neck, he wore about fifteen pounds of gold chains, centered with a golden crucifix that hung down into his overly hairy chest, and you could see the overflowing chest hair, because his black button-up shirt was open down to his mid-chest. His left ear sported a single gold post earring. He was no more than five-feet four or so, even with the shoes on, and from my towering position behind the bar and from my height, I almost needed a telescope to see him. His hair was long, greasy and wet from the application of some purposeful slick-back goo, and he tied it behind his head in an even slicker ponytail. His nose was long and his eyes slightly bulging. A black leather belt with a gaudy golden buckle pulled his skin-tight black jeans tightly around his waist with a blob or two of a belly plopping and hopping around the belt.

C'mon, now, if you are gonna have a belly, take a clue from old Gilly and go for a giant one like mine is. He required lessons in proper belly making. He arrived at the stool next to Carlotta, glanced around and gently placed his hand upon her back, and then leaned into the side of her face in order to kiss her cheek. Carlotta jumped in surprise and her eyes danced all around the pub. Then to me, then to the old guy on the far side of the bar who did not even look up from his bourbon and cola. The old boy usually fell asleep around this time in the afternoon, anyway. I would wake him up in an hour or so, call a taxi, and send him on his way back home to his wife. Often, I had to round up the crows and take good care of them.

I plucked a bar napkin from the holder and like the efficient bartender that I was, I made my way to the Guido as he settled into his stool next to Carlotta while his fingers danced along her spine and his eyes focused on looking down the front of her dress. I dropped the napkin, and I forced a "can I help you" smile while he finally broke his lust-filled glance, and he noticed my huge body towering above him.

"Hey, there, Carlotta's coworker, welcome to Crows on a High Wire Public House. Whatcha drinkin'?"

He cleared his throat, looked at Carlotta, then to me, and poised his body for his attitude to appear. His cloying cologne stuck in my nose like diesel exhaust.

"Ah, yeah, yeah, yeah, geez, can ya give me a minute to settle in and greet my . . . friend here, pal? I mean, shit, I barely settled my ass in the stool and here is ya big ass hovering over me like a damn friggin' helicopter while spewing drink bullshit at me."

My mind arced with various thoughts. Most of them were not very nice. They ranged from reaching out over the bar and ripping the gold off his neck, to coming around the bar, picking his little body up and dragging him out of the pub and tossing his greasy ass out on the front sidewalk, to plain old stomping the living shit out of him. Oh okay, calm down, big guy. It was quite obvious that big old Gilly needed to establish the ground rules with this clown.

I stared him down, leaned in over him, and smiled. I saw him swallow hard and watched as his Adam's apple bounced up and down in his throat. What a punk.

"Sure, but, first, let me set the ground rules for you. I am Gilly, and I own the joint and I am in charge, and you are not. I am not yet, your pal, so don't jump to conclusions. One more rule, don't cuss at me or be rude, otherwise, my three-hundred pounds plus a few more pounds here and there will pick ya little skinny ass up and haul ya outta here and you will find ya ass and you both sitting on the sidewalk in front of the pub with those chains wrapped around more than just ya neck. Now, you let me know when you are settled, and what ya want to drink, or there is the front door. And pick ya feet up when ya walk with those fancy shoes cuz, if ya leave scuff marks on my floor, then I will make sure you are on ya knees and buffing them out. We cool?"

He hung his head for a second. His eyes went over to Carlotta's face and her expression pronounced her displeasure with his statement and behavior. His huge ego ordinarily did not allow an apology, but I knew that if he wanted this meeting to end where he planned it to, he needed to apologize and try to mend fences.

"Ah yeah, sorry. My apologies to you."

He lifted his fist to fist-bump into mine, and I ignored him. There was no way that I was fist bumping with this greasy joker. His fist bump embarrassingly faded after lingering for a few seconds in the air, and then he placed his hands on the bar counter and folded them together.

Apparently, the old boy at the bar, was not yet asleep in his bourbon and cola, because he stirred, shook his head and he huffed out a laugh at the scene and mumbled, in his best, I have been at the pub too long voice, "What a dope."

He stole a quick glance at Carlotta's amazing chest, then tilted over and slowly faded away over his cocktail.

"Ah, okay. No fist bumps. I get it. We are cool, Gilly. It has been a little stressful here since of late. At work. Please, when you get a chance, I will have a gin and tonic. The house gin is fine. Whenever you have a chance."

I nodded and asked, "Lime wedge?"

"Please, yes, thanks."

I walked away and my ear caught the first wave of Carlotta's displeasure at his behavior.

In an unsuccessful whisper, Carlotta, let Guido have it. "See, Dino, this is what I mean. You really are no different than *he* is. Controlling. Acting like a jerk. We find a nice place to meet where no one knows us and right away, you attract attention to us because you have to be the big man. Gilly has been so nice to me and you screw it up, acting like some smug hotshot. He owns the place, and he is not just a bartender. You always act as if you are so much better than everyone else is and look down upon people. It is obvious that the big man does not take crap like that and now, you had to apologize. Not everyone takes your bullshit and attitude. I am rethinking everything. I am just not sure we need to act out on what we feel. Now, I am not sure what I feel for you."

I knew the disdain in her whisper for the simple pronoun of he, meant that "he" was her husband.

"Ah, sorry, baby, I was just a little on edge and he flew up on me before I could make a proper greeting and all. You told him we are coworkers?"

"Well, we are."

Her eyes checked around the pub and I could feel them burning into me to check my status. I simply prepared his drink and acted as if I did not hear a single word of the conversation. Over my many years, I developed an exceptional peripheral vision and keen hearing. Superman and I share common ground. The super guy might have me beat in the muscles department, but Kryptonite has no ill effects upon me. Now, sweet peas do. And liver does too. Very high on the kill Gilly list. I despise sweet peas and liver, but I am quite sure that I can handle a little dose of Kryptonite. When Erma is angry with me, she purposely cooks sweet peas and liver and tries to feed the meal to me. We all have our weak spots, but other than the cape and muscles, I am very close in overall powers to Superman. I am working on the flying part. Anyway. . ..

"Oh baby," Dino cooed while he reached around and grabbed her by the ass and I could tell by the way his muscles moved in his arm that he was giving her more than a playful goose or two. "In an hour or two, we will be working on many, many things."

Oh brother, insert eye roll here. In a gentle glide, just delayed enough to allow the squeeze to finish, I made my way over to where they sat. I dropped the drink; he reached out his hand and extended it while formally introducing himself. Guido man was mending fences.

"Hey, there, Gilly. Thank you and no hard feelings. I am Dino Costa. We are cool, right?" I decided to cut the guy a break and ease back on him now. I shook his hand and his small hand disappeared inside of my large mitt.

"We are cool. No worries, Dino. I am Gilly Gilford. As I said before, I own this joint. Enjoy the drinks. You two, let me know if you want food or refills." I pointed at Carlotta's glass of wine and asked, "You good, my dear?"

"I am. Thank you, Gilly."

I took two steps away and Carlotta cleared her throat and asked me, "Ah, say, Gilly. One question. I am a vegan. How is the black bean burger?" She pointed at the menu and at the offering of the black bean burger listed there.

"It is great. All the food here is great. Pub food. It is right there on the comfort food list with pizza and soup and mac and cheese. We offer comfort here, our regular crows are a family, and our not so regular crows are welcome to join at any time. We are more than just beer and booze and cocktails . . . we are an experience."

Upon hearing my words, Carlotta smiled widely and just above a whisper said, "I will take a black bean burger and the experience too."

"Not big bad, Dino," Dino the Guido said with his now already very annoying smirk planted on his face, "I am a meat man. A normal meat burger there, Gilly, medium to well, some cheddar cheese and fries. Yup, meat for me. I like 'em round and plump . . . so that I can bury my face into 'em."

"Coming up," was all that I could muster up. I heard of shitty roundabout innuendoes, but that reference to the size of Carlotta's chest sure sucked. While I was asleep, I could come up with a better pick-up line than that one was. This guy was a clown and a heel. Carlotta seemed lost and nervous and perhaps, this guy was preying upon her situation, whatever it was, but even if she was not a Hollywood bombshell, with her chest and that gentle and engaging smile, I knew she could do a whole lot better than this grease ball. Now, old Gilly is not judging, but if ya gonna have an affair, which the jury was still out on, but close to reaching a verdict on, then at least pick a winner.

There you have it! That is how I first met Carlotta and Dino the Guido. This first meeting to plan their initial hook-up was an adventure of rather interesting ebbs and flows in activities. As the alcohol worked some magic on their inners and their moods shifted and changed, they alternated between arguing over what seemed to be where to have their first hookup and then shifting to sharing the reasons why this affair was justified. Then after another glass of red wine and Dino downing a few more gin and tonics, the interaction really grew intense. After a long interlude of whispering interlaced with Dino deeply squeezing Carlota's ass, the conversation moved to some more verbal sparring, then to all out loving, and even sharing a long kiss right there at the bar, a kiss that Carlotta was obviously very nervous about sharing in public. She looked around a hundred times or more to see if anyone saw it. No one other than old Gilly and his fantastic peripheral vision spotted it . . . the pub was still dead. The gang of elderly men remained gathered around the dartboard as if it was a campfire on a January evening, but as far as pub patrons go, that was about it for now. Even sleepy bourbon and cola packed it in an hour earlier and I stuffed his old ass in a taxi and sent him on his way.

Ashley arrived for the beginning of her shift and Carlotta and Dino were deep into the romantic-alcohol-induced-la-la-land by now. I guess going back to work was off the table now, as it was past four o'clock in the afternoon. Ashley carefully reviewed the performance and event list for this evening's entertainment, the dinner and meal specials and the logbook, all the while keeping her eyes peeled out of the strategic corner of them on the Carlotta and Dino show.

After reviewing the information for the beginning of her shift, Ashley walked over to me, smiled, and greeted me, "Good afternoon, boss. Everything under control?"

Her shoulder-length blonde hair danced all around her, her slim but amazing figure leaned into the bar and with her left hand, she rubbed at her sleeve of tattoos on her right arm. It was a nervous habit; the tattoos did not itch or bother her, at least, as far as I knew they did not. Ashley had begun work on another sleeve of tattoos on the left arm, but it was a work in progress. Her eyes were a deep blue, her facial features perfect, and Ashley was a looker. Tight jeans, a great backside, some canvas sneakers on her feet, a black blouse open just enough to catch a glimpse of her ample and amazing cleavage, enticed by a sterling silver y-type necklace that pointed the pathway to her breasts. And she wore no wedding band.

As of late, Ashley's luck in the romance department

sucked. I told her that she had a broken picker. The last young man she went around with ended up on his ass in front of the pub. One night, while waiting for Ashley's shift to end and chilling at the bar, the dope drank too much, decided to forget about our dear Ashley, and forcibly grabbed the ass of one of my regulars—a married woman, who was older but a knockout. Ashley broke into tears, punk-ass got a slap in the face from the woman and I picked his scrawny ass up like a bag of trash and tossed him out of the pub. Old Gilly was like a bulldozer and once my three-hundred-pounds rolled, ain't too much stopping me.

That night, we crossed another joker off the Ashley list. It was becoming a routine thing to do. Someday, she would find her man and her world would be complete. I loved her like a little sister and protected her as such, too. Speaking of protecting Ashley, my peripheral vision caught Dino the Guido checking out Ashley's ass, and this guy made my blood boil a little more. In retrospect, perhaps I should have tossed his ass out when I had the chance to do so. The Gillster was rather good at it after all these years.

"Hey, baby doll, glad you are here. I have had it for today. Everything is under control, Ash. Under control and it is all yours." With those words, I stood up tall and stretched my back out. That persistent dull ache from standing for so many hours and so many years generally settled in hard in the late afternoons.

Ashley gently touched my arm and concern washed over her face, "Back hurting? Gills, ya gotta go get it checked out. Maybe a chiropractor could fix ya up?"

I waved my hand in the air to display my stubbornness. "I dunno, maybe. Mostly, it might be something that losing one hundred and fifty pounds will help to cure. I am a fat ass and all this weight takes a toll. Gettin' old now too, Ash. Old. As in very old."

"Oh, no you're not, Gilly. You are still a giant, lovable,

teddy bear and the epitome of the handsome bomb.com. I love ya, man. Love ya."

"Love ya too, baby doll."

Ashley smiled; she leaned in and with a coy look over her shoulder with her gorgeous baby blues, a gentle whisper rolled out of her, "Speaking of love, Gills." Her eyes danced in the direction of Carlotta and Dino the Guido, both of them currently riding a wave of love in their various mood swings and staring into each other's eyes.

"Ah, lookie here at these two love birds. My illicit affair radar is blipping like crazy. Totally scandalous, huh?" Great Lord in Heaven, this young woman was beyond remarkable. If my past was not my past and I never met my wife, never loved my wife and daughter more than I love air, Irish whiskey, beer, food, and water, then, despite our fifteen years of age difference—I would marry this gal. Smart, gorgeous, hip, and groovy, all in one glorious package. Ashley just invented the perfect tagline for these two crows. The title of "Totally Scandalous" . . . perfectly summarized them. The fact that Ashley within a few minutes of observation could peg the relationship and label it with such a perfect tagline made me realize that Ashley had now reached the peak of her skills as a bartender and assistant manager of Crows on a High Wire Public House. This business was all about knowing your customer and Ashley was on top of her game in that regard, as well as many other aspects of the business. Her life experience earned her a special psychology degree, and it required a final stamp of approval. I was going to make a split-second executive decision here. It was time for a change.

"Perfect, tagline! You are truly amazing. Yeah, looks like a full moon fever for those two. I will tell ya 'bout them. . .. Later." I paused and thought. Then I spoke. "Say, Ash, baby doll, c'mon here because it is quiet now and we can take a minute or two here without ignoring the handful of patrons in here right now. This is spontaneous and all, but your tagline statement made me realize that you are where you need to be and where we all belong. These two crows won't miss us for a minute and," I threw my arm around her shoulders and tucked her into my huge body while saying, "I have to tell ya that it is time for a promotion for you. How does the title of general manager sound?"

At first, Ashley seemed shocked and her face indicated the emotion. After a few seconds, it sunk in of what I just proposed to her and she smiled widely and then threw her arms around my neck and kissed my cheeks repeatedly while shouting in joy, "Hell, yeah! This is so awesome and amazing." Ashley then stepped back and grew pensive for a few seconds; she posed, sticking her right hand on her hip while tilting in towards me. Her pointy finger on her left hand went out, and her voice changed a little. She was confident and forceful and those were only two of the reasons that Ashley was going to be a huge success in her new position, as well as in her life. Once we fixed her broken man picker, then that would help too.

"I have worked really hard here, Gills. I deserve this." She relaxed, her hands went back to her side, and then she folded them across her beautiful chest. "Right?" She was so adorable.

"Hell, yeah, you work hard! Hell, yeah, I am promoting you because you are smart, hard working, amazing and great with the customers and with managing our staff." I then changed my voice and lowered it a little, and with a sly grin, I added, "Plus, ya a knockout chick too!"

Ashley rushed into my arms and hugged me, and I hugged her back. Tight. Really tight. "I love ya, Gilly! Ya da bestest!"

Now, we had the full attention of all the patrons of the pub. The retired clan looked up from their darts and debates. Dino stopped his distant fondling of Carlotta's right breast with strategic rubs of his nearest elbow and Carlotta blinked rapidly and tried in vain to recover from the power of covert love.

"A round of drinks on me! Gather on in now, everyone! I want you to meet the new general manager of Crows on a High Wire Public House! Ms. Ashley Stahl." The bar filled with joy while I poured the rounds, and Ashley wiped away tears of joy while her pub family congratulated her.

Yes, even Dino the Guido. We accept all kinds. No bias here. Honestly, maybe just a little bias.

In looking back on the evolution of what became a most interesting pair of patrons for our pub, as Carlotta and Dino slowly evolved into regular crows and our humble establishment became their official or unofficial sort of, kind of, secret rendezvous place, I came to understand that their relationship was tumultuous. Perhaps that is a major understatement of sorts. Up and down, as if it was a wooden roller coaster ready to hurl off the tracks, might work better as a description. One minute, they were snuggle-poo and staring into the calm pools of love swimming in their eyes, and the next minute, it was hellfire and brimstone shooting massive electric sparks out of their eyes to inflict injury upon each other's souls. One minute, they would be lip locked, the next minute, they would be screaming at each other and arguing over where to plan the next romp in the sack. (yeah, sometimes, I wish they spoke quieter and I did not have Superman powers. I would willingly concede defeat to the super guy) and when they should leave their respective spouses. As they became more comfortable with meeting at the pub, their efforts to hide the not-so-secret relationship faded as they trusted Gilly and Ashley more and more and timed their visits perfectly when the pub was quiet and the retired clan paid them no attention. Crows on a High Wire Public House became the perfect covert enclave for their meetings. There were plusses and minuses to our hosting their not-so-secret liaisons. Carlotta was cool, but Dino was a major pain-in-the-ass. Since Dino was working so hard to impress

Carlotta and keep the panty dropping afternoons flowing, the greasy dope always tipped us rather well and they did buy a ton of drinks. And Carlota's chest was a huge bonus too.

I used the word huge on purpose.

"What can I get you?" I asked a tall skinny man, wearing a faded black or what was now grayer than it was black, dungaree jacket, faded black dungarees, a plain black tee shirt, and bright red basketball sneakers on his feet. Unusual garb. The man's black hair was slick and combed back and over his head in a shiny mess and he looked as if he smelled something really bad. As in super bad. He was slimy. His demeanor oozed slime.

He leaned into the bar counter, placed one red sneaker on the rail in front of the bar and said, "Information."

Oh, no. Gilly does not like the word, "information." Especially in New Jersey. The word comes with baggage and with a black bow of trouble interlaced between the letters and tied up on top.

I leaned in close too, and my hulking presence caused him some pause. He leaned back from the bar counter just a bit.

"Okay, well, I am Xavier Gilford. Friends and acquaintances call me, Gilly. I am the owner of this establishment and I need to tell you that we serve pub food, beer, wine, and booze and the occasional fancy-ass cocktail with an umbrella stuck in them to the not so pub-like crowd, but generally, I do not serve any . . . information."

The sleazy guy leaned back, pulled his wallet out, took a

business card out of the wallet along with a fifty-dollar bill and dropped both on the bar counter while saying, "Okay, gotcha, Gilly. Here is my business card and some inspiration for you to serve me just a taste of some information. I need you to mix me a cocktail of information. I think that fifty bucks covers that rather nicely."

He slid the business card and the fifty-dollar bill across the bar in my direction. The slime from his hands helped to make the items glide effortlessly across the surface of the bar counter. I left the fifty-dollar bill sitting upon the bar counter; however, I did pick up the business card and glance at it.

I read it and I am quite sure that my lips moved while I read it aloud, "Roger Fortunate, Private Investigator, and a friggin' telephone number. No address, no email." I dropped the card on the counter, slid it along with the fifty-dollar bill back to Roger and said, "Nice. I am not interested, nor am I inspired. My name is Xavier, or you may call me, Mr. Gilford. As I said, only my friends and acquaintances call me, Gilly. You are neither."

He picked the card up and tucked it rather neatly into his jacket pocket. The lower pocket. On the right side.

He left the money and smiled while slyly talking out of the side of his mouth, "I see. Well, money talks and bullshit walks."

He unzipped the zipper on the upper left pocket of his jacket and slowly reached inside and pulled out two photographic prints. They were pictures of two people. A male and female. I glanced at the pictures and immediately recognized that the photos were of Carlotta and of Dino.

"I am looking to see if ya might just happen to know these two folks who might, and I emphasize just might, stroll in here on occasion. They might, they just might, drink wine . . . wine that is for the woman, and the guy . . . might, just might, suck down a shit load of gin and tonics.

He also squeezes her ass and rubs on her rather substantial breasts. In public, they do this. Now, I am just sayin'. He and they . . . might do all of this. I am lookin' for a person to collaborate all of this . . . might stuff."

When he finished speaking, he reached for his wallet again, and I surmised that he was pulling out more inspiration.

I held my hand up while simultaneously telling Mr. Fortunate, "Keep it. I don't retain dossiers on my patrons. Many people come in and out of here. They deserve to enjoy themselves here, not have some barkeeper retain tabs on their behavior. Cash money does not motivate me to divulge information about people's lives. Hit the pavement, pal."

I walked a few steps down the bar, picked up a bar rag and began wiping down the bar top while, Mr. Fortunate smiled and picked up the photos and the fifty-dollar bill and managed to keep his smile planted on his face even while asking, "Okay, well, Mr. Gilford, can I have a beer, then? For say, one-hundred-dollars? How about two-hundred-dollars?"

I threw the bar rag aside and walked over to where he sat and leaned in and over him even more forcibly than I did before and said, "You can get the hell out of here, either on your own or with me chucking your ass out of here. Your choice."

"You are refusing me service?"

"I own this joint and reserve the right to refuse anyone anything that I want to refuse them. So . . . your choice."

"I am licensed in New Jersey for private investigations and I will call the cops if you touch me," the slimy private investigator said, while reaching into his pants pocket to pull out his golden private investigator's badge. He held it in the air as if it was a badge of courage.

I stood up taller and said, "I'll dial the phone and stick that tin badge up your ass while we wait for the police to arrive."

He meekly placed his badge away in his pocket, held up his hands, stood up, took sunglasses out of his pocket, and smirked at me. A small audience of regular crows now gathered around him and they all joined forces to protect the pub family once they overheard and understood the discussion and intensity of it.

Ashley walked out from the back of the house and she studied the situation, glanced first at my very red face, and then, at my throbbing temples and sensing that, I was a little more than just upset and that I was angry, Ashley walked over, stood next to me, and placed her hand upon my shoulder. "Easy, big guy. Easy, now."

Roger studied her with lascivious intent, while his slimy eyes walked all over her body. He was undressing her in his mind.

He licked his lips and winked at Ashley, who then promptly and loudly said, "Never in your best dreams, jerk."

He put his sunglasses on and took two steps, turned, and said, "Ya know, these guys are cheaters. Their spouses' attorneys hired me to prove it. They are destroyers of families and lifestyles. I am just doing my job, but they ain't good people."

I cleared my throat and felt as if that deserved an answer, "I can't say that I agree with you nor can I say that I disagree. It is none of my business. That is not for me, nor is it for my staff to decide. People chart their own courses in their own lives and we here at Crows on a High Wire Public House do not judge them. We see many things. Happy people, sad people, people in love, people without love, and people in grief and filled with sorrow. Lonely people, social people . . . we see it all here. We serve them beer, wine, booze and food and provide entertainment. Mostly, local musical acts pursuing creative dreams. We support creativity. We offer an experience, and perhaps, an escape from reality. Temporary escapes, but an escape nonetheless. And, our integrity means that we don't take cash for a payoff for knowing certain things. What I am saying is that you have a lot of nerve to come in here and lay cash down on my bar, in my place, for me to divulge some inside scoop on two people's personal lives and behaviors. It insults my integrity and I might be a lot of things, but I have my honor. Cash for information is not part of the deal. You are the private detective . . . go get your proof someplace else."

Roger nodded and tucked his hands in the front pockets of his dungarees and said, "Fair enough. I getcha. I will go sniff around somewhere else. This ain't the first joint that I got chucked out of and it won't be the last one. See ya. Thanks for nuthin', Mr. Gilford."

"Well now, forgive me if I don't say thank you for stopping in. However, you are welcome . . . for nuthin'."

Roger, the slimy private investigator, stomped out and disappeared. The gathered crowd of supporters collectively shook their heads and went back to their darts, drinks, and chatter.

Ashley looked at me and her face told the story.

"I guess some people think there is a price for everything, boss. I am so proud of you."

I picked up the bar rag for what seemed as if it was the millionth time and rubbed the same spot on the bar counter for what seemed as if it was the millionth time.

"Ashley, in this wild world, there really is a price for everything. In his defense, he is really just doing his job and his job requires digging up dirt. Old Gilly, well, I rather wipe this same spot on the bar than give that slime ball any information. He ought to rethink the red sneakers for sneaking around in, though."

Ashley nodded and grabbed another bar rag and smiled while saying, "Ha! Hell, yeah. Not the best choice for footwear when ya trying to blend. Anyway, as far as the cleaning goes, well, Ashley, rather clean too, boss. Yup, Ashley too. How about you wipe over here and I will wipe over there?"

"It's a deal, Ash. I need to wipe this spot right here where he sat, in order to get rid of the slime and dirt. If ya know what I mean. Damn, Dino the Guido and Carlotta sure did end up turning into totally scandalous. Your catch phrase was perfect beyond description. Didn't they?"

Ashley stopped wiping the bar, picked up a used cardboard coaster, and tossed it into the trash bucket behind the bar.

"Sure did, Gills. I might need to up the phrase a notch or two after this. Perhaps, into the super scandalous range."

It was Tuesday and as we crept a few hours past noon, we reached into what Ashley and I somewhat playfully labeled, "Totally Scandalous Time." Perhaps, our sense of humor at their relationship was slightly insensitive and certainly ill advised, but nonetheless, we kept it to ourselves and it sure turned out to be the perfect label. Dino and Carlotta usually had a routine by now. They had been Tuesday regular crows for the best part of nine months or thereabouts and not too much changed. They had three or four of their usual drinks, ordered some food, argued, they loved, they kissed and they argued some more and then made up before heading out to do whatever it was that they did. This particular Tuesday was about a month or thereabouts after the visit from the creepy private investigator and either, he was Sherlock Holmes, or he was a total bust. At this point, it was difficult to determine. Both Ashley and I expected that some Tuesday it would all blow up for them. We could feel it. We surmised a scene of pandemonium looming. A scene, when Dino and Carlotta were head over heels in layers of love, when suddenly, an entourage of irate and deceived spouses led by Mr. Fortunate would burst into Crows on a High Wire Public House and create a raucous scene of turmoil in a climax to rival any Hollywood movie.

Our expectations for the anticipated climax might have been set too high, but not by much.

Through general conversation and a certain amount of supposition, Ashley and I determined that these Tuesday rendezvous were in lieu of out of the office sales calls that both Carlotta and Dino were supposed to be making on Tuesday afternoons. They must have been exceptional performers at their jobs and performed sales calls in some other manner, because money did not seem to be a concern and their tips were more than fair. In fact, they were generous. I think they both appreciated our keeping out of their business and tolerating their slightly wacky behavior. We never determined where they worked, but we knew it was not close to the pub, because it was far enough away that they decided upon the pub as a location in order to meet off the beaten path. I surmised Newark was their office location and Ashley thought that it was Clifton. They were in sales and marketing of some sort, but once more, we never really knew the exact business they were involved in with the marketing.

The usual Tuesday routine remained unbroken. Wine for Carlotta, small talk with her, the grand entrance by Dino the Guido, his pose, his arrogance, his gin and tonic. A salad or bean burger for Carlotta, a big hunk of some type of meat for Dino. A little tushie squeezing, a not so covert rub on Carlotta's mountainous breasts, a kiss or two, followed by arguing and then make-up to break-up.

Sometimes, the arguments became angry and forceful, and one of them would even walk out of the pub, only to return a few minutes later and engage in a classic makeup session. Then there might be another break up session. It was a vicious cycle of weirdness, often fueled by wine and a gin and tonic intake. Then, after the final makeup and a round of deep kissing, they would pay their tab, then dance off to what was most likely a session of lovemaking somewhere. Who knows? Who really cares?

All within three to four hours or so.

This particular rendezvous on this fateful afternoon was an extra weird one. Their public passion even managed a rise out of the retired clan over by the dartboards, between some putts on the golf television feed.

Right when old such-and-such, whose last major win was ten years ago, sunk an impossible shot, Carlotta and Dino's totally scandalous behavior caused two of the retirees to look over to the bar and one of them mumbled, "I think that they both need to go and get their room early today."

Then it was back to the golf game. The retirees had seen this all before and it was old hat. Carlotta's amazing breasts and bursting cleavage of love enticement did not take priority over the impossible shot.

After the lovin' subsided, it was time for Carlotta and Dino to fight over whatever it was that they fought over all of the time. It was a rotational cycle, first love, then fight, then love in an endless cycle of wackiness. I tried not to listen and pay attention any longer. At one point, Dino stomped off, tugging away at his greasy hair, stomping around the pub, then out the door he went. Carlotta remained unshaken, gently sipping her wine and when Dino returned, he was calmed and now, after a few muted whispers, Carlotta went off spinning into unhappy land. They alternated episodes of weirdness. She left the bar in a huff. Dino waved for his tab and I closed them out and cleaned up. I never asked a question or offered a comment and Dino did not say a word other than a mumbled, "Thanks."

He stomped out of the pub and I nearly fell over. When a few minutes later, the both of them returned. Now, they were both laughing and happy and their hair was all tousled and their clothes in disarray. Sex in the back seat of a car while parked in my parking lot? Maybe? Makeup to break up. Once more, I do not judge. The wife and I tried it a few months ago with our car parked in the driveway and in the middle of the night. The wife was feeling rather adventurous and risqué and well, it was a little bit of a struggle with my size and huge girth, but we pulled it off rather well.

It cost me a few bucks because I had to replace the shocks on the car the following week.

Back they were for another round of bizarre behavior and I had just sat the new drinks down; when I spotted a handsome, middle-aged man walk into the front door of the pub, followed by a tall, attractive woman. The man carried a white cardboard box. The type of box that the bakery provides for you for carrying a pie or a cake inside of, tied up with a white string with red stripes. I had a bad feeling about this, and my "oh-oh senses" were tingling, but since a regular crow on the other end of the bar required a refill, I needed to hustle over and refill his drink. Ashley had just hired a new server, a young, part-time college student named Courtney, and she stood in the server station waiting to see what table and seats this couple chose. They did not choose any place to sit; instead, their eyes jointly scanned the interior of the pub and settled upon the Dino and Carlotta show. I poured the drink as fast as I could and watched the scene unfold. The man pointed to where Dino and Carlotta sat, and the woman nodded. He tore the string to the box open, and the man and woman whisked by poor Courtney, who stood somewhat confused in the center of the dining room, while she held menus and silverware in her hands.

Courtney babbled, "Ah, ah, you can sit anywhere you want . . . oh, okay, going to the bar, well, Gilly will. . .." They went by her in a flash. I dropped the drink, thanked the regular and I watched as the couple, without speaking a word, headed to the scene of the impending chaos.

It takes old Gilly a little while to gain speed, but once I roll, then I become a runaway freight train. I was not fast enough. Too slow out of the gate. Within seconds, the man reached the side of Dino and the woman reached the side of Carlotta.

He removed a cake from out of the bakery box, balanced it in his hand (rather expertly, I might add) and in one motion while saying, "Hello, I am, Mr. Mateo Mulatto, Carlotta's husband," he forcibly smashed the cake into the face of Dino the Guido.

It was a strawberry-vanilla cake with fresh strawberries on top. The cake had multi-layers of strawberry glaze between the cakes. My fave! Damn, Dino was right in the middle of squeezing Carlotta's ass, too. The dumbass turned right into the cake smash! Full force, smash!

Simultaneously, the woman picked up the glass of red wine and dumped the balance of the contents of the wine over the top of Carlotta's head. Too bad that Carlotta was more of a sipper than a guzzler, and the glass was almost full of wine. It did not matter much because while the shock overtook Carlotta, the woman picked up her seltzer water glass and dumped that over Carlotta's head too.

Damn a wine mixer!

"Hello there! I am Mrs. Irene Costa. Dino's soon to be ex-wife. You deserve each other!"

Wow! A perfect ambush.

The retirees ran (as best they could. Okay, a slow walk or maybe a trot is a more accurate description) over to the scene of the crime. Screw the golf game and darts! This was awesome! Much better than a random glimpse of Carlotta's often seen breasts! A crowd gathered and poor Ashley, who had just arrived to relieve me, burst out of the back of the house along with our head chef, Renaldo. Dino jumped up, and I made my way out from behind the bar to get between all of them and became the referee.

"WHAT THE HELL? YOU ASSHOLE!" Dino screamed as he plucked some cake out of his eyeballs. Ashley giggled and put her hand over her mouth and shook her head to indicate her faux remorse at her reaction.

One of the retirees shamelessly pointed at Dino and loudly proclaimed, "Ha! Who is the real asshole, there, Dino? Ya just got nabbed, you clown!"

"Okay, okay, now, calm down everyone!" I shouted while I held my hands in the air and plopped my huge body between everyone. "Calm down now! Calm down. This is a place of business and we need to settle down here."

Carlotta took the fresh and unused bar rag that Ashley handed her and wiped her hair and face and Ashley handed another bar rag to Dino, who did the same. Cake remained splattered all over the bar counter and the floor and Ashley giggled once more. I turned my head away from the angry combatants and winked at Ashley.

I smiled while pretending to be serious, and said, "Ashley, Renaldo, please go get a mop and bucket from the back room."

Ashley nodded, grabbed the chef by the arm, and the two of them hustled off to laugh at the scene in the privacy of the back of the house. On the other hand, ah, I mean to obtain the clean-up supplies.

I pointed at the group of retirees and said, "Youse guys, please, I think what's his face is attempting a putt. Why not check it out and finish your darts? Okay?"

Since the action was now over, and at the prospect of missing a strategic putt, they all glanced at the television screen and off they went to study the intrigue and analytics of the game of golf.

Carlotta burst into tears and loudly wailed, "I am so sorry! I am so ashamed!"

Mrs. Costa shook her head, put her hand on her one hip, fluffed her long hair over her shoulders and confidently said, "Don't be, you floozy. Because of your carrying on, I met your husband and while you have been enjoying Dino, on your little Tuesday interludes, I have been enjoying Mateo. It has been the best sex of my life! Thanks for giving him up. He is so much better equipped than miniature-penis, Dino is!"

Ouch. Touché. What a tangled web we weave.

Miniature-penis, huh? Who knew? Between a splatter of cake in the face and revealed secrets of his anatomy, it seems as if Dino the Guido's macho image took a major hit here today. Apparently, poor Dino was all sparks with no fire and a legend in his own mind.

Carlotta wailed even louder, she turned and ran out of the front of the pub screaming and Dino looked around, tore his sunglasses out of his pocket, flicked some random chunks of cake out of his eyes, placed his sunglasses over his eyes, turned around and hustled out the front door after her. I looked around as Mateo and Irene laughed and embraced at their victory.

They kissed and high-fived each other, and Mateo looked at me and said, "I am sorry about all of this. I will help clean up and something tells me that these two dummies and the soon to be ex-spouses skipped out on their tab."

I stood with my hands on my hips and I surveyed the scene. Splatters of cake, wine, seltzer, and spent love were all over the floor and bar counter of Crows on a High Wire Public House. I deeply inhaled and then sighed while Ashley arrived on the scene with the mop bucket and with Courtney's help; they began the clean up detail.

"Oh well, yes, they did, but it is all right. Ash and Courts have the clean up covered. Thanks for the offer." I dipped my finger in a large blob of cake sitting on the bar counter and stuck it in my mouth, and smacked my lips at the sweetness of it. "At least, youse guys bought my favorite flavor."

"I will cover their tab, and say, can we have that table over there? I could use a few belts of Irish whiskey, and Irene will take a few vodka martinis. Dirty. As far as food goes, what is good on the menu here? Ah, ah. . .."

I put my huge arm around Mateo and said, "Hello there, disruptive, but redeemed, Mrs. Irene Costa and Mr. Mateo Mulatto. Welcome to Crows on a High Wire Public House. I am Xavier Gilly Gilford. All of my friends and acquaintances call me, Gilly, and you may do so too. I am the owner, bartender, maintenance guy, bookkeeper and general all-around schlep. The gal working the mop is our amazing general manager, Ms. Ashley Stahl. The gal working the bar rag is Courtney Winslow. Senor Renaldo Lopes is in charge of the kitchen. All the food here is great. Pub food. It is right there on the comfort food list with pizza and soup and mac and cheese. We offer comfort here, our regulars are a family, and our not so regulars are welcome to join at any time. We are more than just beer and booze and cocktails . . . we are an experience. This afternoon, we sure all had some kind of experience."

We all shared a few smiles and a round of laughs at the scene, we cleaned up and our new crows chose a table and had a great time. Such a good time that I called them a taxi.

Oh well, all's well that ends well. So, they say. In this case, it was more than our imagination that led us to witness a happy conclusion to all of the madness and mischief.

We never saw Dino or Carlotta ever again, however; Mr. and Mrs. Mateo Mulatto became semi-regular crows at the pub. More crows joined the group on the high wire after two flew away for a new life and a new direction. Totally scandalous gave way to totally blissful. The Mulattos seemed deeply in love and very happy. It is funny how some pain and deep hurt can somehow bring about joy. We never asked about the final fate of Carlotta and Dino and the Mulattos never mentioned them. It was none of our business.

That is how it goes around here. As I grow older and my back hurts a little more each day, I always think that I have seen it all. Aliens landing in the parking lot, sauntering into the pub with all kinds of eyes and tentacles, and asking in some weird language through a communicator-translating box to order drinks might give me a slight shock. The aliens might, but chances are they would not give me too much of a rise. After all, this is New Jersey, and I have come to realize that you must always expect the unexpected and when you think you have seen it all—you ain't actually seen jackshit. Every time the front door opens, it is another story, another character, another potential adventure, and that is the magic of all of this. Some people see a public house with a cool and quirky name; they see some gin joint with whiskey and beer soaked (and some strawberry cake) floors, an odd cast of characters and some huge fat dude with hoop earrings and a shaved head as the owner, assisted by a gorgeous and totally hot young woman. However, all of us that know better see it as an adventure. An experience.

Okay, now, lookie there, how about that?

The front door just swung open. . ..

Don't think that I am not going to double-check for multiple eyes and tentacles now.

Chapter Five

The Table of Obscurity

True Love, Finally

Ashley plunked her perfect backside down on a stool at the special table tucked in the far corner of the bar. It was the most unpopular table in the joint. It tucked itself into an obscure corner of the main barroom; it was on the pathway to the restrooms, had a poor view of the stage, no clear view of the televisions, and seldom, if ever, did anyone occupy it. We only kept it there because I often use it as a work table that I could type away on my laptop and still keep an eye on what was happening out in the public house. Many years earlier, the amazing Clive Peepers, in his best sense of humor combined with his British eloquence, tagged the lonesome table as the "Table of Obscurity" and the name stuck. It stuck so much that we had a brass plaque made and we screwed it to the wall right above where the table sat in quiet obscurity.

Ashley gently moved my paperwork away, and she sighed rather heavily. She had tied her blonde hair on top of her head in a messy bun of some sort, and she wore very little makeup. Ashley was always immaculate in her appearance and she reported to work always looking hot enough to melt icebergs. As she slowly approached forty years of age, I swear that she grew more beautiful each and every day. Her appearance made the men drool and I am quite sure that her following brought in a substantial amount of testosterone that dropped more than their fair share in the till, all in hopes of attracting the attention of the stunning Ms. Ashley Stahl. Ash strategically played them as if they were fine violins, milking the cows until they mooed in a peaceful bliss. Open wallets and happy patrons. Capitalism at its best.

It was time for my faithful assistant to report for her shift, and judging by her appearance, Ashley was not doing too swift today.

It was late in the afternoon on a Friday, in mid-summer, and we had a local headliner band that was very popular playing the pub tonight. They usually brought in a good crowd, and if the early gathering descending upon the pub was any indication, this was going to be a very busy evening. We were going to need our beloved Ashley in peak form tonight.

I dropped a few drinks, checked on the assembled regular crows, glanced at the clan of retirees getting ready to wrap up for the day and head home for naps, and decided that I could break away for a second to check on Ashley. I walked over and looked at her and she raised her head and then folded her arms and placed them on the tabletop. She then dropped her head into the folds.

"Hey, Gills. Sorry, boss, I am not at my best today."

"I see. Can I help?"

"Not sure, anyone can help me, Gilly."

I placed my hand on her back and when I did so, she tucked her head deeply into her hands to cover her face, and poor Ashley began to weep rather violently. Oh no!

I decided to take an odds-on favorite guess at the reason for her breaking down and sobbing and I leaned in and whispered, "Is this because of Kyle?"

A sad and weepy, "Yes," emitted from the cover-up, and I knew what to do. Punt.

Kyle was the latest in what was now a long, long, long string of failed relationships for our beloved Ashley. I knew that he was a loser when I first saw and met him, but with our dear Ashley and her, what I called "broken picker," love was blind.

Ashley lost her mom to breast cancer when she was only eight years of age, her dad was a hardworking guy, who did the best that he could to raise her and her aunt jumped in on motherly duties, but our lovely and amazing, Ashley, did not always receive the best guidance and have an easy childhood. Now, her dad was gone, the poor guy worked himself to death, her aunt was old and feeble and being an only child, Ashley only had a few cousins, her small circle of friends and Erma and Gilly. And her pub family. A bunch of crows on a high wire and all of us cared deeply for her.

One of the old retired guys wobbled up to me and held his pint glass in his hand, and upon noticing Ashley with her face covered while in the middle of a meltdown, said, "I will come back, Gilly. I am so sorry. Is Ashley, okay?"

I noticed his furrowed brow and the look of concern across his face and reported, "She is not too swift right now, but she will be fine in a few. Ashley is the bomb.com, and she always bounces back. Thanks for your patience. Please give me a minute or two and the next round for you and the boys are on me."

He nodded and wobbled back off to join the geriatric gang. Just another crow amongst the crows.

My mind burned with thoughts of the loser who hurt our dear Ashley. I wanted to take my giant body and stomp the air out of him like a faded party balloon. Kyle was another bum, an unemployed hipster with a penchant for laziness, an intense love of weed, and the warped idea that a productive day was spent sitting on his ass playing video games. He wore a wool cap on his head, even if it was a friggin' hundred degrees out, he needed a cat to lick his face to remove his baby whiskers and often he needed a good scrubbing in a hot bath to remove the dirt and the stupidity. When you have a super-hot girlfriend, who works her beautiful ass off every day, and you can show her off to your buds, and sit on your ass all day, smoke weird shit and drink rot-gut booze, and live off her hard work and hard-earned money, and have awesome rolls in the sack with her, well, life is pretty damn good.

After they dated for a month or two and the bum still did not have a job, but he knew all the cheats on the most popular video games, Ashley begged me to give the punk a job. Because I love her, I gave the clown a job and put him to work as a laborer in the kitchen working under Renaldo so that Ashley did not have to manage him on a direct basis. I thought that maybe old Gilly was being too protective of Ashley and too judgmental of Kyle, and that he deserved a chance. Perhaps Renaldo could teach him prep work and cooking.

Perhaps.

I was not being too judgmental of Kyle. Always go with your gut, Gilly. It certainly is big enough.

The bum quit after two days and told me that the job was, "Not what he expected it to be. It is dirty and hot and greasy and when he went home at night, he smelled like food."

I asked him, "What the puck did you think it was?" Only I did not use the word "Puck." Instead, I used a rhyming word.

Back to my decision to punt. My apologies because I digressed in my emotional testimonies of what a bum and loser that Kyle was.

Since our daughter was now deep into her studies at a university for her Master's degree in English (thank you, Clive) my amazing, remarkable and glorious wife, Erma, had some free time. Utilizing her accounting degree and love of numbers, Erma often jumped into the office here and there and assisted with bookkeeping and with other office duties that I struggle with and I am not very good at performing. Erma was here today, and I needed her assistance with this mess.

I patted Ashley on the back and then rubbed her neck a little to ease her tension, but she kept her head down into the folds of her arms while I mumbled, "It's gonna be okay, Ash. Be right back." I rolled my three-hundred and whatever pounds in the direction of my office and found Erma nose deep in files that I did a lousy job of organizing and burst into the office. Erma looked up. And at first, I knew that she was going to let me have it about my poor office organizing, but my wife of almost thirty-five years carefully studied my face and she knew that something was wrong. Dear Lord in Heaven, how I love this woman!

"What's wrong, Gilly?"

I thumbed my huge right thumb in the direction of the "Table of Obscurity," and explained, "It's our, Ashley. She just reported for her shift and she is a damn mess. Weeping uncontrollably, and I need you. I don't know what to do." Erma nodded; she pulled her eyeglasses off and stood up. Her hands quickly tapped the piles of files to stand them neatly upon the desktop, and her brilliant mind easily surmised the trouble and cause of the emotional distress with Ashley.

"Let me guess, that the smelly hipster fool went astray somehow or somewhere and broke her heart?"

"Yup. I want to break him in half like a pretzel and sit my huge ass on top of him until he is dust."

Erma brushed by me while I stood in the doorway to the office and my wife stood on her tiptoes and motioned for me to lean over and then puckered her lips and begged for a kiss. I happily obliged. What this gorgeous little petite chick with a great figure, a gorgeous face, and a heart of gold saw in my disgusting hulking frame and ugly face always amazed me, but once more, thank you, Lord.

"Nice image, Gilly. Thank you for that. Easy, big guy. I have this. By the way, you suck at filing. In fact, you suck at all forms of office work."

I smiled and slapped her on the ass as she scooted off to render assistance to Ashley.

"Yeah, I suck at many things, but you keep me around."

Erma's head whipped around and a coy smile waved across her mouth, "Office work is not a priority, Gills, and you don't suck at the things that really count."

Erma winked, and my heart melted. Again. Still.

"Ash is weeping at the Table of Obscurity. At least, she is sort of hidden there and the pub is still mostly empty, except for a few of the good old boys."

While I prepared a round of free drinks for the retirees, and Erma spoke with Ashley, I found myself deep in thought. I knew that within a few minutes, my incredible wife will have worked her magic on Ashley and all will be well. Ashley will be sad, and for a few weeks, she will carry some remorse over falling for and becoming involved with Kyle the smelly loser, but this glorious young woman will rebound, she will be stronger and more independent and someday, her man will walk into her life and she will be happy forever. I know this in my heart because it is going to happen. We are a team. All of us. We are a family that cares about each other, and who looks out for each other . . . through thick and thin. When one of us is down, we all are down together. It is not always, or only, about making money and stuffing your bank account with dough. Oh sure, we all need to make money and we all love to live our lives comfortably, but I for one, and Erma too, we have all that we need. We do not need big houses, or some exclusive vacation retreats, or fancy cars. We are content with what we have, with what comes to us, and money does not drive us. Our daughter is obtaining her education, reaching for her dream, and now, as we suddenly can see the golden years looming in front of us, we have come to feel peace with it all. If you think that you can standalone in this world, without teamwork, and run a business or run a company successfully, then you are sadly mistaken. You will fail. Life is about human relationships, and I am aware of the fact that I have received so many blessings.

When it all boils down to the paste at the bottom of the pot, Crows on a High Wire Public House is all about the crows.

It was late on a Friday afternoon and the day was now giving way to the evening. Friday was a big night for us here at the pub and as the usual evolution of the day crowd spun into the nighttime crowd, the Friday night buzz of the pending entertainment began to grow. A new and younger crowd slowly filtered in for the night. Tonight's performers were a local band that Ashley booked and they played indie rock, as well as they moved in and out of the cover band circles by playing some of their own music. The beat on the street was that this band was very good and while I seldom devoted much attention to the performers and the bands that Ashley booked, this one might draw some of my attention. They must be solid because this late afternoon and early evening crowd grew rather quickly. I watched as the retired gang waved goodbye and went home to their naps and television game shows and they gave way to the new crowd that was now filing in for the performance. A constant evolution was part of the magic of the pub.

This particular Friday was a few weeks after Kyle left out of Ashley's life and slowly, we witnessed an improvement in our glorious Ashley's spirits. Thankfully, it seemed as if Kyle was in the rear-view mirror. Erma constantly checked on her, spent time with her, and the two of them even went on a shopping spree that seemed as if the resulting charges of that adventure somehow mysteriously ended up on my credit card, but I was not complaining. Erma suggested that Ashley needed a slight image adjustment and the clothes they purchased seemed as if they reflected on that fact. Ashley lost just a bit of the hipster garb, and now, she wore a selection of more traditional clothing, still tight in all the right places, and she was looking fine as fine can be. There were more blouses as opposed to hoodies and tee shirts, and no hats, but Ashley allowed her golden hair to hang loose and straight. Her jeans no longer had rips, tears and fades. Now, her jean selections leaned closer to designer styles, and they were still tight, but conservative and fashionable. Moreover, they were comfortable for our line of work. Erma's influences were all over this fashion change and new statement. For footwear, Ashley alternated from wearing her usual canvas sneakers to low-top leather boots. I was so used to seeing her wearing the sneakers that, at first, the boots seemed out of place, but when I grew used to them and her look combined with the change in the rest of her clothing, I grew to love her look when she wore the boots. She recently completed the sleeve of tattoos on her other arm, and as of late, she also regained a little confidence, and her sense of humor returned too.

This evening, Ashley wore the boots, a long sleeved, blouse, that she unbuttoned at the cuffs and rolled up the sleeves to expose her tattoos and she left a few of the top buttons to her blouse undone too, to show just a tease of her remarkable cleavage. She had an awesome pair of jeans on tonight . . . jeans that clung to her hips and to her amazing backside perfectly. She oozes sexiness, and I knew that she would attract a crowd of drooling men tonight. I might need to calm a few of them down, and beat a few of them down too, but Ashley knew how to handle them.

Old Gilly usually did not work on Friday evenings, these days, my lower back began to give out around four in the afternoon, but about one hour ago, I swallowed a few pain relievers, strapped my back brace on and was buckling in for a long night. I was going to work behind the bar this Friday night with Ashley, because not only did I want to keep an eye on her, but I also wanted to check out the band. As I mentioned, Ashley booked our entertainment and her high praise of this band roused my curiosity. The name of the band, "Years Go By" had me intrigued too, because that is somewhat how I felt these days! Also contributing to the Friday night bartending gig by Gilly was the fact that Courtney, who Ashley recently promoted from a server to a bartender, was out for a week or so after having her wisdom teeth extracted. Ouch!

I was individually checking the identification credentials of a group of young men who just piled in and bellied up to the bar while ordering a round of brews, when I saw the front door open and the man walked into the pub.

Even after all these years, I still always looked up when the front door opened, it always was good business to greet patrons, either by name if they were a regular, or if they were newbies, I always extended a welcoming greeting whenever possible. If we were busy, then our staff knew to pitch in and greet them too. Our servers always were greeting them for a table inquiry, asking if they had a reservation, or if they were going to the bar, and most of all, thanking them for joining the flock of crows.

One of our newest servers, Tim, nodded to the man, and greeted him with, "Welcome to Crows on a High Wire Public House. Are you heading to the bar, or would you like a table, sir?" Tim did a nice job of reading the man's direction and purpose, and I smiled. I knew by the manner in which he focused his eyes that he was heading for the bar.

"The bar is fine. Thank you," the man replied in a voice laden with a heavy New Jersey accent.

Tim flowed in effortlessly, "Certainly, thank you. Enjoy. Gilly and Ashley are working at the bar. They will take very good care of you this evening."

We are not fine dining, we are a pub, but Tim was very cool, and he was going to be a good one. He worked two jobs, one in retail and the other here with us at the pub. He was a hardworking young man, and he even managed to squeeze in some college courses part-time. I could tell that he was a solid guy and was going to be a success at whatever endeavor he chose to pursue in life. Right now, we were happy to have him with us. Tim was reliable, had a cool demeanor, worked hard, and seemed as if he floated effortlessly while working the tables scattered across the dining room floor and the outlying high tops.

I handed back the identification card to the last young man in line. I went to pour their frosty mugs while out of the corner of my eye while using my Superman vision, I watched the man make his way towards the front of the pub and the bar area. The barstools were rapidly filling up across the high wire with multiple flocks of crows, who were chattering in their secret languages of the crows. I poured the last mug, slipped my fingers through the handles, and dropped them on the bar counter in front of the thirsty young men. One man handed me their credit card to open the tab, and I looked at the first name on the card and typed it into the keyboard on the cash register computer. Things sure have come a long way from the days when I began, with pads and pencils, handwritten tickets and cash and metal push button cash registers! It is all wonderful when it works, but when it goes south—it sure sucks. Luckily, I keep pads, pencils, and tickets handy.

While I ran the credit card, the man stopped in front of the bar and I watched his eyes while he scanned the bar for an open stool. I handed the card back to the young man and leaned in on the bar counter and studied the man up close and carefully. There was no way that he was interested in being one of the crows and squeezing in on the high wire. It was not his style. I could tell that crowds were not his thing. This guy was a loner, and he was content to be alone.

Now, my many years of standing behind the bar working the body languages of untold numbers of people passing through this pub . . . helped me to peg this guy right away. Pretty women might be my favorite study, and Erma understands because she checks out handsome men too, but I have to admire a guy with style. Now, this guy he had style. Head to toe. Confident, conservative, proud, tall, lean, and mean, with a hint of muscles under his polo shirt, and arms with muscles but not bulging in any way, shape or form. This guy was in fine physical condition, but he was no gym rat meathead. He dressed all in black, a black jean jacket, an untucked, but neat black polo shirt, black jeans, black boots and dark black sunglasses over his eyes, which as he now studied the bar and his eyes adjusted to the interior lights—he perched on the top of his head. Over his right shoulder, slung in a casual but stylish manner, was a small, black leather bag, which I surmised held a laptop or a tablet or a notebook of some sort. Yet, with all my experience, I could not determine the nature of his business, but there was little doubt in my mind, by the way, that he carried himself that whatever his business was . . . he was very good at it. He had very little hair, his head was not a bowling ball as mine was, but instead, he shaved what was there, high and tight. A number one razor comb, if I had to wager a guess. He wore full facial hair, and in the lights of the bar soffit, his hair looked as if it was a light brown, leaning toward hints of auburn or red in there and his beard was shaved to perfection, high and close and it fit his face perfectly. This guy was as handsome as a movie star is, but not a pussy as most of them are. This dude looked as if he just had enough of an edge that if you messed with him, you just might find yourself on your ass. I guessed him to be in and around his mid-forties, but with this guy, his exact age was difficult to tell. His facial hair had very few licks of gray in there, if any, and usually, the beard is the first to turn. It was not dye—it was genes.

I watched as his eyes, which seemed to waver between gray and blue in the lights of the bar, moved past the bar scene and settled upon the Table of Obscurity. Immediately, he clicked his heels and made his way to the dark corner where the table, of course, remained vacant.

Yes, indeed, right again, Gilly, because I pegged this guy right on the head. The table was perfect for him, no one around, no one to bother him, no one to interact with other than the server.

His eyes glanced at the plaque proclaiming the renowned title and status of the table, and a hint of a smile crossed his face. He pulled the stool out from the table, hung the shoulder bag over the back of the stool, unzipped it, and pulled out an electronic tablet. While he settled in at the Table of Obscurity, I tended to a refill of a Scotch and water for a regular crow and it was then that I noticed how intensely that Ashley studied the man.

Oh boy, Ashley enjoyed what she saw! An older, conservative man had caught her eye! Very unusual for our dear Ashley. Usually, this type of guy was not her style. Then again, maybe the Kyle incident and experience had changed her type of guy and she had finally adjusted her picker. Ashley had not dated anyone since dumbass left her life, and right now, as I watched the glow in her eyes, I knew that her mind whirled with potential. When I dropped the drink and greeted another group of young people gathering in the last remaining stools along the bar, I stole a quick and careful study of the man, who now had his tablet open and was tapping away on the device. No wedding ring on his finger. Confirmed. I knew that Ashley already scouted that out, too.

Technically, the Table of Obscurity landed within the dining room area of the pub and one of the floor servers would attend to it. When Ashley met eyes with Tim, who had grabbed some drink coasters, a menu, and silverware and was already heading that way, Ash intercepted Tim and with hand signals, indicated that she would handle the table tonight. With a nod and a smile, Tim went on his way. The young man understood because he too, recognized that the guy had style. Ashley almost ran over to where we kept the pile of drink coasters and after she picked one off the pile, she glanced at the exposed tattoos on her arms. Ashley dropped the coaster back onto the pile, and she proceeded to roll down her sleeves to cover her tattoos. Oh no, oh no, not good. I walked over and put my arm around her; she looked up, and when she knew that I had seen her study of the man and her decision to serve, the Table of Obscurity, Ashley put it all together. Her blue eyes twinkled, and I smiled at her.

I turned around and told the group of waiting young men, "I will be right with youse guys. Beer or drinks? Have ya i.d.s ready, Okay?"

They all nodded simultaneously and reached for their wallets while announcing in unison, "Beers."

"My heart just went thump, thump, thump, as it never has thumped before, Gills," Ashley said in a voice just above a whisper, "he is friggin' stunning."

I nodded and asked, "Then why ya pulling down ya sleeves, baby doll?"

Her eyes licked around the bar, and a look of pause covered her face. I thought, how damn, this woman is so gorgeous and her spirit was so kind and generous. Ash deserves the best.

"Cuz, it might not be his style . . . he seems conservative. Squared up. Tight. However, he is not uptight. Does that make any sense?" Her skill at analyzing patrons was dead-on now. Ashley was a pro and it might work to her advantage quite well in this case.

I gently touched her right arm and pushed at her sleeve while suggesting, "Perfect sense. Yup. Then be who you are, Ash. Always be who you are. Don't hedge on all that you are. Tats are part of you, he likes them or not. You are amazing, totally gorgeous, and you need to display all of you with pride. My best advice is to display them with pride." Now, I lowered my voice and added, "With the way ya ass looks in those jeans, he ain't gonna focus on the tats. After all, if ya two hit it off, he will see them and the others, sooner or later," I said with a wink. Ashley laughed aloud and held her hand over her mouth, and I pulled her in for a hug.

While she pushed her sleeves back up her arm and carefully and neatly folded them in a gentle tuck, Ashley whispered, "Damn, I love you, Gills."

"I love you too, Ashley. Now, go knock his socks and other things off him."

And so, she did. No fake prancing, no extra wiggle of her fine as fine can be hips and backside, just a genuine and perfect walk. I needed to work the bar here and carefully checked the i.d.s of the group of young men, while leaning in as best that I could to hear how Ashley made out on the initial approach. Strategically, the men all sat on the far edge of the bar nearest the infamous table, and I could lend an ear to the discussion.

"Welcome to Crows on a High Wire Public House and to the Table of Obscurity. In my humble opinion, the best table and seats in the house." Ashley leaned back as if to mimic the actual seating and in doing so provided her own testimony to the attributes of such, "You can peek around the pole here and catch the stage and the performance. You can lean this way and see the televisions over the bar and those over by the high tops and you are out of the way of the chattering but just close enough to hear what's happening. No one will bother you here. That is . . . unless . . . you want to be involved."

Her glorious body moved in all the right ways as she flexed and turned to duplicate the testimony of how wonderful it is to sit at an obscure location. All the young men on the end of the bar turned and carefully studied her move in those tight jeans during the demonstration. Oh, wow! Ashley was killing it tonight!

The man studied Ashley. He smiled at her remarkable introduction, and as I poured beers and attended to the now overflowing bar scene and demand, I smiled too. I did not mind that right now, I was running hard and my pain relievers long since gave out on working and my back was screaming at me. My back was emphatically reminding me that I had been on my feet for the best part of nine hours or thereabouts, but something told me to suck it up and let Ashley run a little longer and linger at the table for this handsome stranger. Something told old Gilly, and nowadays, I always went with my gut feelings.

"I am, Ashley, and I will be taking care of you tonight."

The man smiled and tapped the plaque on the wall and said in that same New Jersey accent, "I read the plaque and while I have not tested out any others, it seems as if you are correct and this is the best seat in the house. I like it here. It is obscure and I like to hide a little and remain obscure. Nice to meet you, Ashley. A pint of stout, please. That's it for now. Please, you can hand off a menu when you return . . . not sure, if I will eat . . . but maybe. Thank you. For now, the plan is just for some sippin' and tappin' here on this tablet while finishing up some last-minute work."

"Gotcha. I'll be right back with the pint and a menu. We have a great band playing tonight. Starting around eight or so. Please stick around . . . you will not be disappointed in the band or the food or the service and the . . . company."

Ashley winked while she strategically laced the invitation with duplicity and when she turned away, I watched for the man to study her rear-view, but to my disappointment, he went right back to his keyboard. Damn! Is this guy blind or what?

I met Ashley at the beer taps and while I poured lagers, she poured the stout and whispered, "Gills, please, turn the air conditioning down to about fifty-five because I am overheating. Damn, his eyes are the most amazing eyes that I have ever seen. Gray, blue, green, or whatever. I can't say exactly what color they are. They sparkle and change and he is hotter than hot is hot and steaming my damn makeup off my face."

"Whoaaah, Ash. That is hot. I will adjust the air to cool ya down a little. Just cuz I love ya and care. Old Gilly is just gotta add here, and it is a guess on my part, but he is much older than you are, Ashley. I am not trying to be a jackass and kill the vibe, but I am just sayin'. Be careful, love."

"Thank you and I get it. I can't tell how old he is, he looks so good it is impossible to determine, and honestly, I don't really care in the least," Ashley said as she poured off the foam and topped the pint off, "I bet he is experienced . . . in all the right ways." Ashley grabbed a menu and the pint and went to turn away but she stopped and leaned back into me and said, "Maybe it is time to be with a real man and give up on the boys."

I laughed at the statement and watched as the group of young men drooled over Ashley while she passed by them, and they studied her ass and whispered catcalls just loud enough to be heard.

I gave them a little stink eye and a subtle warning with my facial expressions, and they immediately quieted.

Satisfied that they understood the big picture, I whispered an agreement. "Yup, it is time, baby doll. Time."

The band rocked the joint, and the stranger stayed through to the end of the first set. He quietly sipped pints of stout, watched and listened to the band, and while he did so, he sporadically tapped away slowly on the keyboard of his tablet. It was apparent that he was not overly social because he did not say or interact with anyone other than when Ashley stopped by and tended to his order and made her best attempt at small talk. Since the pub was rocking so hard and was crazy busy, Ashley did not get to spend a lot of time with the handsome stranger. He was so quiet and unassuming that I knew she was more than just a little disappointed at not making much, if any, headway with him. Ashley did not try too hard. She knew when to ease off on a patron when they wanted to be alone, and after all, despite her personal attraction to the man, she was the general manager of the pub and respected his wishes.

Yet I could sense her disappointment.

Occasionally, he stopped typing whatever it was that he was working on, folded his arms across his chest, and intentionally focused his attention upon the band while he studied their performance. Then he tapped away thoughtfully upon the device. He was difficult to read, with not displaying much, if any, expression in his face, very few reactions, and he remained hidden in the perfect corner of the pub at the Table of Obscurity. He sat there quietly, while not saying much of anything, just politely thanking Ashley for dropping the pints and for her attention and for her service. I knew that Ashley's disenchantment was profound, and it grew even deeper when he asked for his tab and prepared to leave after the band's first set.

She grumbled, while processing his credit card, and studying the name on the card, "Ryan Griffith. It figures that he would have some damn sexy-ass name."

The bar was quieting down as the band prepared to

resume the next set, and I leaned in with my foot on the bar rail to take a little pressure off my aching back. I did not say a word, while Ashley delivered the card, thanked Mr. Griffith by using his last name and the mister title and added, "I would love to see you again here at the pub. I not only tend bar and serve, but I am also the general manager here. I hope you enjoyed the performance and the cold pints."

He nodded, mumbled a thank you, and while packing up his gear and placing his jean jacket over his shoulders added, "I did. The band was excellent, the pints were cold and your service was awesome. You manage a top-notch place. Thank you."

He left it open ended as to his willingness to return, and Ashley looked as if someone peed in her cocktail when she returned to her post behind the bar and stood next to me. She folded her arms across her chest, leaned back on the tap rail and sighed while she watched Mr. Griffith wander through the maze of the jam-packed dining room of the pub; he briefly stopped in front of the stage, studied the band, and then, with a glance at his watch and a quickened pace, slipped out the front door.

Her disappointment made her supposition as to his evening's plans run wild, "Did you see him look at his watch? I bet he has a date tonight with some gorgeous chick. A man who has it all together as he has is not going home to be alone. No, no, no . . . he most likely has his pick of the herds of women chasing him around. Damn, I blew it. No reaction at all from him. What a tough nut to crack. He made no move, was just polite as all get-go and did not flirt with me at all, not even a harmless flirt or a coy word back at me."

I still did not say a word but hoped that our Ashley did not slip in her spirits once again.

She turned and looked at me and asked, "You watch everything, so I know you studied this . . . did he even check out my ass or my chest? I left this blouse open and I think that I look pretty good tonight."

I did not react or answer her right away; I could not lie and did not want to disappoint Ashley. Instead, I stumbled for words, and fiddled with bar coasters and scanned the bar for refills.

"Ah, ah, ah, yeah, Ash. No doubt that you look super-hot. Ya always do."

Ashley called my cards in rather quickly, "Gilly, you are avoiding answering my question. You never fudge anything. Don't start now. Did he, or did he not, check me out at all?"

I waved my hand in the air in a feeble attempt at a dismissal of the situation. Ashley was just climbing back up the romance hill to give it another slide down on the other side and I did not want to impede her progress, but I could not lie to her either.

I attempted an excuse, "Well, Ash, maybe his work was important on the tablet thingy that he was banging away on and he had some type of a deadline to meet. You know, the work might be a priority for him tonight and he just stopped by here to chill and relax and clear his mind a little. He really needed to remain focused on . . . his work."

"You are still not answering my question, and are fumbling around with your words, so that means no. Damn . . . not even a quick glance?"

I fessed up now, "Sorry, baby doll, honestly, I did not see him checking you out. However, I got really busy and might have missed it. It was rocking in here during the first set."

A crow called for a refill and Ashley waved to acknowledge the request. She walked down the bar and picked up his mug, dropped it in the wash rack and pulled a frosty mug from the cooler.

Ashley continued her lament, "Shit. This. Really. Sucks. I can't believe that he did not even check me out once."

"Well, I did, and so did every other man and maybe even some of the women in here tonight."

Ashley began to fill the mug from the tap and laughed while saying, "I am pretty sure that you saying that you check me out is some type of sexual harassment, boss."

"It is, but what the hell, it is true. I don't lie and I think that we are way past that point in our relationship here."

"Well, we are, and thank you. You are not really my boss, you and Erma are my family, and if it helps at all, I check out your ass too."

I began to mix a margarita and laughed while saying, "It is big enough. I am sure you cannot miss it!"

"More for Erma to love and hold on to. Sometimes, a girl needs handles, ya know."

I grew serious as I flipped the drink into the stainless-steel shaker and allowed all my parts and pieces to jiggle along with the liquid.

"He will be back, Ashley. I can tell."

Her eyes flashed, and she blinked a few times before asking, "How can you tell?"

"I dunno, but I feel as if he is just a quiet guy, recovering from something. A solitary guy with maybe a touch of loneliness in his soul. He is searching for something or someone. He just is . . . hurt and recovering."

"A gorgeous man like that . . . hurt and lonely? Really?"

"Yup, I watched him select the Table of Obscurity. It caught his eye because he wanted to be alone. The table was perfect for his mood. He is pensive." I poured the drink into the glass and smiled while reiterating, "I know these things. I have a useless degree in psychology and I am an expert observer of people. Not only am I sure of his returning to our amazing pub . . . well, old Gilly guarantees it."

Her smile lit up the entire world, and just a little bit more.

Honestly, her smile chased away every inch of darkness.

It was late on a Friday afternoon and exactly one week after the handsome stranger first appeared and stole Ashley's heart. When the front door opened and he walked in with that same cool demeanor, his sunglasses on over his eyes, all dressed in black and his looks that could force lust and desire and allow him to bed every woman within a mile or so, I smiled at knowing my prediction came true. I glanced at Ashley who had already spotted him and she was trying to hold on to her heart and not faint.

I lifted one eyebrow and said, "Told ya so."

Ashley looked at me and smiled and said, "I love how you are always right, except when you are wrong and I am right, Gilly."

"Sure, sure, thank you for that profound observation, but here he comes, so chin up, turn your smile on and push those beautiful breasts out, baby doll."

"Hell, yeah, Gilly. I have this one. Damn, everything on my body and within my mind is going, thump, thump, thump."

I watched as he took his sunglasses off, perched them as he always seemed to do, on the top of his head and after a quick glance around the interior of the bar, and while allowing his eyes to adjust to the interior lights, he took a few strides towards the bar. While he passed a few tables, the women seated at them glanced up and studied him while he walked by. Not only had this guy caught Ashley's eye, but a few other women in the pub this afternoon noticed him, too. He spotted me and smiled, and then he glanced in Ashley's direction and lifted his hand in a friendly wave. His smile was wide and while he walked closer to the bar, he adjusted the backpack strap slung over his right shoulder.

"Hello," Mr. Griffith said to me while the big man leaned into the bar, reached over with his hand extended and with that heavy New Jersey accent leaving his lips, he extended a greeting, "nice to see you again, Mr. Gilford. We did not have a chance to meet last week, but Ashley mentioned your name and the fact that you are the owner of the pub. I am Ryan Griffith."

I shook his hand, and his grip was strong and powerful.

"Please, call me Gilly. It is nice to see you again, Mr. Griffith. Yes, I am the owner of this fine establishment, but I would be nothing without Ashley here. She is my general manager and the most important person in the management chain." I leaned into Ashley and put my arm around her and pulled her in tightly to my big body while adding, "Behind every haphazard, barely functional man, is a great woman. I am lucky because I have three exceptional women in my life to keep me in order. Ashley, my wife, and my daughter."

"Okay, Gilly it is. That is an awesome testimony and, yes, I can tell that Ashley is on top of her game here and that she is simply amazing . . . in *so* many ways." Ryan turned and smiled at Ashley, and I felt her wobble a little in my grip. I squeezed her shoulder to let her know that I had her. "My pleasure to see you again, Ashley. I have been actually looking forward to this Friday night visit." Ryan pointed at the Table of Obscurity and seeing it vacant, as it usually was, asked, "Okay, if I sit there? I enjoy the obscurity factor."

"Yes, of course, Mr. Griffith. Sure, I will grab you a menu, and a pint of stout. Is that what you wish for tonight?"

Ryan turned, smiled, and with a lowered voice, still

laced with his accent, said, "Yes. Amongst other things. Thank you and please, Ashley, call me, Ryan. Please, you too, Gilly. Please call me, Ryan." He turned and walked to the Table of Obscurity and slung his backpack off his shoulder, opened it and began to pull his tablet out. Ashley watched him carefully, and then she grabbed a pint glass and walked over to the taps. I smiled as I listened to her words and watched her reaction.

"Oh. My. Aching. Heart. My legs are wobbly, parts of me are hard, and other parts are, well, I can't say because that is too much information, Gills. Even for our relationship."

I laughed and held my hand up while telling my faithful assistant, "Yes, too much information for certain but even without the detailed explanations, I totally understand."

Ashley pensively paused for a second with her hand on the tap handle while waiting for the foam of the stout to settle into the pint glass.

Her eyes danced around and then she stared out of the corner of her eyes over near the Table of Obscurity while commenting, "I feel like a love-struck teenager and in a few weeks, I will be forty years old. I feel such a connection to him, yet, I am so hesitant. I guess that men have played me for a fool too many times and I am gun shy."

"You are no fool, Ash. Anything but. You are brilliant, smart, gorgeous, and as Ryan said, amazing and on top of your game."

She tugged at the handle again to top off the pint, and the dark brown stout spilled out into more layers of glorious foam.

"Thank you, but you are biased."

"Maybe I am, but I am always factual. I always tell you when you have to wipe your nose or adjust your bra strap or when your amazing breasts are waving hello to me, cuz ya neckline is down near Camden."

Ashley laughed aloud and nodded, while obviously still

replaying the grand entrance of Ryan Griffith in her mind. I thought how this was one helluva long pour. She kept overflowing the glass, pouring it off, and wasting expensive stout, but I understood her nerves were on edge and she was love-struck.

"You certainly do. Factual is one of your many attributes. Gilly, I think there was dual meaning in what he said. Don't you, boss? I think he came here tonight to see me. Or, is that just silly wishful thinking on my part?"

I shook my head and agreed, "I agree with the dual meaning and of course, he came to see you. For sure, he did not come here to check out my fat ass and big, ole, belly."

I had a sudden thought as Ashley continued the never-ending pour of stout, while staring off into la-la-land. I can ignore my screaming back for a few more hours. For our dear Ashley . . . it was worth it. I had a wonderful feeling about Mr. Ryan Griffith. Ryan was a man who no longer seemed as if he was a stranger.

"Hey, take good care of him, and I am staying put for this shift. I have to, so that you can spend as much time as you can over there. It is time for me to suck Tim into life behind the bar, yakking with the crows. The highways and byways and various roads of life have many flattened squirrels spread out on them because they could not make decisions. Go for him, baby doll. I gotcha covered. If it goes really well, then just short shift it and you can quit your shift early. Comp some drinks on me for you and for Mr. Devastatingly Handsome. Tim and I can close tonight."

Ashley's smile and the glint in her eyes upon hearing my words were magical. She topped off the pour of stout, cleared the foam (again), and then poured some off, and just when I thought she was finally finished with the pour, she topped it off again!

"Lord, in Heaven, I love you, Gills."

"Yeah, for sure. That's what all the gorgeous women say to me, but I only have eyes for one woman, or maybe two, or perhaps three or four at the most. Anyway, I love you too, Ash. Life is short, moments in the sun grow dim and cold way too quickly and we only have so many chances at joy. Therefore, my suggestion is to go for joy. And by the way, that glass of stout is full, baby doll. In fact, it was full three foams ago."

Ashley blushed, realized what she was doing with the pint, and said, "Sorry. I am sooo distracted."

Ashley wore a smile a mile wide. She proudly picked up the pint that seemed as if it had a hole in the bottom of the glass, plucked a menu off the pile and gloriously wiggled over to the Table of Obscurity. Tonight, she wore another selection of knockout clothes, with an attractive blouse hugging her bouncing breasts and jeans that fit her more than perfectly. If that amazingly perfect backside of hers and the generous wiggle combined with that perfect smile and stunning blonde hair, did not set Mr. Ryan Griffith off to the moon without a spaceship, then I will recommend an eye doctor for him.

While I poured a light lager for a slightly grouchy and impatient regular crow, who was a short elderly gentleman whose feet did not even reach the floor while he sat on the barstool, I glanced at Ryan's reaction as Ashley approached. Cross the eye doctor off the list, there Gilly. The guy has a pulse, after all. His eyes twitched and I am sure that a few other parts of his body might have felt a twitch, too.

The band playing this evening was nowhere near as talented as "Years Go By" but they were not too bad. The band mostly played cover tunes, some folk rock and some oldies, and they held their own. It appeared as if they did not have a huge following and the pub was not half as crowded as last Friday, but we were not doing too badly. I could handle this crowd and I left Tim out on the dining room floor, since I had no trouble keeping up with the demand. His bartender training will happen soon enough, just not tonight. Rather than teaching a rookie the ins and outs of behind the bar, I could serve the customers and keep an eye on the developing situation with Ashley and Ryan. Old Gilly was looking for some explosions of love here tonight!

Ashley floated behind the bar on occasion and assisted me, here and there, but I gently pushed her back over to Ryan and she stood for a long time, next to his table, listening to him speak, looking at his tablet and what he was working on and engaging in conversation. It must have been going rather well, because when she went to the tap for a third refill of his stout, she checked him first, then caught my eye and fanned herself in a faux display of radiating heat. Perhaps it was not faux at all.

"That's it, Gills. I am off the clock, boss. I am pouring this pint for Ryan and then pouring a double tequila for me."

"Whoooaahhhh, baby doll! You are going for the brass ring, huh?"

"Hell yeah, I am."

"This is awesome. No squirrel-like indecisive action, huh?"

"Nope. He asked me for my number. Then he asked me what I am doing after my shift. I gave him the number and told him that as of right now, because I have the best boss in the entire world, I am off my shift."

Over the top of Ashley's shoulder, I watched as Ryan powered his tablet off. He folded it up and jumped out of his stool, while placing the device in the backpack that he slung on the back of the stool. Then in a super-classy move that was sure to be a panty-smoker (especially combined with the tequila) Ryan held the stool out for Ashley as she dropped the drinks onto the table. Ash eased her gorgeous ass into the stool and he glided the stool underneath the table. Now, I really felt excited about this situation. In fact, old Gilly might even be smiling for the rest of this evening.

Especially, when an hour or so later, after a few more drinks and what was obviously a very in-depth conversation laced with many laughs, they bid me a good evening, Ashley leaned in and gave me a kiss right on my big, old, kisser, and Ryan shook my hand and thanked me as they began to leave.

"Hey, wait a minute there. Be safe out there, you two. You packed away a few drinks. No driving for youse guys." I waggled my finger in the air as a warning.

Ashley posed and put her hands on her hips and if that sultry look did not blow steam and smoke out of a man's ears, then I am not three-hundred-pounds. And, I assure you that I am three-hundred-pounds. Actually, three-hundred and eighteen pounds. To be factual. As of this morning.

"No worries, Dad. We are leaving our cars here in the lot. We are taking a taxi into Newark to pub-crawl and check out some bands. We can leave our cars here and take taxis home. Or, wherever it is that we end up. No driving for us." Ashley's fabulous eyes flashed with some dreaming of where and perhaps, how the night might end. "Ryan wants to check these bands out and take in the shows. He writes music reviews. He is a part-time music critic. In fact, that is why he came here last week. To check out, 'Years Go By.'"

"Very cool on the taxi and super cool on the music gig, Ryan. I guess that is what you are typing away all the time on that keyboard, huh?"

"Yes. I do try to checkout as many local bands as I am able to and write music reviews for some websites, and local publications. Other than music, I do a few other things too."

I nodded, and I thought about how Ashley called me Dad, but I had to be right around Ryan's age or thereabouts. He just looked a helluva lot better than I did. That was an understatement. The guy looked like a God.

"Well, have fun," and while speaking the words, I pointed at Ryan and leaned in over the bar as I half joked and was half-serious, "warning there, big guy, be a gentleman with our precious Ashley and don't keep her out too late. I don't want to hear any tales of bullshit and adventure. You have all kinds of muscles there, but old Gilly can run faster than you figure that I can, and once I get going, then I can roll over ya like a locomotive."

Ryan held his hands in the air and smiled, "I surrender. My preference is to remain upright and not flattened. Thank you for the fair and honest warning. Best behavior. I promise."

"Very cool. Have fun, youse guys. I love you, Ashley."

"I love you too, Gilly."

I waved to them, and off they went. I watched as they weaved through the crowd and Ryan stuck his hand out behind his back as he led the way and Ashley instinctively grabbed it as they navigated what was now an almost full-house crowd enjoying the band. I watched until they disappeared from my view and left out the door.

This band grew on me as they moved deeper into their sets. They actually were awesome. In fact, this entire evening was awesome. Back pain. What back pain?

I walked over to the whiskey display, pulled a glass out, grabbed an Irish, and poured myself a double. Two hours until last call. Hang in there, Gills. Hang in there. Time to toast this one. I leaned on the rail on the inside of the bar and slowly swigged the whiskey. The crows were all lined up and chattering away very happily while sitting on their high wire. In the center of the bar, there was a middle-aged married couple still madly in love and playing a game of squeeze the ass. Next to them, a few male hipsters sat while checking out some hot chicks sitting a few tables away, and plotting when to make a move to their table. On the far ends, there were a few regulars, occasionally listening to the band while checking out the baseball game on the tube.

Then there was this little round guy with a bad hairpiece and a belly that looked exactly as if he stuck a basketball under his shirt. It was perfectly round, and he was happy as all get-go. When a song from the band struck his fancy, he jumped off the stool, stood next to his barstool, and shook his little doodle. He did not have a care in the world.

Good for him.

Life is good, in fact, life is great and, in my heart, I wished and maybe even prayed that our precious Ashley finally found love. Even though they really just met, I had no qualms at all about Ryan Griffith. My loser and clown detecting radar had no blips on the screen. I was calm and felt comfortable with her scooting off with him tonight. Just the looks in their eyes almost brought tears to mine. I cannot wait to tell Erma. She is going to be thrilled with the news. I tilted the glass over and knocked the rest of the Irish down. I felt the gentle burn, just as the hipsters waved at me for refills. They needed more liquid courage before making the move. I don't know why, because those gals sure were hotties and cuties too. All of them were knockouts. Three of them and three of you. Believe old Gilly, when I tell ya, that they checked youse guys out too. Geez, c'mon youse guys, don't be flattened squirrels on some lonely roadway. Make a move, pick a direction, and most of all, don't ever look back.

"Yeah, yeah, yeah. I see ya. Be right there, youse guys," I waved and spouted off in my adopted New Jersey jingo-jango-lingo.

Yup, it is nice to own the joint, and yes, I have a very good feeling about this Ryan guy.

Very, very good.

Usually, I never work on Saturdays unless it is an emergency, such as if I need to fill in for a sick employee or when the heavy vacation time is kicking in during the summer months, or if we have an immensely popular event occurring at the pub. Despite Erma's pleading, I cannot help myself and I stop in every single day, not necessarily to work, usually just to check on things and honestly, to tip a few drinks and grab a meal. Even though I own the joint, I have to say that the food is very good. In fact, for pub food it is exceptional.

Generally, I let Ashley run the weekend show and I always have complete confidence in her and her abilities to handle anything that comes along. I also know that she would call me, or she would text me if there were bombs dropping or disasters looming. We promoted Tim to an opener on the weekends and he was doing a slam-bang job at handling his new position of responsibility. After I told Erma all about the amazing Friday evening and the magnetic connection of Ashley and Ryan, there was no way this side of Antarctica that Erma and I would not show up at four in the afternoon on the Saturday after her date. We wanted to be there when Ashley reported to begin her shift in order to see how things went.

"Soooo?" Erma asked as Ashley lit up at the sight of us settling into the stools at the as usual, (apparently, unless Ryan Griffith was there) vacant Table of Obscurity.

"I have been panting here, since my husband told me all about last evening. Details, girl, details!"

Ashley rushed over, and first, she hugged Erma and then she hugged me while lighting up as if she was a Christmas tree.

"What the hell, no kisses from the gorgeous women in my life?" I asked, with my hands outstretched and my lips standing by.

They both ignored me.

"Oh, guys! He is so amazing! He is hotter than hot is hot

and so intelligent, caring, and thoughtful. I think that Ryan Griffith is the most interesting man that I have ever met. He is great company with an amazing sense of humor, the most amazing eyes that you have ever seen and, well, ya know, put together here and there and everywhere."

Upon hearing the "amazing and put together" part, my instincts kicked in, I leaned in, and gently held our precious Ashley by the arm and her eyes locked on mine.

"He was a gentleman?" I asked as my overly protective forces put the pedal to the metal inside of my soul.

"Unfortunately, yes! I had to do some covert checking out of the vital parts and pieces. After all, a girl has to think about a test drive before getting behind the wheel and buying the car. Ya know, admittedly, I entered some elements of supposition on my part . . . but I know that I am dead on."

I leaned back as Erma giggled and nodded in agreement. I decided not to allow my mind to wonder about the giggles and the agreement part. I took a swig of an Irish that Tim conveniently dropped and I relaxed. This Tim guy was well on his way now. While listening to the details of the amazing evening experience of our precious Ashley, I played the role of Publican and kept an eye on Tim's development. The young man was progressing nicely. I loved his instincts and anticipation of the customer's needs. Technically, I was the owner and not a customer, but what the hell; the guy was on the sticker.

"Seriously, if you saw him, Erma, you would understand. I mean, geez, my panties incinerated when I first saw him, so there was no hope. My bra was going to unlatch on its own. I would have jumped into any bed we could find."

I put my fingers in my ears as my wife looked at me and she laughed while commenting.

"Geez, Gills, it is apparent that the guy is a God. Give her a break."

I perked up when I heard Ashley's testimony laced with a hint of sadness, "But sadly, he did not make any moves. A perfect gentleman."

Now I felt as if I could jump in on Ryan's side. After all, the guy played it cool with a super-hot chick on the first date.

"Well, I think he is very cool, and what is with his accent? Heavy New Jersey there."

"Paterson. He is from Paterson. I looovee his accent. It is sooo cool and sooo New Jersey." Poor Ashley was falling all over every aspect of Ryan.

I still played it cool, "I admit . . . he is . . . tall and he is fairly good-looking, and the guy does have a few muscles here and there, and a cool vibe and a cool accent. Other than that, he is kinda ordinary."

They stared at me, waved their hands in dismissal of my opinion, and for the most part, ignored my comments. Thank goodness that good ole Tim was still aware of my presence and he dropped another Irish in front of me without missing a beat. Tim scurried off to attend to other customers. This kid has major potential. On the other hand, perhaps, he is just sucking up to the boss. On the other hand, perhaps, he was trying to get me sloshed and ask for a raise. Regardless, a few more Irish whiskey tilts and I would not actually care. Ashley was demonstrative and emphatic as she blabbed on and on about Mr. Amazing. I relaxed, not because of the influence of the whiskey, but because I could tell that, last night, I was correct in my assessment of their relationship. This was it. I could tell and by the way that my wife's eye sparkled as she listened, I knew that Erma knew too.

"He *is divorced.* About two years now. They married young, sort of high school sweethearts. He said, maybe they married too young. Who knows?" Ashley flashed her eyes at me and smiled while admitting, "You were right on, Gilly. Ya know, when you said that Ryan was hiding out and recovering from something. Occasionally, you are correct."

I lifted my finger to protest the use of the word, "occasionally," but could not get a word in edgewise since Ashley was so excited to explain everything about her new dream man.

Off she went, "At first, he said that he was very sad over the situation, but he said they just grew apart. It happens, although a woman must be crazy to give him up. Anyway, I did not press him for details, and he did not ask about my past. Thank goodness."

I thought to myself, yes! That is why he wanted to be alone and picked the Table of Obscurity. His soul still ached. However, the gorgeous and stunning, Ashley Stahl brought him out of it. That is so amazing. Ah, the joy of true love! Soulmates connected. I would have enjoyed hearing that he was never married but I guess in this day and age, that might be unrealistic dreaming. Still, I felt no red flags. As Ashley said, sometimes, you just grow apart for whatever reasons. This is so cool.

Ashley went on and on with her excited testimony about Ryan. "He has two older children, but unfortunately, they sided with their mom and Ryan does not see them or hear from them too much. He has been reaching out to them and trying hard to reestablish their relationships. Work wise, Ryan is the vice president of a company that handles property and facility management and repairs. He also writes his music reviews, and he writes some fiction books, and is a professional photographer too. He really is into everything. As he says, he is a renaissance man."

I could not help but to allow my cynical side to surface as some waves of jealousy erupted inside of me as the testimony went on and on seemingly forever. Ryan seemed virtually flawless.

My cynical and jealous side surfaced and I asked, "Did he swim across the English Channel with anchors tied to his legs and in his spare time, did he climb Mount Everest too?"

I mean, after all, a man has his own pride, and I thought that these two important ladies in my life ought not to ignore the handsome giant hunk of intelligent blob that I was.

They ignored me again, and it did not matter, because Tim sailed by and in one quick motion picked up my empty glass, dropped a replacement and dropped a vodka and soda water for Erma (her favorite and usually, I get lucky when she has at least three of them) and a double tequila for Ash. In my opinion, Ryan was well on his way to the same fate if they were meeting up tonight after work. This Tim guy is an efficient machine of drink serving wonder. Now . . . I was feeling a little loopy, and I conceded defeat on fighting against joining in the adoration society of Mr. Ryan Griffith. It seemed hopeless, anyway. The guy was amazing. I rested my elbows on the Table of Obscurity and I rested my head in my hands. I might even have sighed and batted my eyes as I continued to hear of the endless wonders of the extraordinary Mr. Ryan Griffith.

"I think that I am hopelessly in love," Ashley forcibly proclaimed, without any wavering in her voice.

From the look on Erma's gorgeous face, Ashley's words had a major impact on my wife. I felt the sting too, so I dove into the Irish. One gulp.

Okay, cool, here comes Tim.

A look of concern moved across my wife's lovely face.

Erma swigged her drink and said, "Now, honey, please, be careful. Please, take it slowly."

Ashley shook her head in a rather adamant manner and strongly stated, without any doubt, "I can't. I know that you both love me and care, and I love youse guys too, but you need to believe me when I say that . . . I can't. He is everything in a man that I ever imagined and I know that he is into me too. We are going out tonight after closing and on Monday, my day off," Ashley's eyes glanced at me and I nodded in agreement, "we are hiking out in Warren County and doing a photoshoot. He shoots landscapes."

I sighed in relief that he did not do nudes. Until the next words flowed out of Ashley's gorgeous mouth.

"And he does portraits and intimate poses too. Photographic studies of human structure. He wants to shoot my tattoos."

Tim! Suddenly, my head was on a swivel. Where in the hell are you?

Erma posed with unease, washing over her face and infiltrating into her body language while I salivated.

Erma spoke gently, but forcibly, "Ashley, we love you dear, and yes, it sounds wonderful but please, your past track record with men is not too swift . . . and all that we are thinking and suggesting is to be careful and go slowly. He is so much older than you are. . .."

Tim or not, I needed to jump in here. On the tailwind of my wife's words, and to reinforce the point that she had made, I entered reality into the situation.

"If this relationship goes as, you dream that it will and wish it to be, and apparently as you feel in your heart . . . there might come a point in your lives together when you are changing your dream man's diaper."

I blinked at my own words. Strong and powerful in a vision, but I think it needed to be exactly that way.

Upon hearing my words and the words of my beloved wife, Ashley nodded, and her eyes flashed with an understanding of our love for her. Once more, between gulps of tequila (the boss in me was going to remind her that she was working, but what the hell, in this case, who cares?) Ashley spoke from her heart.

In a low voice that was more than just convincing, in fact, it sent shivers down my spine as to the validity that it held within it. Ashley said, "I understand what our age difference means and the reality of the situation. I really do.

His amazing appeal and good looks now do not blur the facts for me. I don't care how old he is. Honestly, I love the fact that he is so much older than I am. I am done with punks and losers. I am sure of this relationship." Her eyes flashed in quick glances at each of us before continuing, "Sure. Of. It. Ryan is the one. He is my man and I am his woman. I know what my heart feels. I would change his diaper, heal his soul, love him, and take care of him forever. And, I know that he would do the same for me. I just know it."

I looked over at Erma. She had tears in her eyes and once that I spotted my wife tearing up. Then, I turned into a cupcake. I pushed aside the Irish, stood up from the stool, and waved my arms for Ashley and Erma to join me in a group hug. They both jumped into my huge arms and we held each other, rocked together, and absorbed our mutual love and warmth.

I whispered, "Then go get your man, baby doll. Let nothing stand between you and your love. Give him your heart, lend him pieces of your soul, and melt into one with your love for each other. Your love will transcend time and space. It will mold you into one person. Now and forever, one person. I can only wish you to have what Erma and I share. It is our greatest wish for you, baby doll. Our greatest wish."

About ten months after that fateful first meeting of Mr. Ryan Griffith and Ms. Ashley Stahl, I walked Ashley down the aisle of a small Lutheran church on the edges of Sussex and Passaic County. Ryan was Lutheran, and this church seemed to be perfect for the two of them. Hidden and slightly obscure. Last night at rehearsal, I drove past the church a few times and kept missing it until Erma knocked me on the shoulder and pointed it out to me. Erma was Ashley's Maid of Honor, and our daughter, Connie, was a bridesmaid along with two of Ashley's close friends. Ryan had some boyhood buddy as his Best Man and some other buddies as his ushers. It was a small, simple service, and if not for the pub family in attendance, then the number of butts in the pews might have been lean and mean, but all the crows flew in and landed to watch one of their favorites take the plunge. I did not expect anything less from our loyal flock. Ryan's adult children attended the service and while it seemed as if they had grown apart after their parent's divorce, they were very cool with his remarriage. It seemed as if they knew in their hearts that their father had found his soulmate and perhaps this happiness would spark a new bond in their relationships. Time would tell.

When Ashley asked me to walk her down the aisle and give her away, my big body rippled with love and many other emotions.

"It is my honor to do so, Ashley, but do you think they have a tuxedo large enough to fit me?"

She laughed and said, "I am sure they will dig one up. I would not want anyone else to give me away, Gilly. You and Erma are my family. My best friends and such a huge part of my life that I am not sure of where I would be right now without the two of you."

Her poignant words brought this big man to tears and almost to his knees.

It felt as if the entire world was watching us as I held Ashley's arm in mine and we took the stroll down the center aisle of the small church. She looked beyond gorgeous. Beyond captivating. Ashley looked out of this world with beauty and so did my precious Erma, who was holding back tears as best that she could. Our amazing daughter was quite the looker, too. Thankfully, she did not inherit her old man's looks.

I stared at the groom, and Ryan's eyes were wide with love and captivation at the stunning woman about to become his wife. When we approached the altar and the pastor began the service, I did my best to focus on all this meant to me and to us and to Ashley and Ryan. The beginning of the journey. The ups and the downs, the hills and the valleys and all that life throws your way. I knew in my heart that it was a real love and that they were going to be forever.

True love, finally.

"Who gives this woman away to enter into Holy Matrimony," the pastor asked.

"I do," I proudly answered.

I turned and gently leaned over to kiss Ashley's cheek while the stunning bride whispered, "Don't make me cry, big guy. My mascara will run. I love you, Gills."

"I love you too, baby doll. Be happy. Please, be happy always and forever."

I kissed her cheek. Then turned to Ryan, shook his hand, and gently touched his shoulder. He was as tall as I was, just in a helluva lot better shape. I have to admit the guy was better looking than any Hollywood movie star was.

"Take exceptional care of her, Ryan. Please, make her happy forever."

"I will, Gilly."

I nodded and took my seat in the first pew and did my best to fight back the tears.

I lost that battle.

As I sat there and took it all in, I thought about how Coatsie is going to be so proud and happy to hear this news. I usually called him once a month or so, but I would call him tomorrow to give him the details on this one. He used to visit a few times per year, but now he was too damn old to travel anymore. I was not sure, but he had to be in his mid-eighties or thereabouts. Yes, indeed, as the pastor spoke the final words of the service and pronounced them man and wife, and the happy couple kissed, I thought how special that old storefront of about eight-thousand square feet of space in downtown Bloomfield, New Jersey was. How amazing it was that those crows landed on that electrical high wire and how it all came about in Coatsie's mind so long ago. I thought of all the marvelous things that have happened because of that special place and how it was where we all belonged. All because I could not find a job and had a useless college degree and met a knockout chick who stole my heart forever.

And, every day, I thank the good Lord in Heaven that it all happened just the way that it did.

About two days after the wedding, I screwed in a brass plaque to the edges of the Table of Obscurity. This table was very special. To say the least. I saw no reason as to why this table could not have two special designators. The Table of Obscurity plaque hung on the wall right above the table and this new plaque was going right onto the outward edge of the table.

The new brass plaque stated, "Ashley and Ryan. True Love, Finally."

Chapter Six

The New Jersey Defense League

You Don't Mess with the Crows

It was a Tuesday in the late summer and the dog days of August were in the rear-view mirror. Since I resembled the girth of a blimp, I am always rather thankful when the heat and humidity go bye-bye and my socks are not soaked with yuckiness at the end of my shift. Erma appreciated it too. Doing the laundry with a clothespin perched on her nose seemed as if it was rather uncomfortable.

Our general manager, Mrs. Ashley Griffith, was in early today for a special training mission that was vital to our success as a business. Those were not my words, but that was what the insurance representative for our business liability policy told me. I hung up the telephone and Ashley leaned on the bar and looked at me with a puzzled look on her lovely face. Since her marriage to Ryan, a year or so ago, her contentment in life flooded over her, and she was even more gorgeous than she ever was. I did not think that was even possible. I never saw her happier and that fact gave immense and indefinable joy to my heart.

Ashley overheard just enough of the phone conversation to piece it together.

Ashley blinked a few times and then asked, "Well, is he coming or what? He is an hour late and all the staff is waiting. We open in fifteen minutes and even if he arrives soon, we will need to break up the training into small groups."

I shook my head to indicate that the first aid instructor that my new insurance provider insisted we hire to teach us CPR, basic first aid, and such handy aids such as the Heimlich maneuver was not showing up today. In fact, based upon the phone call that I just hung up on, this particular instructor was not showing up here, there, or anywhere.

"He is not coming today, or in fact, any other day, Ashley. Unfortunately, the poor guy is dead. He keeled over from a heart attack last night."

Ashley's gorgeous face contorted into a series of amazing twists, very similar to a twisted pretzel. One of those hard, crunchy, suckers baked out in Pennsylvania Dutch Country that knock your teeth and any fillings that you have in your choppers right out of your mouth on the first bite. I watched as she at first tried to hold back the laughter and then as she lost the battle, Ashley burst into uncontrollable laughter, and then, while watching her, I too lost it. Our bodies heaved in great sobs of laughter and we hung onto each other, trying to stabilize our bodies to prevent us from falling on the floor, holding our bellies and kicking our feet in the air while we laughed. The staff gathered around from their seats in the dining room to see what had their two bosses laughing so hard.

Ashley recovered a little, held her hand over her mouth, gasped, and panted as the words barely popped out of her mouth, but they did.

"I am such a horrible human being! The poor man! His poor family . . . and here I am, enveloped within hilarious, uproarious laughter. Laughing at . . . the death of a fellow human being!"

Initially, I could not speak because the laughter was still arriving in great waves that shook my body. Instead, I just waved my hand in the air and dismissed her self-loathing.

After mustering up immense strength in order to gather my wits and after successfully doing so, I managed to squeak out a few words that entered some more facts into the situation, "Here *we* are laughing, Ash. Me too! No, no, no, we are not horrible human beings. I bet when this guy arrived at the Pearly Gates, Saint Peter, did a double take and said, Really, pal, really? There was no one around that could save your ass? He had to go straight to Heaven being a lifesaver and all. Don't ya think so, Ash?"

"I think so, yes. But, geez, I mean, Gilly, the irony of it. He taught CPR . . . and he died of a heart. . .."

Ashley lost it again, and now the rest of the staff had overheard enough of the conversation to put together the root of our laughter. The man hired to teach us life saving first aid had died of a heart attack. This was no laughing matter . . . but it was. . ..

At some point, Tim slipped away and unlocked the front door. At least one of us had the best interest of the business in mind. We all slowly recovered at our wretched display of sympathy to our poor, fallen, lifesaving instructor. Now, while trying hard to be stoic and serious and render heartfelt sympathy at the news, Ashley and I were fine as long as we did not look at each other. If we did so, then the laughter and hilarity began all over once more.

At one point, we burst out into another round of laughter while we were setting out the glasses and mugs for the day, and Ashley pointed her finger at me and rather strongly said, "Stop! You are so bad! Don't tell Ryan about this!"

"Me? I *am* bad! Who started laughing first, Ashley?"

Ashley did not answer. Instead, she screwed her mouth up like a corkscrew to prevent any more laughter from spilling out of it.

I stopped and toyed with a footed mug and had an idea to quell the uncontrollable and somewhat inconsiderate hilarity.

"Deal, if you don't tell, Erma."

Ashley nodded and leaned over and stuck her pinky finger out to me, and I nodded and grasped it.

"Deal. Pinky shake on it."

We were very silly at times, but I loved every ounce of this amazing woman. The day that she walked into this pub, looking like a bed of roses, and asked me for a chance at a job was one of the greatest days of my life. She had no experience, no training, no resume, but she had desire and presence and she had a spirit. Thank goodness that I was able to recognize her for her.

I still recall her surprise when I said the word, "Hired" and she answered with a puzzled face and a loud, "Really?" The economy was very rough sledding at the time that Ashley applied for the position, and she was so used to rejection that it was commonplace. Fortunately for us, or perhaps, unfortunately, depending upon your perspective of life, but when the economy sucks, people tend to drink even more to escape their woes. Anyway, there is no doubt whatsoever that this business would not be where it is without the efforts and talents of the remarkable Mrs. Griffith. Erma and I discussed it many times, and even though Ashley now had financial stability with her marriage to Ryan, we would handsomely reward her contribution someday in the future. We would not overlook all the success that Ashley brought to this business and to our lives.

"Irish coffee time, Ash?"

"Huh?" Ashley looked at me, blinked a few times and then looked at the footed clear glass mug and pondered my offering.

"Yupper, Ash. Come on now, baby doll, a little caffeine and booze in the morning. I think a little buzz will take down our emotions or it might do the opposite and elevate us to more silliness. Besides, we should drink a toast to the expired instructor, and try to offer some repentance for our abhorrent behavior.

She smiled and said, "I am in."

Here at Crows on a High Wire Public House, we did not mess around with our Irish coffee. No wimpy Irish crèmes in our mixture. We went straight for the Irish whiskey. Irish whiskey, strong-ass coffee . . . strong enough that it almost sprouts a few stray hairs on my bald dome; we add a dash of some brown sugar, and a generous topping of cream. You suck the mixture down right through the layer of cream. We serve the drink in our special clear glass-footed coffee mugs. It is a magical drink!

I just finished mixing two Irish coffees for us and handed one off to Ashley and we toasted in memory of the poor first aid instructor, and prayed for forgiveness at our lack of profound sympathy, when the front door opened and in walked our first customer of the day.

I almost forgot that Tim had unlocked for the day, and I squinted to peer through the rays of bright sunshine that pounded through the front windows. I had sunshades installed on the front glass a few years back, not only to cut out the glare but also to make the air conditioning more effective. But Tim had not pulled them down into position yet.

While peering and squinting my eyes in order to shut out the sunlight, I spotted a tall man entering into the pub. Ah yes, the first patron of the day. At first glance, I thought perhaps it was a salesman making a cold call. This man seemed too well dressed to be a patron stopping by for an early drink, or maybe our legendary Irish coffee or an early lunch. As the man approached and walked out of the glare, I realized that he was anything but a salesman . . . and I had a strange feeling that if he was selling something, you needed to listen to his sales pitch very carefully. As in, hang upon every word type of listen. As in, do not dare miss a single syllable, a pause, or a verbally insinuated comma.

The man stopped in the center of the dining room and removed his sunglasses, and his eyes darted all around the interior of the pub. He was tall and lean and he wore a black fedora hat, a black suit with faint silver pinstripes, a white shirt and a black tie that matched the pinstripes in the suit. His black shoes glowed in a high luster and actually reflected some of the sunlight from the front windows. This guy had it all put together. As in very expensively put together. Perfectly tailored—all around. His black hat tilted at the perfect angle and his dark features were faintly visible under the hat. His eyes were narrow and beady and . . . scary. Ashley tapped me on my arm because I had a feeling that my mouth was hanging open as I studied the man.

"Ah, Gills, this is going to be interesting. Screw the coffee. Should I pour us a shot each?" Ashley was on top of her game. As usual.

I mean, can we both spell mobster? Yes, I could. Ashley could too. N-e-w-J-e-r-s-e-y, m-o-b-s-t-e-r. I emphatically nodded and placed the coffee on the counter, and Ashley set her coffee aside and hurriedly made her way back over to the whiskey selection. The man tapped his suit jacket right under his left shoulder and I did not want to know why he did that, but I guess *it was* there.

He first nodded at Tim, who grabbed a handful of silverware and a napkin from the server's station, cleared his throat and squeaked out in a voice that made poor Tim seem as if he was just entering puberty, "Ah, welcome to Crows on a High Wire Public House . . . sir." Tim grew up here and he could spell and connect the dots, too. "Will you be dining in the main dining room or at the bar? We just opened, but I can . . . provide a menu with the lunch specials or breakfast, or Irish coffee, or tea or a shot of hooch, or wine or anything else that you need or want."

Oh brother, poor Tim was struggling here. His needle was stuck in the vinyl record groove. He was sinking into a nervous abyss. The man shook his head, pointed at the bar, turned, and moved in our direction. Tim dropped the silverware, looked at Ashley and me and then crossed himself repeatedly. Tim was a dedicated Catholic and after meeting this guy, I might swear off my heathen ways and join his church.

When the man was a few steps away from the bar, Ashley finished the pour and slipped the shot glass into my hand. She downed her shot in one tilt and gulp. The man watched us, as I had no shame at all while picking up the glass and tilting the contents into my gaping mouth and it went bye-bye. Over the lips, down the drain and away went all the pain. Our first patron of this very strange morning, gently removed his hat and held it in his hand as his dark, beady, scary eyes, first scanned my huge body, then my face, and then his dark, beady, and scary eyes moved over to the stunning Ashley Griffith. First, he scanned her lovely face, and then her amazing chest, and his eyes landed upon her wedding ring. That's right: dark, beady, and scary, she is off the market. With the influence of the Irish coffee and the straight shot working some magic in my bloodstream, I decided to jump into the fray. Ashley wiggled close to me, and I was ready to shield her with my huge frame and layers of weight.

"So . . . the bar, huh?" As soon as I spoke the words, I felt like an idiot. They came out of my mouth as if I was spitting popcorn. Ashley glanced at me and narrowed her eyes and I responded, with a slightly more confident approach, "Welcome to Crows on a High Wire Public House. What can I get for you? Good morning. This is Mrs. Ashley Griffith, our general manager and I am, Mr. Gilly Gilford. I own the joint and Ashley is the brains behind the operation." I smiled and wiggled my eyebrows and added,

"And the better looking out of us." Ashley smiled and I knew that she was impressed with my startling rebound from my previously timid and rather stupid demeanor.

Upon hearing my invitation and introductions, the man almost smiled and finally, words came out of his mouth.

He spoke in a low growl, with a thick, Italian accent lacing his New Jersey English. After many of his words, there was a letter "A" sound that actually came out as a long ahhh, type of sound.

"Can I'a see'a ya, menua? Please'a." He waved his hand in the air and in the direction of the pile of menus sitting next to the cash register.

Ashley picked a menu off the top of the menu pile and promptly handed it to Mr. Dark, Beady, and Scary.

"Here you are. Thanks for stopping by today. Please let us know what you would like to order and for us to prepare for you," Ashley said with a smile.

"You'a welcome. You'a very beautiful lady'a. I like'a ya voice'a. Sweet. You'a husband'a is'a very lucky man'a."

Now, he smiled for a nano-second, picked up the menu, and glanced at it for a minute or two and as he did so, he nodded and flipped the menu page-by-page. After a careful study of the selections, he handed the menu back to Ashley. "Nothing for right'a now'a, but'a I will'a be back. This is'a nice'a place and I see'a that ya carry pasta. On the kids'a menu, but could'a ya' do it on the big'a menua? Do you'a serve Italiano?" He asked, and his eyes became even more beady with the question.

Ashley was feeling it now and since she was a few million pounds lighter than I was, I am sure the whiskey made it into the important inner workings of her glorious body much faster and more effectively than it did for me.

"Of course, we could do pasta for the main menu. Our head chef, Renaldo is amazing. We serve Americano, Italiano, and cashiano too."

Mr. Dark, Beady and Scary either missed Ashley's

attempt at humor or simply decided to ignore it. He only weakly nodded his head, and then his eyes slowly began a scan of our offerings. First, he scanned the whiskey selection and then the tap handles and then all the areas behind the bar. It was obvious that he was searching for a particular drink. Since it was time for me to step up into the game, I let my intuition take over and I jumped into the water and made a big splash. Believe me; this body can make one helluva splash when I jump into the water. As in an emptying all the water out of the vessel type of splash.

My now restored confidence, combined with the Irish whiskey that was finally working through my huge body and they loosened my Flap Jaw Valve.

The words bellowed out of my mouth in an elegant display of master salesmanship, "We have a huge selection of wine too. Reds, whites, sangria, brandy, cognac, anything that you desire. We keep the wines in a special cooler. Temperature controlled to absolute perfection." I touched my lips with my fingers and kissed it off into the air.

I hit pay dirt! Upon hearing my testimony, he nodded emphatically and waved his hand in the air again while saying to us, "Good'a, yes, ya' two'a make a good'a team. I see'a that'a you'a have'a parking in the back'a. Off'a the main street'a. That is'a good'a. Perfecto. I am'a checking out'a places to hold'a our'a weekly business meetings. Our other place'a, that we'a met at'a, well," he paused and then tapped that same area under his left shoulder and allowed his eyes to wander around the pub, then he turned and looked at Tim . . . who immediately pretended that he was folding napkins, and then he leaned in closer to Ashley and me. He waved at us in order to signal that we needed to come in closer. Ashley and I floated into each other and leaned over the bar in unison, and we prepared to listen to every syllable of his proclamation. We just received an invitation into the inner circle of New Jersey Mobster

World! Ashley and I were in! Oh, oh, cement shoes fit everyone.

His voice lowered just a few notches, and he finished his thought, "It's became'a too'a, how do ya say'a" he waved his hand in the air and looked to us to finish the sentence for him.

The brilliant mind of Ashley jumped in and said, "Complicated and noisy."

Mr. Dark, Beady and Scary leaned back and placed his fedora hat back on his head and smiled widely and said, "I think'a ya are'a as smart'a as you'a beautiful'a. Yes'a, complicated'a and too much'a noise'a.

He turned and pointed at a high-top table over in a corner of the pub. Near the shuffleboard but away from the dartboards.

"I wanna reserve'a that'a table ovah'a there'a. Every Tuesday. At'a two'a in the afternoon'a. Four men'a. My boss, me, and two others. Please'a. Not too many'a questions. No noise'a. Lots'a red wine'a. Dishes of pasta. Your'a choice'a. Tomato sauce'a . . . not too'a spicy, but just'a little'a sweet'a. A light antipasta, a light'a tomato sauce'a and after lunch'a, short'a glasses of Benedictine and Brandy." He rubbed his stomach and smiled. "It is'a good'a for digestion-a-nado. No?"

"Yes! Ashley and I screamed in unison.

"Good digestion-a-nado is very important in life," our brilliant general manager added.

"Good'a. We pay'a extra for the private services and sixty-five dollars'a for using the table every Tuesday'a. See ya at two'a."

He tapped under his left shoulder once more. Somehow, I wished that he would not do that, but there was no way in Hell that I would ever tell him so.

Ashley grabbed the reservation book and her pen, posed with her amazing chest out, her hips slanted, and when she did so, her hair tumbled all around her. This woman's astounding beauty could stop a damn high-speed locomotive in its tracks. Ryan was, indeed, a very lucky man. Right after me on the list, he was the luckiest man in the entire world.

Ashley asked *the question* and the imposing man, despite the "too many questions" statement could not resist the gorgeous, Ashley Griffith, while she asked *the question* with her pen poised over the reservation book, "Please, sir, the name for the reservation."

The man nodded, smiled, and almost in a whisper said, "Please'a use'a the name of my boss, but only youse two guya's can'a be'a involved'a. Yeah, yeah, yeah. Ya get it?"

We both nodded our heads as if they were rocking chairs in nursing homes.

"Good'a. Dubani. Dubani Pecorino." After finishing stating the name, he watched us for a reaction and in seeing none; he slipped his dark sunglasses on back over his eyes in one fast sweeping motion and mumbled, "See ya."

Holy Guacamole! Dubani Pecorino! Ashley and I mustered all the power of stoic behavior in our souls and mixed it with the alcohol to remain silent and not to throw our arms over our heads and run away in horror at the mention of the notorious mobster's name. Everyone, and I mean everyone, knew who Mr. Dubani Pecorino was! Geez, Pecorino and his crime family were on the local news most every night for involvement in one scandal, crime, or investigation after another! Ashley and I stood waving goodbye with our feet planted solidly on the floor with stupid shit-eating grins on our faces while our minds were bordering on explosion. Dubani Pecorino, okay, yes, thank you. Never heard of the guy. Just another patron. Ho hum. Just another day at Crows on a High Wire Public House.

Somehow, we pulled it off.

Satisfied at our reactions or lack thereof, Mr. Dark, Beady, and Scary turned on his heels and walked out into the sunbeams. Only the gentle bang of the front door told us that he left. We could not see jack-diddly squat, with that damn sun streaming through the front glass.

"Is he gone, Tim?" I managed to squeak out while Tim held onto the edge of the server's station for stability.

"Yes, boss. He is gone."

Ashley and I looked at each other and I exclaimed, "Dubani Pecorino! Holy Pearly Gates of Heaven! Pour us a shot, Ash. Tim, ya want one too?" Tim nodded and hustled his way over to receive his medicine. After some small talk and downing our shots, I said to Tim, "Tim, please, go ahead and pull the shades down, will you? Ash and I are going blind back here."

"Gotcha, boss. Besides the sun glare, we don't need prying eyes with Mr. Pecorino coming in here. Don't all those joints where the mobsters hang out on the television always have the shades drawn down? Ya know, the mobsters always tilt the blinds to the side and peer out and pull their weapons and say, 'Damn! It's the Coppers!'" Tim said while he made his way to the front of the pub.

"You watch too much television, Tim, but you do have a point."

No sooner had I finished speaking the words, when we heard the door swing open once more and all three of us held our collective breath. We were all a little jumpy. Right now, I so wanted to be Renaldo and hide in the kitchen with his new prep assistant. The new assistant was a little short guy but for the life of me . . . I could not recall his name. Nevertheless, he had cool hair and a tattoo of an Italian flag on his neck. I made a mental note that I needed to ask him if he was born in Italy or America, but for now, I focused on the front door swinging open. Was Mr. Dark, Beady, and Scary returning? We all breathed a huge sigh of relief, when old, and reliable, Mr. Anderson waddled around the corner and his presence confirmed the fact that it was indeed, Tuesday. It was nearly eleven in the morning and Mr. Anderson was here. He was a regular crow for years upon years. While he painfully and slowly shuffled his way toward the bar, and I answered his wave with a wave, I noticed Ashley grab one of the plastic table-tent signs that stated, "Reserved," she waltzed her perfect backside over to the high-top table that was now reserved for Mr. Dubani Pecorino and rather elegantly dropped it onto the tabletop.

I mixed Mr. Anderson's signature cocktail of "Trilogy-Brand, Extra Reserved," bourbon and ginger ale with four ice cubes and greeted him warmly, thanked him, and dropped the drink while typing in the order for his usual grilled cheese sandwich. On whole wheat bread, with two tomatoes and an extra pickle on the side. Twenty-five cents more for the extra pickle, however; every other Tuesday, I gave him the extra pickle on the house. Okay, now, I know what you are thinking that geez, Gilly, ya charging extra for a damn pickle. Let me assure you that those suckers added up. In addition, old Anderson always counted the ice cubes because it had to be four ice cubes. No more and no less. Therefore, even though old Anderson was an awesome guy, the pickle charge was really me covertly adding just a hairpin of a pain-in-the-ass-count-the-ice-cube-fee to his charges. However, I remained a decent Publican with the occasional discounts on every other Tuesday. Even better, on his birthday, I bought him the entire shooting match. We always took good care of the regular crows.

Ashley returned, she leaned into me and batted her gorgeous eyes at me in a rather dubious form of jest mixed with seriousness, while saying, "Now that we worked a deal with his head henchman and we are hosting the most notorious organized crime legend in these parts every Tuesday, can we have another shot, together? It frazzled my nerves beyond description. Wait until Ryan hears this one!"

I changed my voice to imitate the Italian laced New Jersey growl of the head henchman and Ashley looked up at me while I said, "Yeah, yeah, yeah," I waved my hand in a further mimic of his actions, "Pour'a it'a, baby doll'a. Make it a double'a. We are already'a half'a in the bag'a so we might'a as well'a be all'a the way'a in'a the bag'a."

Ashley chuckled and pointed at me while she wiggled over to the whiskey selections. "Better be very, very careful there, Gills. Cement shoes fit everyone."

Most everyone in and around our neighborhoods here in this part of New Jersey knew of the reputation of Mr. Dubani Pecorino. His status as a supposed crime boss operating in and around the metropolitan area was the talk of street legends. Here in New Jersey, there were quite a few of those types of legends. Some had validity and some did not. I suspected that Mr. Pecorino's status was not subject to very much in the way of exaggeration. He was in the rubbish carting business. His trucks zoomed up and down the streets of all the major cities in these areas, in Newark, in Jersey City, Paterson, all over. As luck would have it, they hauled our rubbish. The bright red truck with "Pecorino Carting" stenciled on the side was distinctive and familiar. I imagined that the head henchman already knew they hauled our refuse. . ..

Promptly at two in the afternoon, the entourage of Mr. Dubani Pecorino wandered into the pub. The head henchman was in the lead, a short, bent over elderly gentleman with a baldhead; a head, as clean of hair as my own head was, walked behind the head henchman and then two other men fell in line behind the elderly man.

They were all dressed in suits and ties and wore similar types of fedora hats. Some hats had different bands and slightly different styles, but they were all black. In fact, everyone dressed in black except for white shirts. All the men, except for the elderly man, scanned the entire pub and tapped that same spot under their left shoulders. The elderly man remained bent over and propelled his frail body in slow but steady steps. His beady eyes remained focused on the table that the head henchman was leading the group to in the corner of the pub. Mr. Dark, Beady, and Scary approached the bar, removed his hat, and nodded to me. There were a few patrons in the pub, but for the most part, it was a usual Tuesday afternoon. Fairly quiet. There were a few groups of businessmen finishing lunch and talking business in the dining room and one young couple oblivious to everything but staring into each other's eyes and playing grab-ass and grab-the-other-part under the table. The bar had six or seven crows sitting on the high wire. There were a few regulars, including a lingering and now very tipsy, Mr. Anderson and a few other retirees. The rest of the retiree crowd gathered over by the dartboard and they were debating a dubious call by an umpire in the Yankee baseball game.

Mr. Anderson looked up at the head henchman and pointed at him and warbled, "I like your suit and your hat. Very nice to see a well-dressed young man."

"Yeah, yeah, yeah. Thank you'a old timer. It is'a . . . expensive."

No one, except the harmless Mr. Anderson, even paid any attention to the group entering the pub and slipping into the reserved table. I had a strong feeling that this is the exact reason why they selected our establishment. Now, I was somewhat surprised that the Table of Obscurity did not catch the head henchman's eye during his scouting mission, except for the fact that it was near the kitchen door and the restrooms. My mind wandered and since I felt as if

I could write a damn good crime novel, I made a supposition as to the real reason that the Table of Obscurity did not make the cut. Mr. Dark, Beady, and Scary already staked out our joint and the layout and determined ahead of time that any seating over in the corner allowed for a front ambush and rear ambush from the delivery door in the back of the house. Solid walls bordered the table that he selected and all the watch had to do was to keep their eyes glued on the front door and hallway leading to the delivery door of the pub. Yes, indeed, I nailed it!

He turned his attention to the reserved table and smiled. Ashley had set a candle in the center; the wine glasses were set out, and the menus set at each seat. This was not fine dining, but it was fine service.

"Is'a the beautiful'a young lady'a available? We only'a want'a her or you'a to serve us. We prefer her'a. No offense meant to you'a."

I nodded and reached out my hand, and he grasped it and shook it.

"I don't blame you. She is a stunner and my ugly ass is efficient but not too pretty to stare at when compared to, well, most everything. No offense taken. It is a fact. Ashley is in the kitchen checking on your salads and working with Renaldo. She will be right out. We spoke earlier after you left, and usually, Ashley comes in around four in the afternoon and stays until closing. We assumed you would want limited servers at your table, so from now on, Ash will come in at around one on Tuesdays."

He nodded, but did not say a single word.

I needed to open up the conversation a little more. After all, I owned the joint.

"I did not catch your name, sir."

"Sal," was all that he said, with his dark eyes glowing. I understood. No last name required. While turning in the direction of the table, Sal added, "Good'a. Thank you'a. Perfecto."

Ashley appeared, and she waltzed over to the table. Her glorious appearance caused all the men to lift their eyes and admire her. I pulled the wine that we selected out of the cooler, handed it to Ash, positioned my huge body on the edge of the bar, leaned in, and observed.

"Good afternoon, gentlemen. Welcome to Crows on a High Wire Public House. I am, Mrs. Ashley Griffith and the big guy over there on the edge of the bar, is the owner, Xavier. . .."

The elderly man interrupted Ashley, and he spoke in a clear and loud voice. A surprisingly powerful voice for what seemed to be a frail and elderly man. His sunken eyes peered out of many wrinkles around his eyes, and they stared down the slope of his hawkish nose. Unlike his right-hand man, Sal, his accent was mostly pure New Jersey with just a gentle hint or two of Italian lacing within his voice.

"Xavier Gilford. Everyone calls him, Gilly. We will too. I like the fact that you added your marital status to your name, Ashley. Very classy woman, and Sal's description of you did not do you justice. I am Dubani Pecorino. He motioned for Ashley's hand and gently reached for it as Ashley extended her arm. He gently took Ashley's hand in his hand, lifted it to his mouth, kissed it, and smiled. I lifted an eyebrow to the fact that Dubani Pecorino knew everything about us. No surprise, but I did lift an eyebrow upon hearing the testimony. And from the look on Ashley's gorgeous face, she sort of, kind of, expected it too.

"You are lovely beyond comparison and I agree with'a Sal here, your husband'a is a very lucky man. Married about a year, now. Correct?"

"Yes," Ashley squeaked.

Mr. Pecorino continued to spout off the inside scoop on our lives, "And your husband, ah, Ryan, he is in real estate. Maintenance and management of properties. Commercial ones, correct? He is very respected and successful."

"He is, and he also writes a little fiction in short stories and novels as a sideline hobby and is a professional photographer."

"I bet he takes many photos of you. Correct? Such a gorgeous subject that you are," Mr. Pecorino waved his hands in Ashley's direction and she blushed as she admitted that Ryan did.

"I would too. His pride overflows at your love and your beauty. He worships you and so he should. Hard working, gorgeous, smart, and gentle in your mannerisms but forceful and independent when you need to be so. I bet he is overwhelmed with admiration of how lovely you are."

"Thank you, Mr. Pecorino. He is a wonderful man. I am madly in love with him more and more each day. He treats me as if I am a queen."

"As he should. He is very handsome, so in many ways, you are very lucky too'a," Mr. Pecorino said and then he focused his eyes on me and waved in my direction.

'Oh no! I thought. My turn in the barrel of Italian mobster wonder. Be nice to me, Ash. I love you!' My thoughts ran ramshackle over me, while those beady eyes all stared at me. All sixteen of them.

"Your boss'a he is a good'a man, too. Right?"

Ashley smiled and turned in my direction, and she toyed with the floor. She looked sultry and cute all at the same time.

"Awwww, he is kind of all right," Ashley laughed and stumbled back into the conversation, "no just kidding! He is amazing. I love him to the moon and back. He is more than just a boss to me! He is my best buddy in the world. And his wife is one of my best friends too. His wife is amazing. Gilly walked me down the aisle and gave me away at my wedding. My father and mother are both dead and my family is all mostly gone from this world. But I have my giant teddy bear of love."

I injected rather loudly, "I gave her away rather

reluctantly, I might add."

Mr. Pecorino laughed and smiled and his companions took the guidance, smiled for the first time, and nodded their heads in unison at my statement. They did not laugh, but they did crack smiles. At least, they displayed some type of emotions.

"I don't blame you, Gilly," Dubani Pecorino said and then spoke with a rather serious tone in his voice, "Ashley, I am'a sorry about your'a family and your parents passing, but all of this," he waved his hands and arms in the air to indicate the entire pub. "Is this not'a your family? Not just Gilly and Mrs. Gilford. All of the, how'a do you'a label them? The crows. Here. This is love to you. Correct?"

Wow! I leaned in now and watched carefully as the emotion filled our dear Ashley's eyes and thought, how this man, mobster or not, had a heart and soul of pure gold. He nailed it. He felt it. He understood.

"It is a very special place to me and for many others, Mr. Pecorino. It is where my heart always remains. I met my husband here. I met my glorious and amazing Ryan . . . right over there." Ashley pointed to the beloved Table of Obscurity, and Mr. Dubani and all his men followed her hand with their eyes. Mr. Pecorino smiled at her outward display of love for Ryan. He felt what words did not have to say.

"My heart thumped with immense love from the first moment that I saw him. The stories of the people that I have met and their individual adventures and lives and love, will fill a book someday. My Ryan, he makes a very good living and honestly, I do not have to work anymore, but he understands that this place is a part of me. It is not just a workplace . . . it is a safe haven in the storm of life. The crows are all my family, I love them, and they love me."

"I understand'a. I feel how special it is. Sal'a did an amazing thing bringing us here'a. This location is different for us and sometimes, different . . . is very good. This is pure Americana. This is the real, New Jersey. This is life."

It seemed as if Mr. Pecorino sensed that he needed to change the emotions for Ashley, and he did so with a rather pointed question directed at old Gilly.

"So, Gilly, he pays you well'a and treats you with honor?"

"Very well, and very honorable. He is the greatest."

"Good. Perfecto." Mr. Pecorino touched his fingers to his lips and smacked a kiss into the air with them. "I will not ask any more questions. Please, forgive me, but due to the nature'a of my business, we always investigate'a whom it is that we do'a business with in this world. You cannot be too careful these days. Often, it is not a fair or pleasant world out there and you need to do . . . certain . . . things to adjust'a the attitudes and conduct of people. I am sure that you understand."

He leaned back in his chair and folded his arms across his chest. All of his henchmen at the table nodded in agreement and they tapped that same location under their left shoulders. Sal tapped it twice.

Honestly, I wished that they would not do that.

Sal's two companions said not a single word; they simply stared at their boss for directions. Both of them with dark black hair, pointy features and tightlipped mouths. They could have been brothers. One was stocky and his muscles rippled under his jacket, and the other was thinner, a little taller, with slender hands and wavier hair. He might have been more studious, but he had the eyes of a no-nonsense type of guy. No doubt, they were the muscle of the operation, but somehow, they served as lead men in the operations, too. They were more than just meatheads. As Sal recommended, we will not ask too many questions.

"Of course, we understand. I mean, Gilly and I understand. So," Ashley held the wine bottle in her hand and explained, "your antipasto is coming right out. Please, your choice of dressings?"

"Red vinaigrette. All around," Sal responded without hesitation, and Ashley mumbled a thank you while displaying the bottle of wine for all the men to observe.

"Is this wine acceptable?"

Mr. Pecorino leaned in, studied the label, and then said, "Perfecto."

Once more, Mr. Pecorino touched his fingers to his lips and smacked a kiss into the air with them. Ashley handed me the bottle and while I felt the burn of their collective eyes, studying me for the potential of slipping a Mickey, I worked at uncorking it, and then handed it back to Ashley, who poured all the glasses of wine for each of the men.

"To your immense and incomparable beauty, Ashley," Mr. Pecorino said as he lifted his glass in the air. His companions did the same. They toasted Ashley who smiled and once more squeaked out a thank you, and then she turned heels to pick up the salads.

"I will bring out the antipasto and dressings and check on the main meal."

As Ashley hustled by me, our eyes met and she stopped, leaned into me, and motioned for me to lean over so that she could reach my cheek. She wrapped her arms around me and she kissed my cheek, and we followed it with a peck of a kiss on each other's lips.

"Well, done, baby doll," I whispered, and I knew that the Pecorino table witnessed our exchange of mutual love.

"One more, Gills! Then I will take a taxi to downtown Newark and shop for one of those fancy hats," Mr. Anderson bellowed out and pointed into the direction of Sal. "I think that I will look good, right?"

Mr. Pecorino laughed and pointed at me and proclaimed, "Please, his drink, Gilly, put it on my tab. Yes, sir'a, you'a will have all the ladies chasing you all over town'a. Cheers." He and his companions all lifted their wine glasses in a toast.

"Philip Anderson is my name there, sir. I am one of the crows on a high wire here. I have been a widower for over thirty years now. Lost my glorious, Mabel, way too young. It was so long ago that I hardly even recall many details other than how beautiful she was. Her eyes were the purest green color that you will ever see. Pure and clear, like green glass with a candle behind them. Nowadays, I dance, but because of this place, I never dance alone. Thank you kindly for the drink and the words. I am quite sure that I would not run if a woman chased me. That doesn't happen too often at my age, so I would just let her capture me and have their way with my old ass. I would date a few women, but most of the women that I knew are dead. Nice to meet youse guys. I am retired now, after I worked for fifty-seven years in a garment factory. I have my pension, my Social Security, air-conditioning and heat in my apartment, a color television, a table radio, old Frank Sinatra records to play on a damn, fine stereo system, most of my hair, and we all have the crows. I could not ask for anything more than what I have now. Life is great."

"It is, Mr. Anderson. It is. Dubani is my name. Dubani Pecorino and this is Sal, this is Mikey, and this is Francesco. Here is a toast to your wonderful, Mabel."

I dropped old Anderson's drink in time, and they all toasted to Mabel's honor and memory.

I hoped and prayed that old Mr. Anderson did not react to the mention of the name of Dubani Pecorino, but he did not bat an eyelash. Old Anderson knew who he was, but he also knew the rules of the pub. Don't go poking around where you did not have to be.

"Thank you for that. She was a great woman and a wonderful wife. Enjoy your lunch. You will love this place. It is the best."

Mr. Dark, Beady, and Scary did not seem so imposing now. He and Mr. Pecorino, and Mikey and Francesco, all seemed as if they were just some more crows that flew in.

The meal went very well. Perfect, in fact. Ashley was spot on, and after dropping their meals and checking on the wine levels, we left them alone. Luckily, everyone else gave them space, too. Mr. Anderson left with a thank you and a gentle wave in their direction, but for the most part, they received exactly what they wanted. Privacy, space, good food, excellent drink and superior service. The retirees yelled and hollered a bit at the baseball game on the tube, but Mr. Pecorino simply smiled at their reaction and it did not seem to bother him in the least. In fact, I even caught his eyes following the game a little here and there. At times, the group was deep into discussion in low voices just above a whisper and other times; they sat in quiet and enjoyed their meals and drinks.

It was close to four-thirty in the afternoon. Soon the tide will roll out, and a new wave will roll into the pub. When Ashley scooped up all the plates, poured them the B&B drinks and set them out, Mr. Pecorino requested that Renaldo and his kitchen assistant come out to meet them.

"I want to'a thank them'a for the amazing pasta and the sauce. The sauce was . . . mild, sweet, not too sweet, but charming on my palate. I would never have thought'a that this was not fine Italian dining. It was perfecto."

Ashley nodded and retrieved a rather shy Renaldo and his assistant, who I now knew his name. I even knew his title now too! Mr. Dennis Cuccinelli, Assistant Chef at Crows on a High Wire Public House. When they approached the table, it was then that I once more spotted the Italian flag tattoo on the young assistant's neck, recalled his last name and made a solid connection. This should go rather well.

After introductions, Mr. Pecorino leaned back in his chair and addressed Renaldo while Dennis stood silently at his side. I watched as all the men at the table studied the tattoo on the neck of young Mr. Cuccinelli.

"My compliments, Renaldo, for such a fine meal. Where

did you learn such amazing recipes? You are'a not Italiano?"

"No, sir, Mexican-American. My grandmother taught me to cook. All kinds of cooking. That sauce is her recipe. Just a touch of sugar. Not too much but not too little, either."

Mr. Pecorino leaned back and waved in the air and did the now familiar finger kissing and lip routine while proclaiming, "Magnificenti.' Perfecto. Your grandmother. Such love. Your gravy, it is the best'a I have'a enjoyed in forever." Mr. Pecorino nodded and then turned his attention to Dennis. "And something tells me this young'a man'a had something to do with the homemade cannolis for our dessert?"

Dennis nodded his head, pointed at Renaldo and said, "Ditto for me. My grandmother's recipe. I thought it would be an enjoyable touch."

"Parli Italiano?" Mr. Pecorino asked while pointing at the tattoo.

Dennis nodded his head and answered, "Parolo Italiano."

"Da dove vieni in Italia?"

"Roma."

Mr. Pecorino nodded and off the two of them went, speaking in Italian for a few minutes until they finished and Renaldo and Dennis shook hands with everyone at the table and prepared to retreat to the kitchen. Dubani Pecorino nodded to Sal, he held his fingers up in the air, first, he held five fingers in the air, and then curled his thumb in the shape of an "O." Sal nodded, leaned back and pulled his wallet out of his suit jacket and looked at Dubani as his boss pointed first, at Renaldo, and then to Dennis, and nodded. The two men had an intuition between them. Sal peeled two fifty-dollar bills out of his wallet and gave each man a fifty-dollar tip each. Thankfully, our two employees were overwhelmed and gracious at the extraordinary generosity of Mr. Dubani Pecorino. Our two cooks retreated to the kitchen. The men all stood up from the table, and Dubani slowly walked over to me.

He leaned over the bar counter and reached his hand out and said with warmth in his voice, "There is not too much better in this world than fine drinks, beautiful women, fine food, homemade desserts and great conversation. You sir, have a remarkable business here and even better people working for you. Ashley here is a wonder of life and you have my gracious thanks. What did that very wise man, Mr. Anderson, say?"

"Life is great," I answered without hesitation.

He gently nodded, waved, and said, "See you next Tuesday. Ashley, peace and love. Please, enjoy life and always be very tolerant."

He nodded to Sal. Sal removed a wad of cash from his suit jacket pocket, plunked down a crisp one-hundred-dollar bill, and pointed to Ashley. He then peeled off four one-hundred-dollar bills from the wad of cash, placed them on the counter, and pointed to me. Sal smiled, waved, tapped under his left shoulder and marched in line with the rest of them. Only the front door slamming told us they had left. I picked up the receipt checkbook, opened it, and read the total tab. Ashley had not even had time to deliver the tab to the table before they left. It was only one-hundred and forty-dollars. Ashley floated over and whistled, and she already had the Irish in her hand. She poured two shots and down they went. Over the lips, down the drain and away went all the pain.

The monumental weekly Tuesday lunch meetings with Mr. Pecorino and his companions went on in about the same manner for over a year or thereabouts. Dubani Pecorino and his companions showed up every Tuesday and enjoyed the meals, drinks and the atmosphere. If Ashley took a rare day off, or was a vacation, then I filled in for her. Almost immediately, Mr. Pecorino became part of the family. More crows. We never discussed anything out of the ordinary. They received their space, and we never tread on it. The tips were always as generous, and the man and his companions were always just as gracious. The Christmas tips were particularly astounding. Sal occasionally spoke, but Mikey and Francesco seldom spoke to us. Their conversation remained hushed with the group after we had the general greetings. We understood what they wanted, and they respected us as we respected them.

Ironically, it all happened early on a Tuesday morning in late October. Of course, it would be a Tuesday. First, there was a contracting crew installing a heavy chain across the driveway entrance between the pub and the adjoining building next door. Then there were reflectors hung on the chain along with a "No Trespassing. Private Driveway" sign hung on the chain. When I opened the pub for the day and spotted the crew, I was naturally quite puzzled and very upset. The owner of the building and property next door to the pub owned the driveway and one-half of the parking area behind the pub and their building. For all the years that we were in business, going all the way back to when Coatsie first opened the pub, we had an agreement in place to share the common driveway and some of the spaces in the parking lot between our buildings. I paid a monthly fee to utilize the driveway and a portion of the parking lot, to the owner of the building next door, which first housed a law office for many years until the attorneys retired, then an insurance agency, and now, it was office space for an I.T. company. There were two apartments above the offices and parking in the rear for everyone. Tenants and the office workers could access the rear parking from the other side of the building. That particular driveway had a gate and electronic pass cards, which controlled the access to the parking.

When I spoke with the foreman of the contracting crew, he knew none of the details of the work order. The owner of the building next door hired his company to install the chain and signs and that was all he knew. This was serious. We had a loading zone in front of the pub for loading, unloading, and deliveries, but most of our patrons, deliveries and employees, including Ashley and I parked in the rear lot. For us, there really was no other way into the rear parking lot and our loading dock other than this common driveway. On-the-street-parking in this old city was haphazard at best, the city had parking meters, and a few city parking lots for fees, but we always boasted, "Free parking in the rear of the pub." Our website stated it and we even printed it on our menus. Not to mention patrons such as Mr. Pecorino who insisted upon it! The rear parking lot was where most of the daily regular crows and newcomers parked. The evening crowds were younger, and they did not mind the city lots and the city ordinances stopped collecting money in the parking meters after six in the early evening. In addition, most businesses along Main Street, except for the service businesses, closed down for the day and parking along the street freed up considerably.

This situation could be a huge blow to our business. Especially so, since it was so sudden, and I knew nothing of it until arriving for work on this fateful Tuesday.

I tried not to panic and thought at first that my wretched bookkeeping skills had caused a missed payment and the owner of the property closed us off for non-payment. That seemed feasible but lousy of them—I would think they might give me a past-due notice, but these days, you never know. As I scanned through my general ledger spreadsheet on the computer, I knew that was not the case. I had sent them a check as usual and while I stared at the name that I wrote the check to, it was then that I recalled the original owner of the property had passed away, his family assumed the property about one year ago and the parts and pieces began to fit. I bet they were selling the building and the land and they did not want the hassle of explaining the lease of the common driveway to potential buyers. Still, where was my advance notice?

Sure enough, when I sorted through the recent mail delivery, it brought the confirmation. In the pile of mail was a letter explaining in detail exactly the reason that I surmised was driving this situation. The building and land were on the market and until they finalized the sale, the common driveway access and shared parking spaces needed to remain closed. Liability, insurance reasons, and property protection and blah, blah, blah. No notice, but at least they were decent enough to prorate the fees and issue me a refund check for the unused portion of the monthly use of the driveway and parking. Wow! Yes, they sent a letter, but they sure pulled the rug out from under us. The letter came from an attorney representing the family in the property sale and the estate of the deceased original owner, so I am sure they did not mail it late on purpose. I suppose the letter was a victim of the daily flow of the business of selling the property. A small detail that they left until the last minute. Now, I sure could begin to negotiate with the new owners, but in the meantime, I now officially panicked. I looked at my watch. It was almost ten o'clock, and soon, daily business would roll. Ashley would be here, the regulars, new customers, old customers, deliveries, Renaldo and Dennis. Everyone, including me, all confused by the chain and most of all, Sal and his black four-door sedan with the blacked-out windows could not park in his usual spot right next to the kitchen. Damn, why did this happen on a Tuesday? Of all days, and I had no contact information for Sal to even give them a heads-up about the situation.

Shortly thereafter, the entire crew was onboard for duty and I was doing my worst job at throwing up smokescreens to downplay the impact of the loss of the rear parking lot behind the pub. Fifty spaces, actually forty-seven, and I hoped that no one asked me how I knew that . . . because I did. I did because; I went out there at least ten times this morning and counted them. And the turn around for the trucks to back into the loading dock space. And the reserved spot right next to the building for Mr. Pecorino's sedan. And two motorcycle spots and five slots for bicycles in the bike rack.

With Renaldo, Dennis, and Tim gathered around the bar, Ashley slowly read the letter and her eyes told the story. Tears brimmed the edges of them, and I melted whenever I saw her upset.

She handed me the letter back and asked, "What are we going to do, Gills? Our regular crows during the day count on parking in the rear parking lot. It is so important to our business and what about the deliveries. Out front, deliveries suck. And it is Tuesday and Sal and Mr. Pecorino will be here in a few minutes. You know the deal . . . no way can they park out on the street. Exposure."

I waved my hand in the air and answered, "I know, I know, but don't worry, Ash. I have a plan."

Her eyes brightened for a nanosecond and surprise washed over her face, "You do?" She then studied my face carefully and read the truth. We had worked together for a long, long time. With a shake of her head and her hands on her hips, Ashley dismissed my proclamation, "You don't have a plan. That was a load of bullshit."

"Well, I sort'a do have a plan," I stomped my foot on the floor behind the bar. "Erma was on the phone this morning with our attorney and we were working to see if we can afford to purchase the building and property."

"How much?" Ashley asked in a dubious voice.

With Ryan's connections in real estate, it was obvious that Ashley knew that the price of real estate in northern New Jersey was ridiculous.

"One-point-two-million," I lamented.

"Holy shit! For that place!"

I nodded my head and explained the justification of the price as if I was on the owner's side, "It has the storefront offices, two apartments above it, and a dedicated secure parking lot on the opposite side from us. Moreover, as we already knew, a common shared use driveway, and behind us, coveted, off-street parking with forty-seven parking spaces for cars, the turn around for a truck to access our loading dock space, the reserved spot right next to the building for Mr. Pecorino's sedan. And two motorcycle spots and five slots for bicycles in the bike rack."

All that bullshit was right out of the sales pitch on the realtor's website. I memorized it while I studied the incredible asking price for the building and property.

"Geez, Gills, that was friggin' amazing. How did you know all of that?" Tim asked, but I did not answer him.

"There is no way that we can afford that price. Erma and I are still paying off the note on this building. Damn, I should've negotiated this years ago. I suck at business deals and strategies. Erma is seeing if they would just sell the driveway and the parking spaces on this side, but she doubts they would split the parcel up. They just want to make a clean and easy sale."

Ashley waved her hand at me and propped me up a little, "No, you do not suck at business. Stop kicking your own ass. We don't need a big, wishy-washy teddy bear right now. I mean, what is the back-up plan?"

I answered without hesitation, "Call your husband."

Ashley nodded and mumbled, "I am on it."

Mr. Anderson wobbled in and even though the parking did not matter much to his situation (he did not drive and his apartment was only one block away from the pub) he was visibly upset about the change. He was one of the crows. Change did not go over well around here.

He stood with his hands on his hips after reading the letter and shook his head while spouting off with some anger in his voice, "This is bullshit, Gilly! These people, the family that inherited the building and the property and this shady-ass attorney . . . they don't know the rules! You don't mess with the crows!"

"I know, but Ashley is working with Ryan right now. He is sort of in real estate. We will work something out. C'mon, Phil, sit down here now. I will mix your drink. Relax."

He nodded, pulled a stool out, lifted one eyebrow while looking at his watch, and said, "Mr. Pecorino?"

At first, I only nodded as I dropped the four ice cubes into the glass. Then, I decided to count ice cubes, "One, two, three and four," I mumbled.

Nervous energy. Very, very nervous.

Ashley was still working the angles with Ryan. She sat her lovely ass on a stool at the Table of Obscurity and we had fielded at least twenty-five inquiries as to, "What the Hell is going on with the driveway and the rear parking lot," when the door opened and Sal walked in. He wore his dark sunglasses, his trademark fedora, and he was dressed in his usual perfectly fitted suit and tie, but the look on his face made me rethink his original nickname. He was, once more, Mr. Dark, Beady and Scary. I nodded to him and waved, and in two strides, Sal was standing in front of me. Ashley slid out of the seat and walked over, and Mr. Anderson took a long gulp of his cocktail. Silence ensued over all the crows. No chattering at all. Sal removed his fedora, nodded at Mr. Anderson, and scanned the entire interior of the pub. He then nodded to everyone. With a point and wave, first to me, then to Ash, and it was clear that he meant for us to gather in and explain the situation.

I stuttered and stammered, "I am so sorry, Sal. I would've called, but I had no way to get in touch with you."

"I understand'a. No contact numbers for you'a and Mrs. Ashley'a are good'a for youse'a guys'a. On purpose'a. What the Hell is the deal'a, Gilly?"

I nodded and handed him the letter, and Sal removed his sunglasses and carefully read it.

Mr. Anderson was very upset, and he was already a few drinks into his session and was holding onto the high wire rather precariously.

"It's bullshit, Mr. Sal! Bullshit, I say! You don't mess with the crows!" Phil slurred his statement of profound opinion and yelled the words and upon hearing the old boy's support, the entire pub picked up their glasses and stomped them on their tables in a show of mutual support for Mr. Anderson. The retirees left the golf match right when such-and-such was teeing off. They all clapped and yelled support and Sal looked around the pub carefully.

He nodded and in a low growl said, "Youse'a guys'a are right'a." Turning to me, Sal asked, "Did'a' you'a call and ask'a how much'a they want'a for the sale?"

"Erma did, and it is too much for us to swing. We are still paying off this mortgage. One-point-two-mill, Sal. Ashley has Ryan working on it now and we are trying to see if they will sell us the driveway and the shared space in the lot. We are trying . . . but Erma tried that angle before without much success. Honestly, it does not look too good at this point."

He remained stoic, handed me back the letter, and replaced his sunglasses over his eyes.

"I will'a be back'a. Maybe, two hours. Please, tell'a Renaldo and our paesano to hold'a the meal'a. Mr. Pecorino will be hungry. Ice down'a extra'a wine'a."

"Will do. Thank you, Sal."

Sal smiled and pointed at Mr. Anderson and said, "Ya,

right'a, old-timer. You don't mess'a with the crows'a. We's all'a crows."

Mr. Anderson held his glass in the air in support, and Sal turned and left. Ashley cuddled up into me, and she wrapped her arms around my huge waist.

I tucked her into my soft and generous folds and asked, "What did Ryan say?"

"He said to wait for Sal. He predicted that Mr. Pecorino would have a plan."

"Smart man, ya married there, Ashley."

"He is brilliant, and the sex is friggin' amazing too."

"Okay, nice to hear. A little too much information but good for you and for Ryan. Anyway, I think that Sal has a plan and it might be a lot better than mine was."

Ashley laughed and whispered, "Slightly. Only slightly." She looked up at me and squeezed her thumb and forefinger together to a thin margin to demonstrate the bogus difference between our two plans.

"Shot of Irish?" I asked.

"Shot," Ashley promptly answered.

I poured them for both of us. No one left the pub. None of the regulars and none of the newcomers and none of the retirees. Everyone waited for Sal to return! Mr. Anderson was three sheets to the wind and even though his apartment was only a few blocks away, I would have to call the local taxi to drive him home and make sure that he got up into his apartment safely. Luckily, Walter, the taxi driver, was a regular crow here too.

The door opened to the pub and everyone held their breath, as first, Sal appeared, and then a few other men, all dressed the same as Sal was, then Mikey and Francesco appeared with Mr. Pecorino slowly shuffling in the center of the mass. It looked like a rugby scrum without the ball. Or, I guess that Mr. Pecorino was the ball. Then four other men, all Mikey and Francesco doppelgangers, held up the rear.

Ah, I get it, extra protection. . ..

I called for Ashley and added for her to pull Renaldo and Dennis out of the kitchen and with a nod of acknowledgement; Ashley hustled on her way to do so. We gathered in a group behind the bar and watched as Sal smiled, removed his sunglasses, and motioned for us to meet them at their table. We all moved and as Mr. Pecorino walked slowly by Mr. Anderson; he tapped the old man on the shoulder and smiled. Mr. Anderson smiled back, but even in his drunken state, old Anderson knew better than to say a word.

"My dear, Ashley, please, some wine'a, my dear. Please'a. You look'a extra gorgeous today. You'a husband'a is a very lucky man'a," Mr. Pecorino said with a gentle wave as Sal pulled out his stool and made sure he was steady and seated in it before taking his seat. Mikey and Francesco took their assigned seats. The rest of the men surrounded the table in layers of protection, kept their dark sunglasses on, and they all simultaneously tapped that blessed spot under their left shoulders.

There was not a leftie shot in the bunch.

Ashley poured the wine as Renaldo, Dennis, Tim, and I watched in careful silence. In fact, the entire pub was silent. Even the golf game volume on the television was low, so the retirees could listen. Mr. Pecorino lifted his wine glass. He hovered his long, sloped nose over the rim of the glass and enjoyed the fragrance. He took a sip, did the now familiar finger signal and the snaps of his lips, and mumbled, "Perfecto."

Still, no one moved a muscle or said a word.

He looked at me and said, "Yeah, yeah, yeah. I want'a you to know that'a this little driveway and parking situation . . . is resolved, Gilly. I'a purchased the building next door'a and the parking lot and the driveway, and the property next to it and everthing'a else. The boys cut'a the chain and tossed it in you'a dumpster. Or actually, my'a dumpster that you'a rent'a from me."

My heart thumped in my chest as I saw Ashley turn white and place her hand over her mouth to hold back the gasp.

"No need'a to wait for closings and all that fuss and legal . . . stuff."

He snapped his fingers in the air and pointed at Sal. Sal nodded and reached into his jacket and pulled out a business card and he held it in the air in the direction of Ashley.

Mr. Pecorino explained, "Ashley, my dear, please have'a your husband, call my attorney here. Work the deal to manage the building, the property, the entire asset for me." He waved his hands in the air and smiled, "You know'a collect the rent, maintain the building and do'a repairs, lease the space . . . that sort'a stuff. I don't trust anyone but your'a husband with this. Yeah, yeah, yeah. I have trust issues. I am sure'a that you understand. And tell Ryan that there is no monthly fee to use the driveway or the lot or whatever for the pub. Free'a use."

The joy and euphoria of the news made me lose my mind. I rushed over, and threw my hands and huge arms around Mr. Pecorino and all of his men stood up, but he laughed and waved them all away. I vaguely recalled Ashley's statement that cement shoes fit everyone, but I did not care.

"Thank you! Thank you, Mr. Pecorino . . . from the bottom of my heart! Ah . . . oh, sorry. I lost it a bit."

I stood back up and everyone went at-ease.

"Yeah, yeah, yeah. It is okay, Gilly. I feel you'a joy, but you, and Ashley, and Mr. Anderson, and this place is very special'a to me and to us. To everyone'a here. It is a part'a of our lives. No thank you is'a needed. I understand, but I will'a take a hug from the gorgeous, Ashley. No offense, but you'a kinda big'a."

Ashley laughed; smiled and rushed over with her arms

wide open, and she hugged Mr. Pecorino tightly and kissed both of his cheeks until he blushed.

Mr. Anderson lifted his glass, jumped off his stool and yelled, "Here is to the awesome, Mr. Pecorino! Here is to the crows! Life is great!"

"Life is great, Mr. Anderson. Life is great," Dubani Pecorino agreed.

"Here, here!" Echoed throughout the pub.

Mr. Anderson looked at Ashley and then at me and said, "Sorry, Gills, no hug required here from you, but I sure would like one from Ash!"

Ashley rushed over while saying, "Hugs all around!"

The men lined up, and Sal and the boys kept a careful watch to make sure no one stole any errant squeezes of glorious female body parts. I am sure some of those old boys felt parts of their body awaken that had not stirred in ages.

Everyone shook (carefully) Mr. Pecorino's hand. Renaldo and Dennis hustled off to prepare the meal, and I made the blessed statement that every pub-dweller and crow prayed to hear from the owner of the pub. I tapped the bar counter with my huge hands until I caught everyone's attention.

"Today is a very special day. In honor of this day and a wonderful man who is a special crow and all of his . . . men . . . everything this afternoon is on the house. Food, drinks, everything! Thank you and God bless the great, Mr. Dubani Pecorino!"

Mr. Anderson turned and pointed at Ashley, then Mr. Pecorino, and then me, and proudly slurred, while pointing his right pointy finger in the air, "You don't mess with the crows."

Right on queue, Sal and all the boys nodded and tapped that now familiar location under their left shoulders.

Crows on a High Wire

We lost the amazing Mr. Dubani Pecorino, about one year after he purchased the building and property next door to the pub. A stoic and upset, Sal, delivered the awful news to us one Monday in September of the year.

"A sudden heart attack in his sleep," Sal told us, for the cause of his death. Mr. Pecorino was eighty-five-years of age. We all deeply mourned his loss. In the back of my mind, I replayed the driveway saga. But now was neither the time nor the place to do so. Knowing Mr. Pecorino, there was a plan, and I remained confident in that fact.

The newspapers and news reports were all full of the news, rumors of what he did, what he was, and it overwhelmed us. I considered all of the nasty facts simply a false perception of reality, along with accusations without knowing the facts behind the man. Regardless, we did not care. To us, he was the consummate gentleman. He was Mr. Pecorino, and he was generous and kind beyond description and most of all, he was one of us.

A crow.

On the edges of their high-top table, in the exact locations that they always occupied, I screwed in four brass plaques, "Sal, Mikey, Francesco, and of course, Mr. Dubani Pecorino. Next to Mr. Pecorino's name, I had the engraver add the word, "Perfecto." Underneath Sal's name, the engraver fit in the words, "Don't mess with the crows."

Mr. Dubani Pecorino, was as Ryan was and was originally from Paterson, New Jersey and we all knew that we would pay our respects and attend the services. In honor of Mr. Pecorino, we closed the pub on the day of the funeral.

Ashley, Mr. Anderson, Ryan, Erma, Dennis, Renaldo, and I all attended the services. We drove to Paterson to the funeral, which was in a mega-huge Catholic Church, packed to the rafters with mourners and those wanting to pay their respects. The area in and around the church, crowded with Paterson, New Jersey police officers and New Jersey state troopers. Remarkably, Mr. Anderson outlived Mr. Pecorino, and he fought back tears as he shuffled by the casket, gently touched the edge and bowed his head and prayed.

He finished his prayer with, "Life is great" and went on his way. Mr. Anderson's suit smelled like mothballs and his shoes squeaked, but he, too, was a special man. A crow honoring another fellow crow that flew off the high wire to an higher wire in a glorious place.

We greeted and extended condolences to the family after the funeral service, in what seemed as if it was an endless line of people and, of course, we did not know anyone, until we reached Sal, Mikey, and Francesco.

To my surprise, the normally stoic Sal embraced me and while choking back tears and emotion Sal managed to say, "Thank you'a for'a everything. Mr. Pecorino loved the pub, he loved youse'a guys'a and we will miss'a youse'a. Youse'a guys are all very'a special'a."

I gently put my hand on his shoulder and said, "You are, too, Sal. We love youse guys too. Thank you for you. Please come by sometime," and he agreed, but somehow, I knew it would never happen. He hugged Ashley, greeted Ryan and the rest of the gang, and we shook hands with Mikey and Francesco.

It was over.

On the other hand; we thought it was over.

About two days after the funeral service, Ryan walked into the pub. It was around five o'clock in the afternoon and I waved hello to him and then yelled, "Ash! Your husband is here. No kissy-kissy and ass squeezing allowed in the bar area. Go get a room!"

Ashley appeared from behind the liquor locker, smiled at her husband, and waved a dismissal wave at my stupid humor in my direction. Ryan weakly smiled in return, but his face seemed somewhat ashen. He plopped down at his usual stool at the Table of Obscurity and loosened his necktie. Ryan looked at his wife while taking a deep breath.

"What is wrong, honey?" Ashley asked as she studied her husband and his mannerisms.

"Nothing, my love. It is more as if . . . what is right."

I walked over and placed my hand on Ashley's back and now I was curious too.

"I don't follow you, Ryan. Come on now . . . no messin' around. What the Hell?"

Ryan smiled widely and explained as he pulled out a paper from his suit jacket, and placed it on the tabletop while saying, "Well, baby doll, about one hour ago, I received a call from Mr. Pecorino's attorney and he made an appointment for you and me to come into his office next Monday. At one in the afternoon. You have to sign some papers. Congratulations. You are the proud owner of the building and property next door. Mr. Pecorino left it to you in his will. It is all yours, my love. All. Yours. And as the great property manager that I am," he tapped the paper that he pulled out and placed on the tabletop, "it is my duty to inform you that you will need a new roof on the joint in about a year. This, my dear wife, is the proposal."

Ashley held her hand over her mouth for a few seconds and then as the words and testimony of Ryan set in, she squealed in delight, buried herself into her husband's body, and kissed him generously. As in kissed him all over.

I mumbled, "So much for the kissy-kissy" and when Ryan heard my words and complaint, he reached over; he forcibly grabbed his wife's amazing ass and buried his hands into it. I laughed aloud. Ryan took advantage of the moment. He had a great sense of humor and, yes, his wife had an amazing ass.

Oh, yes, indeed, life is great.

Oh, yeah, one more thing, some words of advice, from these parts of New Jersey . . . don't mess with the crows.

Chapter Seven

An Anthem to Love and to Lemonade

Loose Floorboards Underfoot

Life continued to come at me in giant waves. Some knocked me on my big ass, which is not easy to do so, and others propped me up and gave me endless joy. No one ever said that this life was easy. No religion anywhere on Earth that humankind managed to create ever promises an easy go of it here in life. But if you poke in and around the cracks, if you peer around dark corners before you turn them, or if you take every step of life with your eyes wide open and an awareness of loose floorboards underfoot, then you have a chance of coming out of the madness while smiling.

These days, I tend to smile a lot.

Our precious daughter, Connie, just landed her dream job with a magazine and she was living across the river in lower Manhattan, making an incredible salary, while writing for the magazine and on the side, Connie was working on her first novel. Thank you, Clive. You never leave our hearts. Our amazing daughter just has a magical way with words. Clive knew it, and he blessed it too.

It was nearly Thanksgiving and for this big, sweaty and

severely overweight guy, I sure did enjoy the cooler weather. My lower back pain never eases up very much these days, some days it ebbs and feels tolerable, but most days, it is a struggle with the pain. I tried almost every doctor and treatment known to the medical world, back braces, chiropractic adjustments, osteopathic exams, pills, homeopathic bullshit and whooey, new shoes, exercises and electronic pulsing thingy's taped to my back to shock my ass every minute or two. It is hopeless and my excessive weight and being on my feet for all of these years and days on end only makes a bad situation worse. Nevertheless, I muddle through. I do my best to lose weight, but it is not only the fact that I love to eat, but I am just a big guy. It is the way it is and I go with it. At least now, the leaves are changing; the nights are cool and crisp and the days begin with cold temperatures and then gradually warm. It is a glorious time of the year. Back pain or not, I feel better when I am not sweating gallons of sweat. And today, I was about to feel glorious.

The last six months or thereabouts, Ashley and Ryan have been on a quest to add to their family. Of course, Ryan is much older than Ashley is, but apparently, because it is our dear Ashley and she shares everything with Erma and me, Ryan does phenomenal in the lovemaking department. But making a baby was a completely new direction. Ashley knew her biological clock ticked towards the last of the baby-bearing days when they first married, but now, five years later, it was really at the end of the road for their hopes and dreams of starting a family of their own. Ryan had his older children from his first marriage and it seemed as if things between Ryan, Ashley, and his adult children seemed to have improved, which was awesome and wonderful, but Ashley loves children and dearly wanted her own child and family. Since Ryan was a stand-up guy, who went into this marriage knowing full well his wife's dream, Ryan was up for giving fatherhood another whirl when most men are thinking of retirement and easy chairs. The guy was the real deal. He was tough, powerful, smart, courageous, solid, honest, and he was Ashley's true soulmate. He loved her with all of his heart and soul and watching them go through life and enjoy their love gives me hope for this weary world. Just the way they laugh, the way they enjoy each other's presence, the way they look at each other . . . it is amazing beyond words. I always hoped and prayed that Ashley would find the kind of joy and love that is similar to what Erma and I have, and it gives me great comfort to know that she did so. She was a complete woman and today, her dream of a family complete with a child was about to come true. Six months ago, Ryan and Ashley had decided upon adoption and last week, they received the final approvals after a rigorous investigation process and deep commitment to the process. They were adopting an eleven-year-old girl. A little girl named Rosalita, who had languished in an orphanage until she was four-years-old, and then, was passed from foster family to foster family, never knowing love for longer than a few weeks, never having actual parents, never knowing of a permanent home. Shadows on the wall of life that never remained. They only flashed briefly across her mind and then before they became reality, the shadows faded away.

Today, there were no more shadows.

We all need a home. No matter what it is, how luxurious it is, or how rundown it is, it really does not matter. Material things all pass away and money cannot buy the things that we really need in this life. We all need a place to rest, a place to feel safe, and a place to put your cares away in and feel as if it is where you belong. A place to call our own. A home.

Today, Rosalita found her place. She found a home.

She was of half-Latino and half-Irish heritage and from her picture; she was going to be a knockout. Hell, she already was! Dark features, long black hair with a glorious sheen to it and a round face with perfect features and the blessing of green, almond shaped-eyes. Something told me that Irish blood mixed with Latino; this little beauty was going to be a spitfire.

Ryan would need a stick to beat off the drooling guys.

Uncle Gilly already had one picked out.

Ryan and Ashley were picking Rosalita up today to bring her home, and they promised to bring her by the pub to meet her other family. Erma and me, and Renaldo, and Tim, and Dennis, and all the crows. We all are her other family. We all sat and stood here watching, waiting, and holding onto our high wire for dear life. We could not wait.

I yelled for Erma and kicked open the swinging door to the kitchen and yelled for the boys in the back of the house, the second that I saw the door to the pub open and a beaming Ryan, a beaming Ashley, and a wide-eyed, little Rosalita, enter the pub. Rosalita was in the middle, Ryan held her one hand, and Ashley held her other. I almost fell on my huge ass from the raw emotion at the sight of them. That is not a good thing. I mean, to clarify, me falling on my ass is not a good thing. The elation of witnessing the joy of the new family was beyond awesome. It was Heaven sent. Thankfully, I held onto the bar counter and remained upright. Picking my big ass up from the floor is not fun, nor is it easy.

I rushed around the side of the bar, stopped in my tracks, and pushed back the tears as Erma and the rest of the gang rushed to my side to join me. Erma sensed my joy, and she first tucked her arm in mine, went up on her tippy-toes, and kissed my cheek. Erma then released me and placed her hand on my back. A glorious silence fell over the entire pub. No music, no televisions, no radios, no yelling and debating over the golf game putt, or general noise. Just love. Love has a calming and profound silence to it. All the retirees gathered in and all the crows moved in too. Mr. Anderson, with some assistance, slipped off the barstool, and he wobbled over. Yes, he was still alive. The guy was pickled now and might last another, eighty-years or so.

I kneeled down to Rosalita's level and this amazing little girl held onto her parent's hands; she stopped walking and stared into my eyes, and I fell in love. I mean, I fell in love when I stared into my own daughter's eyes when she first stared at me, and my Erma's eyes when for some reason, Erma thought that I was the man for her and she accepted my marriage proposal, but right now, I fell in love once more. Ashley bent down and leaned in next to Rosalita as I opened my arms wide open and smiled. Talk about a scene—here I was, this big giant man, a huge belly, a shaved head, two golden hoop earrings in my ears, and a river of tears running down my face.

This little girl must have thought, 'Okay, just who the hell is this giant clown?'

"Rosalita, honey, this man here, is Gilly. He is the man that Daddy and Mommy told you about on the ride home. He is my boss, and this is where Mommy works, but he is also my best friend in the entire world. That beautiful woman standing behind him is his wife, Erma, and she too, is my friend. Mommy and Daddy love them with all of their hearts and souls and you can love them too. They love you already. They love like no other people in this world. You see, our dear Rosalita, this is more than just where I work, this is, a second home to me, and," Ashley waved her hands in the air to touch everyone's hearts in the pub, "all of these amazing people here are my family, and they are now, your family too. You can give him a hug if you want to and if you want to, you may call him, Uncle Gilly, and you can call the woman, Aunt Erma."

Ashley lowered her voice to almost a whisper and said with her incredibly soft and magical voice, "I hug him all the time. It is super-awesome. He is all squishy and soft and it is like hugging a big, giant, teddy bear."

Upon hearing those words, Rosalita nodded, smiled, and rushed in. She wrapped her arms around me, I hugged her, and I cried tears of joy. There were greetings of joy and hugs all around and non-stop tears, and now we had a little crow on the high wire. A little crow, dressed in a powder blue dress, with white shoes with buckles on her feet, a blue bow in her hair, a knockout smile, almond eyes, and immense love in her heart.

None of us ever felt better in our entire lives.

After warmly shaking Ryan's hand and hugging him, I hugged Ashley and kissed her cheek. I tried hard to stop my tears from spoiling her dress and raining down upon her back. I did a lousy job of doing so.

"I thought that I was a big sexy, hunk of man and not a squishy, soft, giant teddy bear," I said, while we traded tears, "you know, Ash, to hear that I am squishy is an immense blow to my ego."

Ashley laughed and wiped away her tears and said, "You are a big sexy hunk of man! C'mon, Gills, I can't tell Rosalita that. She is only eleven."

"It's very cool. I have to tell ya that, old Gills, well, I kinda like being a teddy bear. . .."

Somewhere between the loving meetings, the love, the well wishes and the endless greetings, Mr. Anderson wobbled over and he leaned in and extended his hand, and Rosalita grabbed the old man's hand and smiled at him. This little girl had already captured everyone's hearts. Here she was, meeting all these strangers, and she opened her heart to all of us. It was as if it was all part of the stars in the sky. I no longer think of this pub as if it was just a pub, or a gin joint on the Main Street in downtown Bloomfield, New Jersey, or a watering hole for locals, because I knew that it was actually a stepping-stone to Heaven and beyond.

"Hiya, there, beautiful little, Rosalita. I am Mr.

Anderson. They call me old Anderson because I am very old but I am still alive because life is great." His old eyes flickered with magical warmth and his wrinkles made other older people's wrinkles seem to disappear.

"I too, am a friend of your mommy and daddy and I can tell you that you are a very lucky little girl because your mommy and daddy love you very much and are wonderful people. I guess that I am the oldest crow. Please, I would like to be your friend."

Little Rosalita warmly shook the old man's hand and in a strong but sweet voice, Rosalita answered, "My daddy told me that I am now the youngest crow. I would like to be your friend too, Mr. Anderson. I am, Rosalita, ah, ah, Griffith." The little girl stood proudly. She stuck her little chest out and dug her feet into the floor to affirm her position. "Yes, Miss Rosalita Griffith is my name."

"Then, it is my pleasure, Miss Rosalita Griffith, to meet you and to be your friend. Yes, indeed. We shall be crows together on the high wire. The oldest and the youngest," Mr. Anderson said as I watched the old boy wipe a tear away from his eye as he struggled to recover his voice, but somehow, the old man managed to say, "and, your mommy and daddy might just be the luckiest parents in the entire world. . .."

It was now Renaldo's turn and our talented chef tilted his head at the little girl and he greeted her in Spanish, "Hola, Rosalita. I am Renaldo. I am the head chef here and I cook and make good things to eat!" Renaldo knew of her mixed heritage but he seemed curious to see if along her many travels, she learned how to speak Spanish as a venture into a part of her heritage.

"Hablas español?" Renaldo asked.

Rosalita's beautiful face lit up when she heard Renaldo speak and ask her the question.

She immediately answered, "Claro que hablo espanol."

Renaldo smiled to comfort and to reassure her and he

asked, then stated, "Tienes hambre? Te cocino algo." Renaldo was going to do what he did the best. He was going to cook for Rosalita.

"Hazme lo que gustes."

Renaldo paused, smiled and lifted his finger, and then he pulled at his partner's chef jacket to drag him toward the back of the house. Poor Dennis smiled but you could tell that other than it was time to go back to work in the kitchen, he had no idea of what just was said between this gorgeous little eleven-year-old girl and his boss of the Crows on a High Wire kitchen battalion. Dennis was in charge of our Italiano division.

Renaldo nodded his head and said, "Si, un momento."

When Renaldo appeared a few minutes later with a marvelous chicken and vegetable quesadilla, smothered with his special red sauce, with a side of piping hot French fries and a sumptuous garden salad, loaded with tomatoes, diced green peppers, cucumbers, and other amazing things, little Rosalita's face lit up as if Renaldo presented her the entire world on a platter. Dennis eloquently followed behind his boss with a selection of dressings and Pico de Gallo in small bowls sitting upon a wooden platter, and an ice water with a lemon in it, and when the boys looked to me for direction, I waved to the Table of Obscurity. The boys were doing it in grand fashion and I was very proud of them for treating little Rosalita as the princess that she was, and the entire experience . . . was awesome and amazing! Rosalita, first, looked at her mother and father for permission before sitting at the table. It was readily apparent that along her many travels, this remarkable and captivating little girl had learned manners and she was brilliantly intelligent. When they both pointed to the table and nodded, the little girl ran to the table to enjoy the meal. Erma and Ashley settled in at the table to watch Rosalita enjoy the meal and to share in the moment.

I put my arm around Ryan's shoulders and pulled him

in close and we shared a special moment as we watched Ashley sit with her daughter and guide her through the joy of everything that was the Crows on a High Wire Public House. To begin their own journey through life.

It was an immense moment. A moment that lives in our hearts forever. It was the sun and the moon and the constellation of Orion and all the stars and all the galaxies, and most of all . . . it was love.

"How awesome is this moment?" I asked Ryan. "To see your wife and daughter sitting at the very place where you and Ashley first met and fell in love."

Ryan clung to me, and he seemed to struggle for the right words.

For *any* words at all.

After his rather watery and teary eyes wandered the pub and then settled upon his wife and daughter, Ryan managed to capture the moment, and with his heavy Paterson, New Jersey accent barely managing to make the words audible, Ryan spoke, "Gilly, my friend, there really are no words. How does a soul speak when it remains consumed in love? My soul speaks without any words. Because there are no words. Sometimes, silence broadcasts love better than any words could ever manage to do so."

I agreed with his soul and with his words.

Therefore, we both stood in silence.

It is going to be a great Thanksgiving.

It was a great Thanksgiving, in fact, the entire holiday season was awesome. Connie was off from work, so she hung out with us for a week or so. She even took a few shifts behind the bar with her dad. A chip off the old block she is . . . and a whole lot better looking, too. Connie knew how to work the crowd of young men, and her tips were amazing. Especially when compared to the fifty cents some old lady gave me when she told me how handsome I was, and it was a shame that I was a married man. She had to be eighty-years-old and sloshed to the gills. Anyway, Connie took a few shifts for Ashley and that helped the new family have some quality Christmas time together. Of course, Uncle Gilly and Aunt Erma bought a certain little girl some very cool Christmas presents. I might have gone over the top and pulled Erma with me, but what the Hell? I really am an old softie. Now that the holidays were in the rear-view mirror and the cold, dreary, and long days of January settled in, life took on a certain smoothness to it. Rosalita settled into her new family and into our lives rather seamlessly, and this little girl certainly captured all of our hearts. She had an amazing personality that continued to evolve and shape and she took our breath away.

"Please, you can, do your homework over there, baby doll two. We are slap-full today. It is cold and nasty and snowy outside and everyone decided to warm up in here today." I nodded to Rosalita, and pointed in the direction of the Table of Obscurity, as she gathered up her books from her backpack and then dropped them on the blessed table. It was the perfect place to do homework, since few, if any, patrons ever sat there.

Rosalita was now baby doll two. Her mother was forever and always, baby doll.

"Your mother is in the back. I will get her."

"Gotcha, Uncle Gilly. Thank you," Rosalita said as she pulled her books out of her backpack and dropped them with a loud thump on the table. I stopped in my tracks as a sudden thought hit me.

"Wait! How did you get the school bus driver to drop you in front of the pub? It ain't no normal bus stop on the route." I asked, as curiosity captured me. Since the dismissal time for school usually coincided with Ashley's time to begin her shift here at the pub, Ryan usually picked Rosalita from school, but he called earlier to let us know that he was running late on some out-of-town business. Erma offered to pick up Rosalita from school, but Ashley said that they had it all covered with the school bus. Rosalita sighed with a deep and dramatic sigh and she looked at me and quickly batted her eyes together and posed with her hands on her hips.

"Duh, Uncle Gilly, the bus driver is a dumb guy."

This kid had the moves. Just like her mother does.

No further explanation needed.

I waved my hand in the air, laughed at this little eleven-year-old seductress, and said, "I can tell whose daughter you are. Let me go get your mentor. Do ya English homework. I will check it later."

Rosalita mimicked my words and my hybrid living all over the place, New Jersey accent and with a purposeful mumble, the words slid out of her mouth sideways, "Okay, Uncle Gilly. Thank you for checking my English homework. After all, it ain't no regular stop."

Recognizing my total butchering of the Queen's and the King's proper English, I laughed, while I swung the kitchen door open and thought, 'How this little girl is beyond amazing. She just caught me stepping on my own shitty grammar and poor choice of words.'

"Ash! The mini-smart-ass-version of you is here and I ain't helping with her English homework!" I yelled in the general direction of the office.

There. Take that. I just served up a double dose of lousy grammar.

From deep within the confines of the office, I heard my wife's voice echo Ashley's voice as they joined in unison, "Thank goodness. Maybe, Rosalita will get an A on this paper."

Okay, well, maybe my proper English sucks, but if

youse guys and an incredible, once in a lifetime love had not carried me to New Jersey and dumped my huge ass within this hotbed of wild accents and atrocious grammar, then I would have a half-of-a-chance of speaking correctly!

Maybe.

I picked up some ketchup bottles that just arrived and gathered them up into my arms to restock the bar, popped back out of the back of the house, put my huge ass into the swinging door, and walked behind the bar. I saw her standing there in front of the bar and she was staring in the direction of Rosalita. The woman had a look on her face, as if she wanted to say something to Rosalita, but she was not sure of something. This woman was young, maybe in her late twenties or thereabouts. She had black hair with some dyed golden highlights on the tips and she wore large-black-framed glasses. She was very cute and her figure was quite shapely. Generous breasts, flowing hips, and I suspected that she had a nice backside too. While she stood there, wearing black canvas sneakers, a black blouse, unbuttoned to just above her cleavage, black jeans, I admired that she had a nice style, she was solid, not overweight, but solid and she had the kind of figure that was very different and quite attractive. It was nice to see a gal with meat on her bones. Guys need handles to hold on to too.

When she turned to look at Rosalita, I noticed that she had a star tattooed on her neck, and it looked good. Very fitting. This was a hippy chick. I could tell. It was my job to assess the patrons and know their ins and outs. Now, before the reader of this drivel thinks that I am some old whacko, staring at young gals, I had a mission to make sure their experience was enjoyable when they visited here, especially for the first time. Now, admittedly, when it came to meeting attractive young gals, my old ass perked up quite a bit, but I still justified all of this by sticking to my story that it was part of my job. Erma knew that I was harmless. She always told me to look at the merchandise on the shelves, just don't touch it and never, ever, dream of buying it.

On another whim, I guessed from her dark features and facial structure that this cutie was Latino and that was why she was staring at Rosalita. Our precious little Rosalita had those amazing touches of her Latino features, but her riveting green Irish eyes always threw people for a loop as to her exact heritage.

"Hola," the young woman said to Rosalita, who looked up from her homework and smiled.

"Hola," Rosalita answered.

"Quien es ek dueno o el jefe aqui?" The young woman spoke and, not knowing a single word of Spanish, I dropped my ketchup bottles on the bar counter and waited for the exchange to play out. I could sort of follow the inflection in her voice to guess that the young woman had asked Rosalita a question.

"My Uncle Gilly there is the owner, but my mother is the boss," Rosalita answered in English as she thumbed in the direction of me and smiled widely at me with a purposeful toothy grin. Well, sorta toothy, one or two are missing and the new ones are on the way. My darling little Rosalita spoke in English on purpose so that I could follow her statement! This little gal sure was a spitfire, and she already knew the ropes. I could not argue with her statement as to who was the boss around here.

"Gracias," the young woman answered, and she suppressed a chuckle at Rosalita's statement.

At least, I knew that this cutie understood English. I leaned over the counter, extended my arm and hand, and greeted the young woman. "Hiya, there. Welcome to Crows on a High Wire Public House. I am Uncle Gilly Gilford and yes, I own the joint and that beautiful little gal there, *doing her homework,* is correct. My general manager, Ashley Griffith is kinda, sorta, the boss. So, what can I do for you?"

"Well, hiya, there, Uncle Gilly. I am Juana Flores. Nice to meet ya."

"Nice to meet you too, Juana. I cannot quite roll my tongue as neatly as you just did when ya said ya name there with the very cool Spanish inflections, but just go with it. My living all over the place, New Jersey half-breed accent is a mess."

Rosalita piped in, laughed, and mumbled, "Yeah, it is."

I displayed a fake frown and said to Juana, "I am just plain old, Gilly, to you. No Uncle. Even if we are not related by bloodlines and only related through mutual love, I am pondering disowning that little gal over there, *doing her homework.*"

Rosalita stuck her tongue out at me just as Ashley burst through the swinging door separating the Heaven side of the pub from the Hell side of the pub. Literally.

Without missing a beat, Ashley, now in full mother-mode, said, "Rosalita! Don't stick your tongue out at Uncle Gilly. Remember that Aunt Erma and Uncle Gilly buy you all the cool things that Mommy and Daddy won't. Do your homework. Your daddy will be here in fifteen minutes to pick you up and take you home."

Rosalita immediately perked up. She looked over at me, batted her eyes, and blew me a kiss. She was more than adorable, she was more than a colorful and exuberant character, she was more than a smoking gun, she was amazing, and I loved her with all of my heart and soul.

Juana laughed aloud at Rosalita's actions and waved in her direction while saying, "Awesome, Rosalita. Never bite the hand that feeds ya!" Juana then turned her attention to me and asked, "I am curious if you happen to know who owns the building next door to here? I noticed the company on the first floor, with the Main Street storefront, moved out a few days ago and it is vacant but there is no leasing information posted yet. I am interested in leasing the space."

After double-checking the homework status of her daughter, Ashley's ear perked up, and she now was listening in on the question. I waved a thumb in the direction of Ashley, who smiled, and upon hearing the question, she glided over to the conversation.

I explained my thumb wave, "Here is the owner. You came to the right place."

"Wow! Very cool. Timing is everything in life," Juana said while she beamed and held her hand out to Ashley, who smiled and shook Juana's hand. I liked this gal's style; she had a certain ease to her and a gregarious manner of dealing with people, and I could tell—even with life.

"Yes, I own the building. Hello. I am Ashley Griffith and that cutie over there doing her homework is my daughter, Rosalita. I guess you know that already, with some of your Spanish exchanges. My husband's company manages the property and building, but he wanted to clean up the space a little before he posted any leasing information. You certainly are first in line for leasing opportunities."

"Very cool! I have to say, woaaah, you are stunningly gorgeous, Ashley. Stunning and so is your daughter. The big guy there, Gilly, is a hottie too. I like big guys. In more ways than one," Juana said with a wink and I looked over at our innocent Rosalita, who smirked at the double meaning.

These kids grow up too fast these days.

I admired the fact that Juana could obviously determine that Ashley was not blood related to Rosalita, but she never mentioned a word about the relationship.

"Total disclaimer here," Juana held both of her hands in the air and added, "I am totally broke. About twenty-five bucks in a bank account, and that is about it. Not too much more to go on in the ole finance department for Juana Flores." She leaned into the bar, pulled out a stool, and plopped down at the stool while still wearing her effervescent smile. "I will have a double shot of tequila, though."

Rosalita giggled at Juana's actions and words and Ashley laughed a little too, while adding, "Well, Juana, I see that honesty is one of your attributes. Blunt, pure, unadulterated honesty."

"Well, ya know, overall, it pays off in the end. I mean, I don't even have the money to pay for the double shot of tequila that I just ordered, but my boyfriend has a few bucks in his wallet." She spun around on the barstool and looked in the direction of the front door and added, "He is parking the car. The rear lot was full, so he was cruising up and down the street. This place is jam-full today. You two, have a very cool place here. I love the décor and the cool vibe."

Her brown eyes wandered behind her glasses, taking in the interior of the pub. I noticed that she had long eyelashes that added to her beauty. Her boyfriend was a lucky guy, because this chick was awesome. Pretty, honest, a cool vibe to her and her style, and an enchanting personality. First, I tended to a refill of a regular's pint of stout and then I poured her a double shot of tequila. After all, I was going to take her at her word that her boyfriend was the moneybags in this relationship.

"Not sure where he went off to, but he will make it. He can be an adventure sometimes . . . he is from Morocco in Africa, but for the most part, he is very chill. A little confusing, and sometimes, he will babble on and on with talking and lengthy explanations, but for the most part, he is very chill. I think that I will keep him around. For now."

Juana winked and smiled a knockout smile at her coyness.

I heard old Anderson snort a laugh at Juana's comments, but the old man did not say a word. The old man was smitten with Juana. I had a feeling that many of us were about to join him in admiration.

I could tell by the look on Ashley's face that despite the "no money and broke" disclaimer filed by Juana that she was still interested in this young woman's interest in leasing the space and her motives.

Ashley said, "So, you have no money, but you are interested in leasing the space. Please, tell me, Juana, what is it that you want to do with the space?"

I dropped the shot in front of Juana and since I wanted to lean in and share in this interesting conversation, I waved to Tim to come over and step behind the bar for a few minutes to sling 'em and pour 'em. He was now officially our pinch-hitting bartender and officially our floor manager, so he could dip and dive all over the pub. Tim was primarily running food right now because he only had a few tables, and left the rest of them to his server team, so he nodded and made his way behind the bar and began checking on the patrons.

Once more, Juana's infectious mannerisms took over and her face lit up as her reply to the question came out with a singsong melody to her voice.

"I want to open a thrift-store. Gently used items and clothing. All kinds of things, but here is the caveat . . . for the homeless persons, the persons truly in need, the person's down on their luck, we will give them the goods for free. It is going to be a not-for-profit. Sort of. One of the great tragedies of this great country is that we have homeless persons. Look here in New Jersey. Right here in Bloomfield. Successful businesses all over the city, fancy office buildings, a number of affluent law firms there in the corner building. The one with four floors and a security guard watching the fancy and expensive cars parked in their parking lot. Those guys are suing the pants off of everyone and collecting dough while the lawyers drive big fancy cars and wear fine suits. Hey, nothing wrong with that—if they make it, then good for them, but if you walk down the street four blocks, there is an alley with homeless persons living in a box, who have to beg for handouts on the corner. Even today, in this cold and in this snow. Who helps them?"

Her voice lowered with passion and everyone around her leaned in to listen. Even old Mr. Anderson dropped his drink and perked his ears up while adjusting his hearing aid to tune in the conversation a little clearer on his wavelength.

"If I could give away ten free winter coats to ten persons in need on a freezing cold, January day, then my life would be complete. I came from immigrants who wandered up from Mexico to Sacramento, California and found their way. Somehow. I am just a hippie chick from Cali. I smoke too much weed, might drink too much tequila, but I care about people. I know need and I know desperation and it is my dream to help those who need a helping hand."

Mr. Anderson piped up, and he pointed at Juana, and said, "Because you smoke too much weed and drink too much tequila is one of the reasons why you care so much. You have my vote, honey. I am first in line to give you a few bucks for your dream. And I might add," the old man, wiggled his eyebrows and added, "if I were a few years younger, I might give that boyfriend of yours a run for his money chasing after a pretty gal like you are." Old Anderson laughed and mumbled, "You would kill me in two minutes, honey. But I would go out with a smile on my face."

Another crow raised his hand and added, "I am second behind, Anderson. In donating the money, not in chasing ya. My wife would not be too happy with me."

He issued a disclaimer and a clarification.

Then another, "Third."

"Fourth," and so on and so forth. The crows were awesome and knowing their hearts, they were not slinging crow shit. Each one of them meant to honor their pledge. And I am sure that Mr. Anderson meant that he would chase Juana too. He was not dead yet, and his eyes were a lot sharper than his ears were. As if by magic, or perhaps we were too intent on the conversation and ensuing support, but I looked up and there was a lean, medium-height young man standing next to Juana. He was a nice-looking young man, neat, clean, with olive skin, close-cropped hair, dark features. At first glance, he appeared as if he was of Italian descent, or Mediterranean, but I made the connection. Northern Africa. Morocco. Former French colony, right close to Spain, yackity-smackity. The boyfriend found a parking space. He must have been listening into the conversation, and upon hearing the support, he smiled widely and proudly. No doubt this young man was in love.

He spoke with the gentle hint of a French accent, "Well, baby-baby-baby, looks as if you already made some connections. Hi there, everyone," he waved in the air with a whirl-around, general wave, "I am, Younes Bakali. Could I please have a glass of lemonade? Preferably, pink lemonade, if you have it. Lots of ice." He then stuck his hand out to me to greet me and repeated, "Yes, Younes Bakali is my name. Fez, Morocco is my hometown. You spell the first name much differently than it is pronounced."

When I heard his request, I stopped in my tracks. You could have heard a pin drop. No golf games, no sports news, Tim turned the music down in the house, so there was now no more Dire Straits music playing on the overhead speakers. He pulled the plug right in the middle of the Knopfler guitar solo for "Sultans," so you know this situation was radical. All chatter amongst the crows ceased with the pronunciation of the word "lemonade," but it seemed as if all the air in the pub went rushing out with the additional descriptor of "pink" added to the request.

Mr. Anderson dropped his glass hard on the bar counter and he peered over at the young man, who stood silently smiling at me, still holding his hand out to me, while patiently awaiting my reaction. Mr. Anderson gave him a once over and when I spotted the old guy giving him such an intense observation, I leaned over to see what was so fascinating. After all, Mr. Anderson, even at one-hundred-million-years-old, reliving his glory days by flirting and checking out a pretty gal with nice curves, a nice backside, and generous breasts is understandable, but checking out this young Moroccan man was another. Now, I saw it too. Fancy pointy shoes, polished to a high luster, and he was wearing skinny jeans. In fact, he was wearing a rather feminine looking polo shirt too.

Mr. Anderson coughed and leaned back in, picked up his drink and mumbled, "I might have a chance, after all. Hello glorious death while enveloped in the midst of joy."

Sensing that the situation required a bailout of her now suspiciously labeled boyfriend, Juana entered in the ace in the deck, or what she thought might be the explanation card.

"He is Muslim. He does not touch alcohol."

If all the air went out of the pub when the word "Pink" drifted in and amongst the crows, then the word "Muslim" felt as if it made the entire pub spin on its axis. Now, everyone not only leaned into the conversation, but the entire pub stopped chewing, dropped silverware, and stopped sipping their liquid libations. It was not just along the bar, but it was even on the dining room floor. Even the servers stopped in their tracks and Renaldo and Dennis appeared from the kitchen to find out why everything went silent and why Knopfler's classic solo stopped just at the good part. They rock out in the kitchen.

Juana stated with some emphasis and then she added with even more emphasis, while pointing at her ample and rather enticing chest, "I make up with the alcohol intake for the both of us."

With that statement in hand, she grabbed a salt shaker

from the counter, sprinkled a dash of salt on her folded thumb; licked the salt off and then she picked up the shot and downed it in one gulp, dropped the glass hard, and smacked her lips.

"Hit me again, Gilly. Can you please slide some limes in my direction? Damn, that was a great shot."

I weakly nodded, reached out my hand and shook Mr. Bakali's hand and, as expected, it was a rather weak handshake, but, in his defense, I was a rather large human being.

"Nice to meet you. Welcome to the Crows on a High Wire Public House. How did you say that first name, U-niss?"

"Yes, that is correct, but it is spelled rather differently. Please, let me spell it for you letter-by-letter."

Juana reached up, put her hand over his mouth, and said, "Baby-baby-baby, they don't give a rat's ass at how you spell it."

Rosalita, who now completely abandoned her homework and had become engrossed in the conversation, laughed aloud and Ashley turned and gave her the stink eye and waved in the direction of her books.

"El nunca se calla," Juana said to Rosalita, and Rosalita laughed even harder.

I do not know what I expected out of the crows for a reaction to this young man, but admittedly, I held my breath. This crowd was generally a very tolerable bunch. Now, please do not get me wrong, over these many years, I tossed out and landed on their sad asses, many an unruly jackass, hooligan, drunken-ass-pinching-men and even some women with exploring hands, and some foul-mouthed evil guys, but generally, this was a solid crowd of special persons. They were, for the most part, generous, caring, and amicable, but this was a first for us. Obviously, we lived in one of the most diverse places on Earth. Northern New Jersey had a population of virtually every known religion, race, type of person and culture that you could imagine, but right now, the word Muslim had taken the formally congenial and emotional testimony and the support of Juana's wonderful idea to assist the homeless persons and put the crows on the edge of the high wire. My eyes still studied the drop jawed patrons for a reaction and I was anxious for the next step.

Ashley, sensing my thoughts, leaned in close and said, "Gills,. you pour Juana's tequila and please, grab some sliced limes, and Younes, please we only have straight lemonade. We do not have pink."

"Okay. Straight is fine."

Ashley was going to break up the tension and curiosity. "I will get it for you. Lots of ice, right?"

The young man sat on the stool next to his gal and crossed his legs over one another. I thought that old Anderson was going to fall out of his stool.

Younes smiled and fiddled with his hands on his legs while he said, "Please."

Ashley prepared the glass and with her nose, pointed at the tattoo on Juana's neck and said, "I like your star."

Juana immediately pulled up her long sleeve and revealed a beautiful tattoo of a rose on her lower forearm and hand. A red rose, complete with a rose flower, the vine, some leaves, and an outline of the State of California. It was stunning. Ashley finished preparing the lemonade, dropped the lemonade for Younes. I handed her the tequila and a plate of limes, and Ashley pulled the sleeves up on her shirt as far as they would roll up to display her tattoos. The crowd now settled back onto the high wire. Activity returned to normal and the lemonade, fancy shoes, skinny jeans and sort of feminine ways of Younes faded to memory. So did the Muslim part. I was proud of these amazing people. Ashley strategically plowed the road, and they accepted the newcomers as just part of the gang. Juana was in the second that she walked in the joint, and now there were two more crows on the high wire.

Upon studying Ashley's sleeves of tattoos, Juana exclaimed, "Oh, wow. Awesome!" Juana exclaimed, and she tapped her boyfriend in the chest just as he was taking a sip of his lemonade. "See. She is super cool. I knew we were meant to come in here and ask about the building next door."

"What about the building next door?" The question came from that golden voice with the unmistakable, Paterson, New Jersey accent of Ryan Griffith.

"Hi, Daddy!" Rosalita beamed at the sight of her father. She slid out of the stool, ran over and grabbed her father around the waist. Ryan leaned over, hugged her, and kissed her.

"Hiya, honey. Are you doing your homework?"

Rosalita was already daddy's little girl.

"Well. I am trying, but it has been the bomb.com here today."

"So, I heard."

Juana whistled and said with one eye on Ashley and Rosalita, "Woaaah! So that is daddy and your hubby? Oh me, oh, my. *Now* that is one hot man! Luckily, you snagged him first, or I'd be all over that hunk of male goodness. Geez . . . I bet you had to beat the women off of him. And how did ya stop your panties from smoking when you first saw him? But you are stunning too with an amazing body and gorgeous face and hair, so it makes sense."

Juana Flores was honest. Blunt honesty flowed from her mouth at all times without any filters.

"What did you say before about your man? You will keep him, well, I am doing the same," Ashley said as she leaned in and kissed Ryan and patted him on the ass and added, "All of him."

After some introductions, Ryan slid in next to Juana and Younes and carefully listened to Juana's dream and proposal. Ryan hardly blinked at the "no money" part. I think he sensed how much his wife took a liking to both Juana and Younes. You could not help but to enjoy their company. Both of them were infectious.

Younes was a chatty one, but he was very smart. It was easy to tell that he was steady too and Juana was brilliantly smart too. They made an attractive couple.

Since Rosalita was not going home right away, I offered to assist her with her English homework. When Mr. Anderson heard my offer, he picked up his cocktail, walked over to the Table of Obscurity, and slid in next to Rosalita.

"Keep slinging drinks, Gills. I will help Rosalita. Your English sucks."

The truth hurt, but I did not offer a rebuttal.

I poured Ryan a pint of stout, slid in the back of the house and had Dennis and Renaldo prepare Rosalita, a dinner of chicken fingers, a salad and a side of freshly baked scones. I knew this meeting would result in a deal. I could feel it, and Rosalita was not going home right away with her father. Two hours later, and my prediction came true. The storefront space was Juana's and her dreams were underway. She had three months to create the charity, turn up with the rent and based upon the backing she already had mustered with the crows, I had little doubt that this smart, beautiful, gregarious, and bubbly, Latino gal would not be a remarkable success in her quest and in her life too.

Mr. Anderson wandered home to his easy chair and his Frank Sinatra records, Rosalita finished her dinner and she was off beating the old asses of some of the retirees at playing shuffleboard and conning them out of pocket change, when her father gathered her and her books and backpack and homework up and bid everyone goodnight. Of course, Uncle Gilly got a kiss and hug out of Rosalita. Juana was euphoric and mostly half-in the bag, Younes was heading to the restroom every two minutes to get rid of the six glasses of lemonade that he downed and everyone was happy. When Younes wandered off to the restroom for another relief trip, and Ashley returned to her post behind the bar, Juana leaned in, placed her head in her hands, and rested her elbows on the bar.

With that now familiar bluntness, Juana asked while not even moving her chin out of her handhold, "So, girl, just tell me how you managed not to have your panties explode into fire and burn your amazing ass, when you first spotted that gorgeous hunk of what is now your husband?"

Ashley slid another shot of tequila over to Juana, poured herself a shot of Irish, held the shot in the air and answered, "I didn't, girl. The fire was worth it. My goodness, let me tell you, girl, it was soooo worth it."

It was a crazy hot July day. The midday sun on the sidewalk beat the heat back against the front windows of the pub and onto my huge body, and the sweat fell from my head like great drops of water. I swear they made a splash when they hit the pavement. It was a busy day, the rear loading dock was jammed with another delivery, and Dennis was busy helping the driver unload beer kegs back there. Of course, a whiskey delivery had to arrive at the same time, so we set him in the loading dock space right in front of the pub. I was out here helping the driver unload and counting the bottles, and it was not fun. However, the pub had a large crowd, all of the regulars and some newbies and a large group of others, all trying to beat the heat in the air-conditioning, and I could not break anyone else away to help unload. A few feet away from where I was stacking cases of whiskey, the charity store known as "Juana's Closet" was a huge success. Juana's dream became a reality. It not only assisted the homeless, but it was a great addition to the neighborhood. It did a healthy business and even drove some traffic to the pub. Younes would help Juana in the store occasionally; he was now enrolled in a fire academy and trying to fulfill his dream of becoming a firefighter. He turned out to be a solid guy. He would come over to the pub with his Moroccan buddies and they would watch soccer matches, go nutsee-cuckoo over the games and drink gallons of tea, coffee, and lemonade. One of his buddies was a real character. His actual name was Mohammad, but in an effort to fit in, he used the name of "Sam." Because of his light-hearted approach to life, he carried the tag of Sam the Sham, and was not a teetotaler. Sam the Sham could tip them with the best of the crows. He missed the Muslim boat when it sailed, or chose to ignore the rules, but he enjoyed tipping a few. Sam was a real character. He wore these cool sunglasses that were actually not so cool, dressed to the hilt, always had a skirt or two that he was chasing and was always talking smack and working side deals. Once you got used to him and knew him, Sam the Sham was a cool guy and one of the crows now too. We even introduced them to ice hockey, and now they were avid hockey fans.

We tried hard to overlook some of our new friend's peculiar ways. Younes Bakali was a cool guy despite his penchant for wearing the fancy, very questionable polo shorts, the skinny jeans, the lemonade, and the cross-legged sitting at the barstools and the fancy shoes too. Oh yes, we also put deep in the back of our minds, one day, when he told us that he takes their dog to the park and skips with her through the park because, "Skipping is faster than walking and not as tiring as running."

Upon hearing that testimony, Mr. Anderson downed his cocktail in one shot and desperately held the glass in the air for me to refill.

He lifted his eyebrows, shook his head, and proudly

proclaimed, "Gills, please, buddy, I need to erase that vision and statement from my brain. Quickly. Please make my next drink a double. I love this kid, but there is something wrong with the vision of an adult male who has a super hot girlfriend, skipping through the park with his dog."

I made the drink a triple. On the house and poured myself a shot too.

While I pulled out my bar rag from my back pocket and wiped the sweat off my forehead, I debated for a quick minute that I could yell over to the store and ask Younes to help me unload these cases. My back was not getting any better these days, and right now, it was screaming at me. Younes was helping in the store today, but I figured that I might lose a few pounds working out here in this ungodly sun. Rosalita was hanging out in the store today, too. She loved folding clothes, organizing things, and spending time in the store. Rosalita and Juana were best friends now. They chatted away for hours in Spanish and since it was summer vacation and kids got bored within four seconds of school's dismissal, Ashley let Rosalita help out a few days a week. She trusted Younes and Juana, and she knew that Uncle Gilly was right next door.

When I look back on this incident, if I could kick my own huge ass about not trusting my gut judgment, not only this time, but too many times in my life, then I would have a very sore, in addition to a very big ass. My ass was the size of Texas, and if it were a sore ass, it would be a mighty big problem, but when I spotted the two street punks walking down the street, I should have reacted. It might have been the heat, it might have been the sweat, it might have been the fact that I wanted to unload these whiskey cases, grab a hand truck and wheel them in the pub and suck down ten glasses of water, but all of these things were a lousy excuse for my inaction. Yet, in looking back on all of this, not calling out for Younes to help me and sucking it up despite my aching back, well, that was a great decision.

The two punks walked towards me, I looked up, almost said something because of the way their eyes darted around and the way they were acting, then I became distracted when the truck driver thumped the last case of whiskey on the tailgate and said, “Last one, Gilly. Let’s get the hell out of this Hell.”

I nodded my head, looked up, and the two thugs were gone. I looked across the street and they were not walking on the sidewalk on the other side of the street. Where did they go?

I didn’t think that they went in Juana’s store, but when the gunshots rang out and my heart flipped in my chest, I screamed the only thing that I could say, “Puck!” I did not really yell, “Puck,” but that is a placeholder for the actual word that I screamed. The real word that I screamed rhymes with, “Puck.”

I screamed in horror as loudly as I could, and then another gunshot rang out and I started the locomotive engine. The Gilly Train takes a bit to get rolling, but I was going to roll. More gunshots were ringing out from inside the store, and I was within four steps of the front door when the door flung open and one thug looked at me, turned and sprinted in the other direction. I did not care about his sorry ass; I only cared about Rosalita, Juana, and Younes. I flung the door open to see Younes mightily struggling in the center of the store with the remaining thug, and he was holding the thug’s arm in the air as they danced around and around in a test of strength. The upright arm was holding a gun. Another shot hit the ceiling, and I was vaguely aware of Rosalita and Juana cowering in the corner, hugging each other. My brain signaled the fact that they were okay, and now I turned my attention to the fact that I was painfully aware of the blood pouring out of Younes’s shoulder. The thug still had the gun. Younes was hurt, and I needed to neutralize the punk.

The locomotive was full speed, and I pushed my huge body as quickly as I could move it and screamed out a blood-curdling scream, which caused Younes and the thug to turn and both look at me. I launched my body in the air just as Younes let go of the thug and I hit the evil bastard with 324 pounds of fat and fury. The punk hit the wall of the store like a bug hitting a fly swatter, and the gun flew out of his hands and hit the floor. I sat all my weight on the punk and crushed him. All the fury erupted from my inner soul and I pounded the living Hell out of him with my fists. I picked his head up, and slammed it into the wall a few times. I spewed obscenities like a hockey player and was furiously launching my fists into his face when I heard the voice of Ryan Griffith in my ear and felt the tug of the big man at my shoulders.

"Gilly! Gilly! Get off of him! He is out like a light. Ya gonna kill him! He went out when you squished him. He never even knew what even hit him. Please, stop, Gills."

I heard sirens wailing in the distance, and everything was a blur. I stopped pounding the crook who sat underneath me with blood pouring out of his head and his eyes rolled back in his head.

"Ryan! Ryan!" I shouted out his name in surprise. I had no idea why Ryan was even here. What the hell was going on now? My chest heaved and my heart almost erupted out of my chest.

"Ryan . . . Rosalita?"

"She is okay, Gills. Juana and Rosalita are okay. Look!" He placed his hand on my chin and gently turned my head and through blurry and sweat-filled eyes, I saw them standing a few feet away with tears rolling down their eyes while Juana held a cloth over Younes's wound.

"Thank God. Younes?"

"He was shot in the shoulder. He is hurting big time but I think he is going to be okay. The police and medical help are on the way. Any second now, they will be here."

I still sat on the unconscious thug and noticed the weapon sitting on the floor a few feet away. Suddenly, the events of the past few minutes returned to me and I told Ryan, "There was another one. He ran past me when I made it to the front door. I was unloading a truck in the front of the pub when I heard the shots. There were two of them, Ryan. One got away. I let him go because I only cared about getting here to help save everyone. Lord in Heaven, Rosalita. Our precious, Rosalita. And, Juana and Younes. My God."

Ryan shook his head. He kneeled down and put his arm around me and pulled me in close. We were a mound of sweat, blood, and tears.

"No, he did not get away. I was walking down the street to meet a contractor here for an appointment when I heard the gunshots. I ran to the store, and the punk ran straight into me. I nailed him with one punch. Caught him upside the head as he was running, bounced his ass on the sidewalk and took him out. I then saw you fly into the store and I was right behind you. I just looked out the window and right now, there are fifty very pissed off crows surrounding him, with Renaldo, Dennis, Tim, and all the servers, some truck driving delivery guy, and they are all holding him for the police to arrive. Old Mr. Anderson is holding his boot on the thug's throat while the punk is spread-eagle on the sidewalk."

I almost laughed. Fifty pissed off crows, the truck driver, and our kitchen staff and servers, all led by old Mr. Anderson. I should have known the crows would fly in to help.

"Okay, big guy," a police officer said as he and Ryan helped me up by my shoulders, "looks like you got 'em. Between you, the skinny guy here with the fancy shoes, one-punch Ryan, and the wild crowd outside led by the ancient guy with a mean-ass boot, the word is on the street now. Don't pull any bullshit in this neck of the woods."

Another police officer slipped in, rolled the thug over, tucked his arms behind his back and cuffed him.

I stood up, Rosalita crashed into my legs, and I held that precious little girl as if I was about to take my last breath.

Ryan draped over me and I whispered to her, "I love you, baby doll two. I love you with all my heart and soul. I would die if something had happened to you, Rosalita. I would die." She hugged me tightly around my neck, and I could not hold back the tears. "Just do me a favor and forget all those words that I was spewing when I was beating the living Hell outta that evil bastard."

Rosalita shook her head, smiled, and said, "Sorry, Uncle Gilly. I already wrote them all down. I might need them someday."

This little gal was the spitting image of her mother. My love overflowed my love tank.

A paramedic tended to Younes, and another team worked on the unconscious thug. The three of us walked over to Younes, and as best I could without interrupting the medic's work, I hugged this wonderful, courageous and incredible young man.

"I love you, Younes. Thank you for you. You are a hero. Skinny jeans, fancy shoes and all."

"Thank you, Gills. You are a hero too. My shoulder was growing weaker and weaker. The pain became unbearable. I was losing the battle right when you arrived."

"No way, man. You are the hero here."

"Okay, you win. I am the hero. Does this mean that I can have free lemonade?"

"For the rest of your life and the next life, too. I might even order some pink lemonade. I will pour you a damn swimming pool of lemonade and you can dive in and do the backstroke in it. You are going to be a shoo-in for the fire service. You just nailed the bravery part."

Juana still sobbed tears, but when the medic wrapped Younes up nice and tight and he was about to be loaded into the ambulance, we all managed a group hug as a breathless Ashley and then a wild-eyed Erma, both rushed in to join us all. Baby doll and my wife had received the word. We conducted the world's greatest group hug. A hug, mixed with blood, sweat, and tears, and now, my back pain screamed furiously at me. It had been silent until the adrenaline ran out, and despite the pain in my back, there was no doubt that I never felt anything better in my entire life because we were all safe now. My love surrounded everyone.

We closed the Crows on a High Wire Public House for a daylong celebration of Younes, Ryan, Juana's Store and charity, the support of the crows, Mr. Anderson's boot, and of the loves in our lives, the loves of our lives and of life in general. I also received an honorable mention for my now legendary squish of an evil bastard. The word was that the thug was out cold for about twenty hours, while singing to the canaries in his head.

On the other hand, was he singing to the crows?

We partied all day and into the night and into the early morning hours of the next day. Crows sure know how to party. The local police officers who were on duty that day stopped by, the paramedics stopped by, the doctors and nurses from the hospital who helped patch up Younes, all stopped in to say hello and join in the joy. All the wild Moroccans showed up, Sam the Sham arrived, wearing his latest fashion sunglasses, and toting around a new girlfriend on his arm, and we had a wild and glorious time. Mr. Anderson made a toast to the hero who skips, wears skinny jeans, drinks lemonade, and was one brave guy. Mr. Anderson also earned a reward and maybe his greatest dream came true, when Juana planted a big kiss on his old lips, rubbed her amazing breasts on him in a big hug, and let the old boy enjoy a strategic feel or two. Old Mr. Anderson was still alive and ticking, and if he did not keel over right then and there, then the old boy might have a few more hundred years left. Life is great.

We ran right until curfew time, called a fleet of taxis for everyone, and the beer, booze, and wine flowed in an endless stream.

And the lemonade, too.

Pink, raspberry, strawberry, or otherwise.

Chapter Eight

A Wave to the Past

A Look to the Future

I could tell many more stories, because there are so many more that Old Gilly did not tell you. However, I know that it is time for you to go now. Me too. Besides, it is time to create new stories. New crows are flying in and it is time for them to have a turn on the high wire.

Life tiptoed on quiet but still audible footsteps while sneaking up behind me. In fascination, I turned around to look back, but sadly, it was gone.

I had spent a lifetime running this pub and maybe just a little bit more. Erma and I finally had the talk a few nights ago, and I knew it was a long time coming. It was time. Besides, my back was shot. I was not too sure of the exact number of years, but I think it was now thirty-seven years of being the Publican of Crows on a High Wire Public House and time to end this part of the story. At least, it was time to end my side of the story and Erma's side, too.

Coatsie passed away about three years ago. He was in his mid-nineties. He lived an ethereal life. Erma, Ashley, Ryan, Rosalita, and Connie, and I all flew to Florida to attend the funeral. There was no better man who ever lived. There were equals, but none better.

He was the first crow, and in many ways, he might be the greatest crow. We closed the pub for a special memorial service in Coatsie's honor. I knew he was there with us. I could feel him and Clive too, and all the crows that flew off to better places. Near the end of the special service, we gathered around and I screwed in a brass plaque into the edge of the bar where the first barstool sat. When Coatsie was off work and hanging out, that is where he sat. I also permanently turned that barstool around and tucked it inside the overhang of the bar. I retired that particular stool forever. No one but Coatsie could sit there and many days, I felt as if he did so. The words engraved on the plaque were, "Mr. Gregory Coates. AKA Coatsie. The First Crow."

Old Mr. Anderson finally passed away in and around last Christmas. I had no idea how old he was because his family remained tight lipped, but the word was he was over one-hundred-years-old. I think that even his family was not sure of how old he exactly was. He only had a few nieces and nephews left and they were in their seventies! The man outlived everyone. And of course, he had his family of crows. One day, he did not show up for his normal daily shift. There was no answer on his phone, so Ryan and I went to check on him. He had given us a key to his apartment many years earlier.

He said, "If I don't show up for a few days, youse guys better come check on my old ass. I might be croaked or even worse."

We found him in his easy chair, his Frank Sinatra record spinning on the turntable. But the needle had hit the end of the grooves. He had a wide smile on his face because life is great. One more crow was gone, but we knew that he flew off to bigger and better places than his barstool. We closed the pub for that funeral and memorial service, too. This was the amazing part of this special business and place. A crow flew off the high wire and another one took their place. It was fascinating.

Now, a brass plaque was screwed into the edge of the bar where old Anderson sat.

The engraving stated, "Mr. Philip "Old" Anderson. Life is great."

My back was a mess. The doctors wanted to operate and fuse some discs or some other bullshit, but I was having no part of that plan. Once they cut you, then you are never the same after that. It was time to hang up the bar rag. It was all just a blur in time. To think that it seemed as if it was just yesterday when I sat and interviewed with Coatsie. Just yesterday, when Ashley walked into the pub and asked me for a job. Just yesterday, when Clive told me of his many wives and of his remarkable life. All of it, just yesterday.

Ryan was talking of retirement, Rosalita was a teenager ready to begin college, and Ryan was pulling his hair out trying to beat off the young men chasing his daughter around. Ashley, well, she was still my baby doll. Even more gorgeous than ever, if that were even possible.

Connie is a major success as a writer and she actually lived in London for a few years. Across the pond, she met a man, and it looks as if it is a serious relationship. A Scotsman named Duncan. Handsome guy. And they say we have accents here in New Jersey! When they first came over to visit, even though I knew he was a good guy, I still gave him the stink eye. Hell, he is chasing around my daughter. What the hell do you expect? They are both living here in New Jersey now. Connie is writing freelance now and making a ton of money. She was now very comfortable in her life, both emotionally and financially. Duncan is in some type of technology business and he seems to earn a ton of dough too. Marriage looks as if it is on the horizon for next spring. Connie's biological clock might have ticked out, and grandchildren might or might not be on the horizon. Erma and I don't really care because we have such an amazing family that we will forever be blessed and happy for in our lives. We invited Ryan, Ashley, Rosalita, Connie, and Duncan over to the house for dinner one night, and I told them it was time for me to pack it in. It was always our intention to hand the business off to Ashley, and to compensate her with some extra earnings, too. Connie long ago told us while she loved the Crows on a High Wire Public House, running a pub and being a Publican was not in her long-term plans or in her dreams. We understood, but Connie still wanted to remain involved somehow or in some way. We worked a deal, where some money went to Connie and when she wanted to goof off and take a break from her writing or from life; she would always have a place there at Crows. It was all set, and it was a good plan for everyone. Ryan would retire soon, and he would help out and hang out at the pub. The guy was still knockout handsome, he looked even better than he did years ago and I could not help but to be jealous of him. Damn guy, never aged!

The deal was a good one. Erma and I did not want very much money. Just a little monthly stipend for five years, or thereabouts, and for Connie's wishes to be under full consideration. We were very well off and we had earned and banked more money than I ever dreamed of when I first began bartending. To think that this was all because I could not find any other job.

Life is great.

We planned to sell the house and of course, like a million other New Jerseyites, move south. Hell no, I was not going to that flat, swamp-butt-bug-infested Florida! My big ass can't take all that heat and sweat and disgusting humidity. I could handle North Carolina. In the mountains. Yes, where the days might be warm, but the nights were cool and snow arrived in the winter. Yes, a cabin in the woods, on top of a mountain where I could sit on my porch and watch the crows flying in the sky and land in the trees and to chatter to each other. No high wires, just trees.

I knew in my heart that, eventually; the next Publican of Crows on a High Wire Public House after Ashley . . . would be Rosalita. From the second that young beauty's eyes wandered around the interior of that pub, I knew it was going to be her business someday. It was in the stars in her eyes. Eventually, Rosalita Griffith will bring this business to another place. A new evolution. A new phase because, if you stand still, then you grow stale. Young minds, growing trends, fingers in the mixing bowl of life, will taste great things. Rosalita Griffith was the future. Rosalita Griffith is beautiful, gifted, smart, and amazing, and she is destined to do great and wonderful things. Her skills will usher in an entire new murder of crows. Believe me because Uncle Gilly knows.

Once again, we were going to close the pub for an entire day. Invitation only. We would have a grand celebration and I already knew that it would end in a rain of tears, painful goodbyes and joyful celebrations. Saying goodbye to my precious baby doll will be so difficult. Not to see her beautiful face every day will be awful, but it is the next step in all of our lives.

The night will bring much joy, many tears and a few wicked-ass hangovers too. Nevertheless, I will lift a glass and down a shot of Irish in honor of all the crows that flew in and sat on the high wire with me and with us. From Coatsie, to all of our amazing staff, to Renaldo and Dennis and Tim, to Clive, to Mr. Anderson, to Mr. Pecorino, to Sal, to Billy and Noel, to totally scandalous and that wild adventure, and of course, Sam the Sham, and Younes and the amazing and captivating, Juana Flores. I know that I missed mentioning a few hundred crows, but they will forgive me. What a special place and an amazing journey it has been.

They live in my heart forever.

I am Xavier Gilly Gilford and to all the crows, both

present and in the future, I wish you a great life, much joy, love, and I say thank you from the bottom of my heart for making my life as great as a life could ever be. In this crazy thing that we call life, we should never remember the regrets, nor should we recall the missed opportunities. We should only recall the love and the joy.

I will toss down the shot of Irish to remember all the many crows and drink to their honor. I will drop the glass hard upon the surface of the bar counter. Hard enough to make a loud noise. I will grab my precious and glorious wife's hand and we will walk hand-in-hand out that front door and into a new life. A new and glorious life. I will give a wave to the past and a look to the future. Who knows what it will bring? Whatever it does bring; I will have no qualms or arguments. Life has been wonderful to me.

In our places, two more crows will fly in and sit on the high wire.

Because that is just the way it goes. Life is a progressive thing. Perpetual progression.

Now and forever.

Until the end of all time.

THE END

Epilogue

Ms. Rosalita Griffith turned the key in the front door to the pub. It was her first day as the new "official" Publican of the Crows on a High Wire Public House. She was going to nail this one! All of those difficult studies of business management in college were going to pay off. She could do this.

Hell, yeah, she could do this.

While she turned the key in the door, she heard a few crows cawing, and she smiled. Shielding her eyes from the sun, Rosalita looked up, and she carefully watched as a few crows landed on the wires out on Main Street in front of the pub. Not on the lower electric wire, but on the high wire far above the ground. Closer to Heaven. They bobbed their heads and made the calls and the rest of the crows landed on the high wire and scanned their world from their high perch. Rosalita stepped in. She closed the door behind her, and she rested her back on the front door and took a deep breath. Rosalita looked down at the brass plaque in her hands and felt her back pocket for the screwdriver. It was there.

She smiled as she turned the plaque over and read the words with smiling and glowing eyes.

The engraving was in bold, block letters, "Xavier 'Gilly' Gilford. A wave to the past and a look to the future."

Her eyes landed on the retired barstool of Coatsie's, and she knew that the second barstool was officially retired now too. At this rate, she might need to extend the bar counter. Rosalita knew that when it came time to screw the plaque onto the edge of the bar and retire the barstool that her tears would fall like rain.

It does not matter because she cries every day when she thinks of Uncle Gilly, anyway.

Uncle Gilly's huge heart finally gave out on energy, but Rosalita knew that it would never give up on pumping out love. Rosalita held out her arms and turned her palms to Heaven. She walked in front of the bar and spun slowly around and around. Her smile was as wide as the sea, and her eyes shone as brightly as the sun. She felt Uncle Gilly here. She felt him touch her palms, and she heard his laughter and heard his booming voice. His voice spoke in her ears as clearly as a church bell rings on a Sunday morning.

"You go, baby doll two. You go, girl, and go with all my love."

Rosalita stopped spinning and wiped her tears on her sleeve. Her eyes traveled around the interior of the pub and her soul quieted.

Dear Lord in Heaven she will miss Uncle Gilly every single day; however, she knew that he and Coatsie were sharing such a glorious time together, as well as a few shots of Irish. Most of all, Rosalita took great comfort in the fact that she knew that his back no longer ached and that he had some wonderful days to enjoy his cabin in the mountains.

Yes, indeed, she was going to make her mom and dad proud. Yes, indeed, she was going to be a success and set the world on fire. It was her dream, it was her passion, and it was without a single doubt that she was going to succeed in this venture.

And Rosalita was going to make Uncle Gilly and Aunt Erma and Coatsie and Mr. Anderson proud of her, too.

In fact, all the crows.

ABOUT THE AUTHOR

Eons ago, when the dinosaurs first died off, at the ripe old age of sixteen, Paul John Hausleben wrote three stories for a creative writing class in high school. Enrolled in a vocational school, and immersed in trade courses and apprenticeship, left little time for writing ventures, but PJH wrote three exceptional and entertaining stories. Paul John Hausleben's stories caught the eye of two English teachers in the college-preparatory academic programs and they pulled the author out of his basic courses and plopped him in advanced English and writing courses. One of the English teachers had immense faith in Paul's talents, and she took PJH's stories, helped him brush them up and submitted them to a periodical for publication. To PJH's astonishment, the periodical published all three of the stories and sent him a royalty check for fifty dollars and . . . that was it. PJH did not write anymore because life got in his way. Fast forward to 2009 and while living on the road in Atlanta, Georgia (and struggling to communicate with the locals who did not speak New Jersey) for his full-time job, PJH took a part-time job writing music reviews for a progressive rock website, and that gig caused the writing bug to bite PJH once more. He recalled those old stories and found the old manuscripts hiding in a dusty box. After some doodling around with them, PJH decided to revisit them. Two stories became the nucleus for the anthology now known as *The Time Bomb in The Cupboard and Other Adventures of Harry and Paul.* The other story became the anchor story for collection known as *The Christmas Tree and Other Christmas Stories, Tales for a Christmas Evening*. Now, many years and over thirty-five published works later, along with countless blogs and other work, PJH continues to write. Where and when it stops, only the author really knows.

On the other hand, does he really know?

If you ask Paul John Hausleben, he will tell you that he is not an author, he is just a storyteller. His mission is to continue to write and tell stories to warm your heart, make you laugh, and sometimes make you cry, just a little. Most of all, he deals in memories, and helps you to remember the good times of your own life, and the special people who touched you along the way. Paul was born and raised in Paterson, and then nearby Haledon, New Jersey, and began writing at an early age. He revisited a writing career later in his life, and he now is the author of a number of novels, compilations, short stories and audio and video works. Most of his work touches upon nostalgic remembrances of simpler times, and tells the stories of heartfelt, humorous, and special human relationships. Other than writing, among many careers both paid and unpaid, he is a former semi-professional hockey goaltender, a former military radio operator, a music fan and music reviewer, an avid sports fan, photographer and amateur radio operator. He now resides in Somewhere, U.S.A., but his heart always remains along Belmont Avenue in good old Paterson, and Haledon, New Jersey.

Other Work by Mr. Paul John Hausleben

The Time Bomb in The Cupboard and Other Adventures of Harry and Paul

The Night Always Comes, Another story from the Adventures of Harry and Paul

Reunion, A sequel to the Night Always Comes and Another story from the Adventures of Harry and Paul

The Miracle Tree, Another story from the Adventures of Harry and Paul

The Chronicles of Henson

Heaven's Gain
The Final Adventure of Harry and Paul

Geyer Street Gardens
Beneath the Mask of a Hockey Goaltender
Another story from the Adventures of Harry and Paul

Where the River Bends and Curls

Tales of the Quiet Stranger in the Black Hat

And a few others too!

You may write to the author at ctte27@gmail.com

Published by God Bless the Keg Publishing LLC
Henrico, Virginia, U.S.A.

You may write to the publisher at
Godblessthekegpublishing@gmail.com

"Life's simple pleasures are so often the best ones!"

www.ingramcontent.com/pod-product-compliance
Lightning Source LLC
LaVergne TN
LVHW091051080826
845145LV00002B/703

* 9 7 8 0 9 9 8 6 3 0 0 8 3 *